All I've Wanted
All I've Needed

A.E. Valdez

All I've Wanted, All I've Needed

www.aevaldez.com

Copyright © 2021 by A.E. Valdez

Illustrations by Emily J. Fontana

1st edition 2021

For the little girl who fell in love with writing all those years ago.
We did it.

1

Harlow

I SHOULD'VE KNOWN SOMETHING was up when a race red Ferrari pulled up to my house. Hendrix has always been flashy, from his material items to his personality. He commands the spaces he occupies. Hendrix is a man used to going after, and getting, anything and anyone he wants.

Except me. I'm probably the only girl to ever tell him, "No."

Slowly, he rises from the kneeling position he adopted mere seconds ago to ask me this life-changing question.

"No?" he asks, stunned by my response.

"You deserve better than me," I say as tears sting my eyes. I'm aware people are staring now. I thought we were in for an intimate night, sitting at a candle-lit table scattered with rose petals, tucked away at the back of the restaurant. But there's nothing intimate about prying eyes focused on us, watching me refuse my boyfriend's proposal.

He sits back down in his seat and reaches across the table for my hand. "You're my beginning and end, Harlow. All I want is you."

I can't bring myself to meet his gaze. Staring into his honey brown eyes will only make this harder.

He watches me in silence, probably trying to figure out why I would say no to his proposal. We've been together for two years, and things were going great. We're often the couple people describe as "relationship goals." But despite seeming picture perfect, I can't shake the feeling that this isn't lasting love.

"Don't you ever feel like we're just settling, Hendrix? Almost like we're together because we're comfortable, not because we're in love with one another?" My eyes still haven't met his. I didn't want to have to sift through this with him tonight. I hadn't expected him to propose to me. I for damn sure didn't expect him to do it in a public place.

Still not letting go of my hand, he asks, "Are you saying you're no longer in love with me?"

"I love you, I do, but I can't say yes to your proposal knowing that I feel like something is missing from our relationship. I feel like we're together because it's what's expected of us, and not because we want to be together. You're my best friend and..."

He grabs both of my hands and looks into my eyes as if the version of me he fell in love with will reappear. "We can hold off on the engagement if that's what you want but please, please don't ruin us."

A tear rolls down my cheek. He gently brushes it away. There's nothing wrong with Hendrix; he's an amazing boyfriend. But we've always felt more like friends than a couple. I'm unsure if he feels it too and doesn't want to let go of the comfort, or if he truly is oblivious. Or perhaps, he really is in love with me, and I never fell for him.

I hadn't considered that until this moment. *Maybe I'm the bad guy here.*

When we first got together, all I knew was that he wanted me, and I wanted him. The first kiss turned into countless dates and a deepening of our connection. We discovered each other in a new light. When our circle of friends found out we were a couple, they told us they knew we would end up together. It seemed to be inevitable for us. Best friends turned to lovers.

He pulls me back to the present moment. "Harls, say something, please. We can wait if engagement isn't a step that you're ready to take right now."

I exhale a shaky breath. "Hendrix, I don't want to marry you. I love you, but I can't say yes to this proposal." Tears stream down my face as he holds my hand. "I-I didn't mean for this to happen. I thought I loved you in that way but – "

He drops my hands as if I slapped him across the face. Pulling away from me, he sighs and eases back into his seat with his eyes locked on mine. His usually warm eyes have no light in them. For a moment, I'm worried he's going to yell at me. I wouldn't blame him. I'd want to scream bloody murder if the person I had spent the past two years with admitted they didn't love me like I loved them.

Silence falls between us for what feels like an eternity. The people around us return to their conversations and meals when we don't erupt into a fight worthy of going viral. He sits there, examining the black velvet ring box in his hands as if it's a magic eight ball. As if it could tell him an answer that would make more sense than mine.

He isn't crying, but the pain I caused him is clearly etched on his face. "What have we been doing for the past two years? Did you ever love me?" He stares at me, waiting an answer.

I look away from him. "I do love you."

He scoffs and nods his head. "Right, as what? A friend who knows you inside and out, literally?"

Closing my eyes I turn away from him. I deserved that. "Hendrix, I'm sorry. I really am. I love you. I know I keep saying that and you probably don't believe it, but I do care about you. I just can't say yes when I know that I'm not all in."

He continues to stare at the ring box in his hands and then looks up at me. "I'm sorry to lose us," he whispers.

Hendrix's chair slides across the floor, cutting the near-silence of our little bubble. He stands without saying another word and presses a kiss to my forehead. I momentarily melt into the familiarity of him, then miss his warmth as he pulls away. He sets the ring box next to me as he whispers, "I love you, and this will always belong to you."

And then he leaves.

I break into sobs because it didn't occur to me that saying no to his proposal would mean losing my best friend, too.

2

Harlow

STEPPING INTO MY HOUSE, I catch a glimpse of myself in the entryway mirror. My reflection is unrecognizable. Another wave of grief hits me as I lean against the door, then slide down it until I'm a heap on the floor.

I'm not sure I made the right choice tonight. Maybe I just fucked up my entire life just so that I could "find myself" and figure out what I want. I don't know if I just broke his fucking heart for no good reason.

My dad hears me crying and comes to find me.

"Hey, hey, what's wrong?" he asks in a soothing tone, crouching down in front of me.

I doubt he'll understand any words that come out of my mouth, but I try to choke the words out. "Hendrix and I ... broke up." I don't look at him, trying to hide from the judgment I'm sure will come.

My dad pulls me into a hug. Somehow, he helps me up off the floor and guides me to the couch. He leaves me for a few minutes and comes back carrying cups of steaming chai tea. He hands me a cup, and I hug it in between my hands, staring into it as if it can tell me everything will be okay.

"Do you want to talk about it?" my dad asks me sympathetically.

I don't want to talk about it, but at the same time, I know my dad can offer the wisdom I don't have.

I continue to stare at my cup of chai and then I tell him everything: how I felt like Hendrix and I stayed together because we were comfortable, how Hendrix expected my life to revolve around his because he's the next big Major League Baseball player, how I felt like I was suffocating. I tell him about how I really want to do things for myself and not because it's what I feel like others expect of me. I tell him how Charlotte, Hendrix's mom, always tells me what my mom would have wanted for me, as if she knows. I let it all out.

He grabs my hand after I finish spilling my guts. "I'm sorry you've felt that way for so long, kiddo. I had no idea. I can tell you right now that the only thing your mother would ever want for you is to be happy. Whether that's with Hendrix, or alone, or with someone else."

I look at him, and he offers me a smile. "Do you really mean that?" I ask him between sniffles.

"Yes, I truly mean that. Whatever makes you happy, I'm going to support you... even if it isn't a college degree," he says playfully.

"Will you ever let that college degree go?" My lips curve into a smile.

"I support whatever makes you happy, but that doesn't mean I'm not going to bring it up from time to time," he says with a grin.

"Fair enough." I chuckle.

"It will take time for you to feel better, Harlow. You and Hendrix have been an integral part of one another for so long. Don't be so hard on yourself." He rubs my back as he reassures me.

I let out a sigh. "I didn't want to break up with him, but I felt like we're being pulled in opposite directions right now, with him going off to spring training and me being completely unsure of what I want."

"You're doing what is best for you. Don't feel bad. If you two are truly meant to be, you'll find your way back to each other. I think it's good that you want to find yourself outside of him. I love Hendrix too, but I wouldn't want you to feel like you've devoted your life solely to him."

My dad's reassuring words ease my anxiety. "Thank you, Dad." I hug him. "I love you."

He squeezes me back. "I love you, too, kiddo."

I pull away from him and finish the rest of my chai tea. "I think I'm going to go to bed."

"Alright, I'll be here if you need me," he says as he reaches for the remote and settles into his recliner.

I smile at him and make my way upstairs to my room. After I kick off my shoes and strip out of my clothes, I crawl into bed. I check my phone, and for the first time in a long time, there are no texts from Hendrix.

The past few days have been a blur. There have been moments when I thought I would be okay and moments when I missed Hendrix terribly. I still haven't heard from him. It's funny how things change so quickly. He's even been silent on social media. I checked his Instagram, and all the photos he took of us and me are still on there. Maybe he doesn't totally hate me... *yet*.

I sigh and toss my phone to the side. I've considered texting him, but I don't know if he even wants to hear from me. I know he made it back to spring training safely because I heard Will, Hendrix's dad, telling Dad that Hendrix is doing well. I was grateful when my dad didn't say anything about the breakup. Instead, he changed the subject.

I'm sitting in bed with a pile of half-eaten snacks, searching Netflix for something to watch when my door flies open. "Where the hell have you been?"

I bolt upright in bed as my eyes focus on my best friend, Marisa.

"Marisa, how did you –" When I peer over her shoulder, I see my dad grinning at me.

"Thought you could use some company." He shrugs nonchalantly, closing the door.

"I didn't expect to have to hunt you down. What is going on?" she asks as she stares around at all the clutter in my room and then studies me, waiting for me to answer.

Looking down at my can of Pringles, I murmur, "Hendrix and I broke up... a few days ago."

She covers her mouth and gasps. "Oh babe, I'm so sorry. If you would've talked to me, I would have been here for you."

I nod. "I know. I just needed a few days to," I sigh and shrug, "wallow, I guess."

She pulls me into a hug, and I try to remember if I showered today. Pretty sure I haven't brushed my teeth yet and it's nine at night. I guess I'm just a walking biohazard now.

"I'm sorry," Marisa rocks back and forth as she holds me. "How are you feeling now?"

"Not great. I feel stupid for being bothered that I haven't heard from him." I blink back tears because I refuse to shed any more. "Every single thing in my room, my house, the street, my car... it all reminds me of him. Everything. Everything is him."

She doesn't say anything, and I continue. "I really thought this was what I wanted... but now I'm second guessing myself. I've had to stop myself from calling him to tell him that I want to be with him. My dad said this will pass, but it hurts. And I know Hendrix can take the pain away."

"But at what cost?" she asks me as she cradles me.

"What do you mean?"

"Meaning, is he worth losing your sense of self over?"

I sit there in silence, and she rubs my back as she continues to hold me. That's the thing about Marisa, she'll ask you hard questions in a simple way. "He isn't, and that's why I'm in this predicament now."

"Have you showered today?" she asks me and begins picking up all the empty food wrappers and containers. She closes my laptop and sets it on my desk. Then, she starts cleaning, and I stare as if I've never seen someone clean before. She looks at me again as she continues tidying up my room. "If you haven't showered, go shower. Maybe you'll feel better. Then we can talk more if you want. I'll clean up."

The only people who have ever cared for me in this way are my mom, my dad, and now Marisa. I don't know why she decided to show up now, but I'm glad she did. I climb off my bed and glance at her before I close my bathroom door. "Thank you," I say, and I hope she knows how truly grateful I am. She just smiles and continues making my room presentable.

When I come out of the shower, I do feel better. My room is clean, much cleaner than I would have been able to get it, and she even lit a candle. It smells like lavender and chamomile. When she comes back in my room, she's carrying tea for the both of us.

"How do you feel?" she asks as she sets the tray with the tea on the nightstand.

"Better." I smile. "Thank you for coming over."

"Of course. When you weren't at class on Sunday and then again today, I knew something was up. You haven't missed any classes in the two years I've known you. I also wanted to talk to you about something. And after hearing what you're going through, this may be the perfect thing."

Sitting cross-legged on my bed, I wait for her to continue.

"Would you be interested in attending a yoga teacher training with Quinn and I?"

Quinn is our other best friend. We all met because of yoga. Marisa is the co-owner of a popular studio here on Galveston Island. As soon as it opened, two years ago, I signed up. I met Quinn in a class, we became regulars in Marisa's classes, and then the three of us bonded over green smoothies and fruit bowls.

"Me?" I place a hand on my chest, a little shocked. "Doesn't Quinn have school?"

"Yes, you." She chuckles. "Quinn does have school, but she has a month-long break at the same time as the training."

"Oh, I've just never considered becoming a yoga teacher before. The thought of leading an entire class of people makes me nervous."

"I personally think you would be great at it. Plus, just because you complete the training doesn't mean that you need to become a teacher. If anything, it's a nice way to deepen your practice and get away."

I raise my eyebrows, my interest piqued. "It wouldn't be here?"

"No, it's in Bali."

My heart instantly yearns to go. I haven't traveled since I went to Australia two years ago. With Hendrix's training schedule, it was hard to find time to get away. Even when there was time, it wasn't like he wanted to go anyway. "How long is the training?"

"Twenty-two days. The price of the training covers accommodations and food."

My eyes light up for the first time in a long time. "Twenty-two days? In Bali?"

"Yep, the session we're planning to attend is in a month. That gives you plenty of time to think about whether you want to go or not."

"Are you kidding me?" I almost yell. "Of course I want to go!" My whole body vibrates with excitement.

She smiles at me. "I didn't think you would say no. It's been a while since you've traveled. I'll e-mail you all the information when I get home later. I've got to go pick up my brother. Are you going to be okay?"

I shrug. "I will be... eventually."

"You will be." She gives me a hug. "Give yourself some grace. It's okay to not be okay. Plus, you have two amazing best friends to help you along the way."

I let out a sigh, noticing I feel a little lighter after spending some time with her. "I do." I squeeze her back. "You better go before –"

Her phone rings, interrupting us. We both know it's her little brother. "Before I'm late to pick up Killian like I always am?"

"Yes. Thanks for checking on me, babe."

I walk her to the door and wave goodbye as she pulls out of the driveway. I'm not sure what I would have done without Marisa and Quinn over the past two years. I slowly began to feel isolated after Hendrix and I started dating. Everything became about him. The two of them helped me keep a little bit of myself. It wasn't totally terrible being with Hendrix, but I erased a lot of myself to be with him.

Traveling became my life after graduating high school. While my peers sent applications to colleges, I planned trips around the world. At first it was just hopeful planning, adding pretty locations to my Pinterest boards. Then my dad surprised me with paying for my travels as a graduation gift.

I spend the rest of the evening reading up on the yoga teacher training program and Bali, which looks gorgeous. I can't wait to go. Even though everything feels like it's falling apart, I can't help but to also feel like everything is falling into place.

The next morning, I find my dad in his office typing away on his computer. His work never quite seems to be done. He's the president of the university here on the island. Even through loads of paperwork, meetings, and events, he has somehow always managed to make time for me.

I plop down onto a chair and pull one of my favorite pictures off his desk. It's a candid shot of me, my mom, and my dad. I'm sitting between them, smiling at the camera, as my parents look at each other, laughing. Even though it's been eleven years since my mom passed away, it still feels like yesterday.

My dad pulls me from my thoughts. "You seem more upbeat today. Did Marisa's visit help?"

I grin at him. "Yes, it did. Thank you for letting her in, even if I was a mess."

He smiles. "What did you do today?"

"Paid for my yoga teacher training, booked a trip to Bali, and listened to depressing music. You?"

He leans back in his chair, crosses his arms, and chuckles. "Back to traveling?"

I grin. "You know me, Dad."

"Were you able to pay for it all?"

"Yep, I've had nothing to do but save since Hendrix paid for everything, and," I shift uncomfortably in my seat, "I haven't spent a dime of mom's life insurance money." I let out a sigh and look at him. "I'm sure she would want me to use it for something I love. Yoga is something I love."

His eyes glisten with unshed tears. "She would, kiddo." He bows his head. "She would." There's a moment of silence. "When do you leave?" he asks as he clears his throat.

"Next week."

"You know that I'm proud of you, right?"

A wide smile spreads across my face. "Yes, I do." I get up to leave. "Don't work too hard, Dad."

3

Harlow

I COLLAPSE ONTO THE bed and exhale. We've finally made it to Bali and settle into the suite we'll call home for the next three weeks. I melt into the plush bed, happy to finally be on solid ground. Quinn and Marisa crash onto their beds too.

My exhaustion starts to overcome me. I feel my eyes grow heavy. As much as I want to get out of this bed and explore, I know my body needs rest. I kick off my shoes, crawl under the covers, and drift off to sleep.

I awake with a jolt hours later. I'm disoriented because it takes my brain a few seconds to realize I'm not home. The noise that awoke me is my phone ringing. I clamber out of my bed and frantically dig through my bag to find it before it wakes up Quinn and Marisa. My hand lands on it and I pull it out. Hendrix's face is on my screen. My phone almost slips from my fingertips. It stops ringing seconds later.

My heart rate slows, and I relax back onto the pillows. Why the hell is he calling me now after weeks of silence?

I drift off to sleep again, but then my phone chimes with a text.

Hendrix: I miss you, Harls.

I re-read the text over and over as I chew on my thumbnail, unsure of what to say or if I even want to respond. After a few moments pass without any texts, I power off my phone. I don't want to be tempted to engage in a conversation with him right now. Although I hate to admit it, a part of me still thinks about getting back together with him. I can't let that part of me win.

I'm wide awake now, despite it being three a.m. here in Bali and decide to go sit by the pool. Once I'm outside in the balmy night air, I feel like I can breathe. Everywhere my eyes look is lush and green. I feel like I've stepped into another world. Sitting on the edge of the pool, I dip my feet in. The cool water wrapping around my legs relaxes me.

The past two years with Hendrix weren't pointless. We have so many good memories together. Not just from our time together, but even before that. Since our parents are best friends, we were practically raised together. We were born only twenty-four hours and one second apart. When my mom was alive and I asked her if it was planned, she swore up and down that it wasn't.

I can't lie and say that I don't miss him, but a growing part of me has felt at peace since the breakup. I've felt guilty for it because I don't usually say no to people, especially Hendrix. But we all get to a point where we decide we want more, don't we? Even if we seem happy and content. I know there is more out there for me, and I want to find it.

I must have been sitting out here lost in my thoughts for a while, because I see the first hints of the sunrise on the horizon. First, it's subtle and then orange slowly blooms across the sky. Hints of yellow intermix with the orange as the sun continues to rise. I stare in wonder at the picture being painted in front of me. I smile at the sun as a sense of hope warms my body with the sun's rays.

"You've changed since you've been here," Marisa says to me over breakfast one morning.

We've been here for twenty out of the twenty-two days. It's true what they say, time flies when you're having fun.

Quinn smiles at me. "Yes, you're looking very iridescent."

I smile and bite into my mango and juice dribbles onto my hand. I've never eaten this good in my life. The food is all organic and plant-based. It's confirmation that food is indeed a love language. I wipe the juice from my hand.

"Is this an intervention?"

"No, no you just seem more...vibrant here," Marisa reassures me.

"You're more relaxed," Quinn adds.

I shrug. "It's peaceful here. Plus, I feel like I can be myself... enjoy myself and not have to worry about anyone else." I do feel more vibrant and relaxed, but I think our days filled with yoga, meditation, learning, and relaxation contribute to that greatly.

Marisa sips her green juice and continues staring at me. "Have you talked to Hendrix since the breakup?" she asks.

Quinn sucks her teeth. "Please, she ain't worried about that man."

Quinn is always the straight shooter. "He tried to FaceTime me the first night we got here. When I didn't answer, he texted me that he missed me."

"Do you miss him?" Marisa asks.

"Yes and no," I reply honestly. "I miss him, but I also feel relieved to not have to attend practices, events, meetings, and whatever else he does for his career."

"Girl," Quinn scoffs. "You were doing way too much for him. More like a manager than a girlfriend. I know he thinks he's hot shit now after signing that multi-million-dollar contract with the Houston Astros. I'm proud of you for saying no when you knew in your heart he wasn't your forever."

"If he hadn't asked me to marry him," I look away from them, "I think I would still be with him," I admit.

"Sometimes we're forced to make changes," Marisa says.

"What are you?" I ask playfully. "A therapist?"

"I should charge you bitches then," Marisa says.

"We'd be lost without you." Quinn nudges her shoulder with a grin.

I look between the two of them. "I think we'd all be lost without each other."

"Amen to that, sis," they say in unison.

It's our last day before graduation, and we just wrapped up our final session while here. I'm proud of the growth I've experienced in our short time here. The past few weeks haven't been easy, but they have commanded me to bring out a different version of myself. I wipe the sweat off my face with a washcloth when Marisa grabs my arm.

"I want you to meet someone," she says.

"Now?" I ask as I try to tame my unruly curls. She ignores me and pulls me toward a woman with her back to us.

"Now or never." She clears her throat and places her hand on the woman's back. "Celeste, this is my best friend, Harlow. I told you about her a few weeks ago. Harlow, this is my dear friend, Celeste. She owns a yoga studio in LA but is opening up another one in Seattle in a week."

I smile politely although I'm confused as to why I needed to meet her friend when I look a mess.

Celeste extends her hand out to me, "Pleasure to meet you. Have you been to Seattle?"

"Uh..." I side eye Marisa. "No, I haven't. I know my dad's brother lives there but I haven't seen him since I was twelve. Do you like it there?" This conversation is off to an awkward start.

"Let me cut to the chase," Celeste grins. "I've been talking to Marisa, trying to find instructors for my new studio opening next week."

I nod and smile, unsure of where this is going. Maybe Marisa is moving and this is her weird way of telling me.

Celeste continues, "Marisa thinks that you would be a good fit. I pay generously," she gives me a pearly white smile. "You would be teaching a mix of both group classes and private lessons."

"Oh I –" I stare at Marisa with wide eyes. "Why me?" are the only words that come out of my mouth.

"I've seen you grow leaps and bounds in the short time you've been here. I'd love to work alongside you at my new studio in Seattle."

Celeste is a woman about her business. This is a lot to take in. Quinn joins the conversation while I stand, staring at Celeste in stunned silence.

"Honestly, Harls," Quinn says, then takes a sip of her water. "What do you have to lose?"

I look outside at the swaying palm trees. Quinn is right. I don't have anything to lose. My mind races with how I can make this work, even though the thought terrifies me. I would be leaving my dad behind, but it's not like I couldn't visit him. Really, I think the most important piece is finding a place to live in less than a week. I could ask my dad to reach out to my uncle and see if he knows anyone who has a place to rent.

Celeste chimes in, as if reading my mind. "If housing will be a problem for you, please let me know and I would be happy to help."

I get the notion that she can and will make a lot happen for me. "I... would love to work with you." I smile. It's a quick decision, but there isn't anything to think about. Maybe this is how I'll find myself. I'm so comfortable in my familiarity that I've lost myself in it. A change of scenery would be nice.

"Great," Celeste claps her hands together. "We can talk in a few hours after dinner and go over all the details and your start date. I look forward to working with you, Harlow."

I watch her leave. As soon as she's out of sight, Marisa and Quinn squeal and hug me.

"This will be so good for you," Marisa assures me. "Don't overthink it."

"You're going to knock this out of the ballpark, babe," Quinn says and then cringes. "Wait, fuck Hendrix. You're going to make this next chapter of your life the best one yet."

"You two set me up, didn't you?" I pin my arms across my chest, trying to look upset.

Marisa reads right through me. "Oh, please! We know you're excited."

An uncontainable smiles spreads across my face. "I guess I'm moving to Seattle," I say out loud so that it sinks in. "*Holy shit*, I'm moving to Seattle."

I hold up my certificate of completion, grinning when my dad answers my video call.

"I did it!" I squeal while I bounce up and down in my seat with excitement. The past few weeks have been the most fulfilling of my life. "I'm officially a yoga instructor!"

He beams at me with tears in his eyes. "You look so happy, and I am so proud of you!" I'm surprised he woke up to talk to me given the difference in time. But that's my dad. He wouldn't miss an opportunity to ever see me shine.

"Thank you, Dad!" My cheeks hurt from smiling so much. "I'm proud of myself."

"What are you three doing to celebrate your last day in Bali?"

"Exploring, celebrating my new job, and see where the day takes us."

"That's gre –" His brow furrows. "Wait, new job?"

"Dad, I got offered to teach at a yoga studio in Seattle. I took it. I mean, what do I have to lose? And it's not like I can't come visit you. Plus doesn't Uncle West live there?"

It's hard to read his reaction because whatever he initially felt only flitted across his face for a moment.

"Congratulations, kiddo," he says, beaming. "I'm so proud of all that you're doing for yourself. You're right. Uncle West does live in Seattle with his wife, Ava. I assume you'll need a place to stay. When do you have to be there?"

"I do, but Celeste says she could help me if it's difficult to find a place." I cringe. "I have to be there in a week. I know it's short notice, but I don't have much to pack. Having a place to stay is the most important."

"Let me call West and see what he says. I want to make sure you're in a good area."

"You're the best, Dad. I really am so excited to have a fresh start."

"I know, kiddo. I'm excited and happy for you too. Let me let you go so that I can get things in motion with West," he says as he rifles around his desk.

"Alright, Dad. Love you." I grin at him and wave.

"Love you too, and I am so proud of you. By the time you're home tomorrow, I should hopefully have everything sorted out. Enjoy your last day." He smiles and ends the FaceTime call.

Marisa twirls into the room. "Are you ready for our final day in Bali?"

A giggle escapes me. "Yes, you look great." She has her bikini on with a bohemian, macrame-style beach sarong tied around her hips. Quinn appears behind her moments later with a matching sarong in a different color and tosses something my way.

When I catch it I realize it's the same one but in yellow, my favorite color. I smile at her. "Didn't think we'd leave you hangin' did you?" Quinn says with a smirk.

"Never." I grin. "Give me ten minutes to get ready."

After a full day of breathtaking views, delicious food, and amazing conversation, we're walking back to our place as the sun sets.

"Guys, we should get tattoos!" Quinn squeals.

My eyes widen as I look around for what gave her this wild idea. I'm all for living a little, but I'm incredibly indecisive and the thought of picking out a tattoo on the spot gives me anxiety. My eyes land on the little tattoo shop coming into view as the light from the shop spills onto the street. Music becomes louder as we get closer.

"Um, are you sure about this?" I ask wearily. We're only steps away now and Marisa looks as skeptical as I do.

Quinn turns around to face us. "Oh, c'mon guys. It will be a good memory."

"You're tipsier than I thought," Marisa says as she stands firmly next to me.

"Guys, have we not had an amazing time together?" Quinn asks.

When I quiet my anxiety, the thought that this has been the best time I've had in a long time settles in. I nod and so does Marisa.

"Okay, so why not commemorate it with a small little tattoo?" Quinn asks hopefully with her brows raised.

She has a point. It would be nice to have something with—well, on—me, that always reminds me of how free I felt here. To remind me that what I desire matters.

"I'm down," I say.

Marisa's eyes snap to mine, and she smiles when she sees my resolve. "Let's do this!" she replies.

Minutes later, I chew my thumbnail as I flip through the book of possible tattoo options. Midway through the book, my eyes land on a simple yet beautiful butterfly tattoo.

"I want this one," I say without hesitation.

Quinn and Marisa stop flipping through their books and come to see what I'm looking at.

"That's cute!" Quinn exclaims.

"Let's get that!" Marisa adds.

I look at both of them, shocked that they're letting me choose what they want tattooed on their body. "You guys can get whatever you want I just –"

"It's cute, Harlow, and it works for our trio perfectly," Marisa reassures me as she beams with excitement glittering in her eyes. "I feel all three of us are constantly changing, growing, and leveling up. Like a butterfly. I'm proud of us."

I smile at them because I don't know what we would have done without one another.

"Are we getting it somewhere inconspicuous?" Quinn asks.

"I was thinking my hip..." I say.

"Oooh, sexy!" Marisa says while winking at us. It makes me laugh and relax a bit. "So a butterfly on our hips?"

"I'm down for whatever," Quinn says with a smirk.

Not long after our agreement, I sit in the tattoo chair. I'm nervous, but it's an excited nervous. I haven't made a spur of the moment decision since I stopped traveling two years ago. The tattoo artist places the stencil on my skin. No backing out now.

"Ready?" she asks with a smile.

"As I'll ever be." I say, nervously.

Seconds later, the first prick of the gun connects with my skin. It isn't comfortable, but it isn't excruciating pain like I anticipated it being. It's... exhilarating. I don't see myself covered in ink anytime soon, but I can easily see why people get addicted. It doesn't take her long to finish, and I grin at myself in the mirror when she's done. It's perfect.

Bali has been healing for my heart. I've been able to find myself again. Fall in love with myself again. I'm ready for the next chapter of my life. This tattoo is a representation of all that I hope and dream. A representation of my journey for *more*.

4

Harlow

As soon as I arrive home from Bali, I begin packing my things for Seattle. My uncle and aunt have a guest house that they're generously letting me rent. Now all I have to do is pack.

I rummage around my room, realizing I have more clothes and clutter then I anticipated. The overwhelming load of all I have to do before I move to Seattle creeps in. I'm doing my best to keep all the anxious thoughts out of my head. But then I pull Hendrix's sweater from the pile. It's the one he had on the last time he was here.

My shoulders sag as I hold it and rub the buttery soft fabric between my fingers. It's his favorite one. I bring it to my nose, inhale, and close my eyes. The comforting, musky scents of cedarwood and sandalwood greet me. A sadness settles in my chest. I stare at the sweater, wondering if we'll talk again or if the last time I saw him was truly the last time.

I don't have much time to be in my feelings because my dad interrupts my thoughts.

"Are you ready?" he asks as he settles on the edge of my bed.

"Yep," I grin, "I only have a few boxes to pack and then they can be sent."

"Ol' Blue gets picked up tomorrow and will be there soon after you arrive," my dad says.

Ol' Blue is my baby blue 1971 Ford Bronco that my dad and I restored together my senior year. She means the absolute world to me, and I treat her like she's my baby.

"I can't wait to take her to all those amazing trails in Washington." I grin. I've been looking obsessively at things to do near Seattle and there is a plethora of outdoor activities. I'm looking forward to exploring.

"You'll have no problem getting around with her." He looks around my room. "It's going to be weird," he bows his head, looking at his hands, "with you being gone. I know you were gone for a year but that was different." He looks at me and lets out a sigh as his shoulders sag. "I knew then that you were coming back every so often. But now, you're moving. This is all I've hoped for you, but I'm sure going to miss you, kiddo."

I get up and wrap him in a tight hug. "I'm moving, but nothing can keep me away from you. I know it's hard because it's just us." I told myself I wasn't going to cry until we were at the airport but it's too late for that now. "I love you, Dad. This isn't goodbye. I'll be back once I get settled in there. I promise."

"I know you will." He hugs me back.

-&-

My feet are propped on the dashboard of my dad's car as we make our way the airport. I scroll through my phone while he's on a call with his office. He had to take the day off work so that he could drop me off. Marisa offered, but my dad wasn't going to let anyone else take me to the airport. Over the past two weeks, he and I have spent a lot of quality time together. I haven't spent time like that with him in years, and it felt good to be in each other's company.

I decide to post to my Instagram with my Dr. Marten's on the dashboard and a caption that says, "Seattle bound." I've never posted as much as Hendrix does, but people still follow me because I *was* his girlfriend. It feels weird for me to think of us in a past tense. I haven't heard from him since the text, and I haven't tried to reach out to him either.

My phone lights up with notifications, and I check the picture I just posted. It's already received hundreds of likes. Part of the reason I stopped posting is because I felt weird about the "insta-fame" that I had from being Hendrix's girlfriend. Celeste asked me if I had any social media accounts and if I would be willing to use them to promote the studio. She looked like she'd struck gold when I showed her that my account had almost a million followers. I left out the part that it was thanks to my ex-boyfriend who is a rising pro-athlete. Speak of the devil; my heart stops when I see Hendrix has liked my post. I have to remind myself to breathe when I see him share it to his story.

I drop my phone into my bag as if it's on fire and decide not to read too much into it. I must admit that when I posted, a small part of me hoped that he would see it. Okay, a large part of me. But that all fades away when the signs to the airport become visible. We're almost there. The excitement makes me feel like my body is vibrating. I can't believe that I'm leaving Texas.

Once in the airport and checked in, my dad walks me as far as security and then embraces me.

"I'm going to miss you so much, Harlow." His voice cracks. "Know that all your mother and I ever want for you is to be happy. I'm always here if you ever need anything, even if I'm not living there."

I cling to him and tears well in my eyes. "Thank you. For everything. I'll be back to see you before you know it."

"I hope so, kiddo. I love you. Call me when you land, and give West and Ava a hug for me," he says with tears in his eyes as he releases me.

"I will, Dad. I love you." I give him one last hug and then walk towards security. I glance over my shoulder at him as he waves, and I wave back. I turn quickly back around as the tears start to fall. I may have traveled, but there's a different feeling when you know you're traveling to a new place to call home. I'm leaving behind my entire life in the hopes that I can create a new one. Even though sadness grips me right now, I know that I'm making the best choice for myself. I hold onto the excitement that hasn't left me for the past week and look forward to new beginnings.

⁂

As I approach the baggage claim, my stomach is in knots. I haven't seen my Uncle West since I was twelve. His wife Ava and I have talked on the phone a few times over the past week to ensure that everything goes as smoothly as possible. I'm looking forward to getting to know her more. Once I'm closer to baggage claim, I see two people holding a sign that says, "Welcome to Seattle, Harlow Shaw." My face lights up as I see the man and woman holding it.

My uncle resembles my dad except that his eyes are a lighter brown, and his hair is more... trendy. He has faded sides and corn rows up top, which are pulled into a man bun. I wasn't expecting this, but my dad did say that his brother was a "free spirit." His wife looks like she just left her glam team because she is perfect from head to toe. There's not a curl out of place on her head, and her outfit is immaculate.

She waves and bounces up and down when she sees me. I beam at them both, and all the uneasiness I felt melts away. Once I reach them, they embrace me in a hug.

"Welcome to Seattle!" Ava says enthusiastically.

"How was your flight?" West asks.

"It was great. It all went well. Thank you so much for having me."

Ava waves her hand in the air. "Don't mention it, it was the least we could do. When West told me that you wanted to come live in Seattle, I couldn't say no. When I started the renovations on the guest house a few months ago, he told me I was crazy, but I just had a feeling we would need it soon. And here you come!"

West looks at Ava like she's the most beautiful and rare creature in the world. "Ava will make you feel right at home, Harlow," he says, beaming at her. They're so in love. It's beautiful to see. He turns his attention to me. "You know, you look just like Evie."

I smile. "I get that a lot actually. Thank you. It's always nice to hear."

"You'll have to show me pictures of your mama, Harlow." Ava smiles at me and intertwines her arm in mine as she steers us closer to the baggage carousel. She has a southern twang to her voice that's more apparent with some words then others.

"Are you from Seattle?" I ask her.

Splaying a hand across her chest, Ava gives me a surprised look. "Me? Oh, no honey, I'm from Tennessee. I moved out here for West," she says as she looks back at him and winks. "I've lived here for ten years, but the accent will be with me for the rest of my life." Turning her attention to West, she grins. "Let West know which bag is yours, and he can do all the heavy lifting while we sit back and look pretty."

Ava is captivating. She has a head full of golden-brown curls that cascade down her back. Gold bangles wrap around both her wrists, offsetting her rich copper skin. Her honey-colored eyes are wide and warm, immediately making me feel welcome. I've only been around her for a few minutes, and I can already see why West married her.

I slide into the backseat of West's car, and Ava turns around as she buckles her seatbelt. "You'll have to let me know what you think of your apartment. If you want to change anything, let me know."

"I doubt I will. It looks perfect in the pictures you sent me."

"And we have a personal chef," Ava says.

I try to hide the shock on my face, but she picks up on it.

"West and I have done well for ourselves." She grins. "But the chef can make anything you want if you just let him know what you like."

"That sounds amazing." My mouth starts to water as I build a menu in my head.

I haven't stopped grinning since I got off the plane. It feels so good to finally be here in Seattle. I trust that whatever Ava has done to the place will be far better than what I could imagine. While Ava and West talk, I send a text to my dad.

Harlow: Made it safe and sound. Ava and West are amazing. I'll call you when I'm settled in.

He responds a few minutes later.

Dad: Miss you already, kiddo! Can't wait to hear your voice.

Ava wasn't kidding when they said they had done well for themselves. As I step out of the car, I take in the views of their house. It is magnificent and stark white with a sprawling, lush green lawn. A forest surrounds their entire home, and I can't wait to see the backyard because I bet it's gorgeous, too. On the drive here, Ava told me that she owns an interior design company, and that West owns two coffee shops with a third location opening in the next few weeks. He also owns a marijuana dispensary. I now understand what my dad meant by free spirit.

We get inside and the look of awe hasn't left my face.

Ava smiles at me. "I love what I do."

"Love in an understatement. This is art," I say.

Taking my arm, she guides me through the house to give me a tour. Modern yet cozy, there are windows everywhere, letting in lots of natural light. We step into the living room furnished with large plush couches, a fireplace, a bookcase, and a TV. The living room seems like the place they spend most of their time, since it's the one area that looks lived in. Everything else is pretty much immaculate, like Ava. I hope she doesn't think I'm a slob with my organized chaos. I can't help but ask her.

"Do you clean all of this yourself?"

"Goodness, no! If there is someone that can do something for me, I will hire them." She grins. "Why stress about something when I don't have to?" She shrugs. I can't argue with her because if I could hire someone to do stuff for me that I didn't want to, I would.

She continues. "It's big, but hopefully one day West and I can have a few kids of our own." Ava doesn't look at me as she says this. I sense the sadness in her tone, but I don't pry because if she wanted to tell me, she would. I'm sure she and West will be amazing parents when the time comes.

We finish the rest of the tour and step out into the backyard. I was right. The backyard is fabulous. There's a pool, a jacuzzi, and a small courtyard with a firepit and a garden off to the side. I'm grateful that summer is right around the corner because I can't wait to spend my days out here. I was worried that I'd miss being near the ocean, but I think I can get use to the lushness of the Pacific Northwest. As we move through the backyard, I see a small little cottage with lights on, and it takes everything in me not to skip down the path towards it.

As we near it, Ava looks over her shoulder at me. "This is your home. Of course, you're always welcome to come in the house and hang out with me and West, but this also has everything you need."

I'm speechless as I step inside. The living room is light and cozy, much like the interior of the main house, with cream-colored walls and harlequin-painted hardwood floors. A whimsical, antique chandelier hangs from the ceiling over a plush oversized white sofa that looks ready for me to sink into with a good book.

"Is there anything you'd like to change?" Ava asks me.

I look at her like she's crazy. "Ava, what could I possibly change about this? You must not know that I'm coming from my childhood bedroom to a guest house. I'm over the moon happy right now."

"Great!" She smiles. "I had hoped you'd love it."

We make our way into the kitchen, which is all white with black and white marble countertops. I can't wait to cook my first meal here. There's also a small dining space that will be nice to host people when they visit. I think of Marisa, Quinn, and my dad. Hopefully, I make new friends here, but I try not to get ahead of myself.

The loft above the living room is a yoga space Ava designed just for me. I am overwhelmed with gratitude, and I hug her. She made this space specifically with me in mind. "This is perfect, Ava."

Hugging me back, she says, "We're family. I know this isn't Texas, but I sure hope it feels like home."

It does feel like home. I miss my dad, but my heart knows that this is now home. She shows me the bedroom last, which has a blue accent wall behind the white, plush bed. Mirrors sit on both sides of the bed, and there's even a little nook with a vanity where I can do my hair and makeup. Everything is perfect. I'm not sure how to thank West and Ava for even allowing me to stay here. I'm pretty sure if they rented this space out to someone else, they could get a lot of money for it. Then again, money doesn't seem to be a problem for them.

Ava clasps her hands together. "Okay, I'm going to leave you to it. West already set your bags in your room and the boxes that were sent are in the living room. If you need anything at all, let us know."

"Thank you," is all I can muster to say.

Ava turns to leave and then she stops. "Oh, West and I usually have breakfast at seven-thirty. Text me some foods you like, and we can be sure to have them for you," she says with a smile.

Once the door closes behind her, I sigh and look around. I let out a squeal because I cannot believe that this is real life right now. I've been running on exhilaration and adrenaline all day. Now that I'm finally here, I want to relax. I dig through my suitcase and pull out Hendrix's sweater because it's comfortable... and I miss him. I kick off my boots and strip down to my panties and slip it on. I find some socks and put those on too. It's a little bit cooler here, but Ava said the weather will warm up soon.

I flop down on my bed and put some Sabrina Claudio on the Bluetooth speaker. I considered doing a tour of my new place for Instagram, but I figure it will look better in the morning with the light filtering through all the windows. Instead, I post a picture of myself in the mirror sitting cross legged on the floor smiling with the caption that says, "Home" and put my location in Seattle, WA. I silence my IG notifications because I don't really want to chat with anyone. I toss my

phone on the end of the bed and go rummage through the fridge. Ava
has it fully stocked. I've never met a person who is as prepared as she is.

I grab a bottle of water, some grapes, and cheese. Sitting back down on
my bed, I consider calling my dad. My phone chimes, and I expect to see
my dad's name but instead, it's Hendrix.

5

Harlow

My HEART RACES, AND my palms feel clammy. It's been weeks since he last texted me.

Hendrix: *How's Seattle?*

I stare at my screen, annoyed with myself that I'm so happy to finally get a text from him. He must be staring at his screen, too, and sees that I read his text because he sends another one.

Hendrix: *I would have texted you sooner, but I was trying to give you space.*

Chewing on my thumbnail, I try to decide what to say. Instead, I press the camera button to call him over video chat. He picks up almost immediately. At first, all I can see are his inky black curls and then he centers the camera on his face. I smile like a fool as soon as he appears.

"Fuck, I've missed your face," he says. "Harlow Shaw up and moved all the way to fucking Seattle."

I tell my face to stop smiling, but it won't listen to me. Unfortunately, he's still one of my favorite people on the planet, and the past couple of months without him haven't been easy. "I did," I say.

He chuckles and my heart constricts. I've missed that sound. "You look so happy. Do you have your own place? I ran into your dad when I visited my parents and he didn't say much... just that you're happy."

I get off my bed and flip my camera around and slowly turn so he can see my room. "I am. I officially have my own place. Well, it's on my Uncle West's property but... it's mine." I go out to the kitchen and living area to show him those spaces, too. "West and Ava are... perfect." I flip the camera back around so it's on my face and sink into the plush cushions of the couch.

"That's amazing, baby. I'm so happy for you. When do you start your new job?"

"In a couple of days. Celeste wanted to give me time to get settled in. How's spring training?"

He yawns. "Tiring, but you know baseball has always been my first love." A grin tugs at his lips.

I nod, knowing all too well. "Can I ask you something?"

"Anything," he says with his eyes trained on me.

"Why did you propose?"

It's a question that has been on my mind since the night it happened. We had talked about eventually getting married and starting a family. That was after we first started dating, but we hadn't talked about it since. The proposal felt like a rushed decision on his part.

He lets out a sigh as his jaw flexes. "You're going to think it's childish." His eyes are focused somewhere else as he tries not to look at me.

"Try me." I shrug and smile, despite the unsettling feeling in my stomach.

"Alright." He sits up on his bed and he finally looks into the camera. "After I signed with the Astros, and I asked you to come with me to Palm Beach for spring training, you said no."

This isn't what I expected. Right after he signed, he asked me to go stay with him for spring training and then move in with him. I didn't directly say no, but I did say that I'd think about it. An *I'll think about it* to Hendrix Moore equates to saying no to him because he doesn't instantly get what he wants.

"Wait." I cradle my face in my hands. "You proposed because I told you I'd think about it?" I furrow my brows. "Not because of love?"

I've been thinking our breakup was all my fault when he's clearly as guilty as I am. I admitted to Quinn and Marisa that I would still be with him if he hadn't proposed. I guess Marisa was right. Sometimes we're forced to make changes.

"Harls, babe, listen... please." He rakes his fingers through his curls. "I noticed that you pulled away from me after I signed."

He became a different person after he signed. Hendrix has always led a charmed life. His parents made sure that he got everything he wanted. After he signed his multi-million-dollar contract with the Astros, his sense of entitlement was suddenly on steroids.

He looks at me. "I felt like I was losing you and I thought the proposal would help us. I can count on one hand the times you've said no. Look, I know this sounds awful, and I know I fucked up by proposing, but I thought if you said yes that –"

"Let me get this straight," I interrupt him. "You didn't propose because of love?"

He bows his head as his shoulders sag. "Harls, I know I fucked up."

He's still avoiding my question. That's all the answer I need.

"I thought I was crazy for feeling the way that I felt. As if saying no to you was a major fuck up... but it turns out it was the right thing. You're not ready to be married or settle down with me either."

"But... I love you, Harls."

"You can love me, but that doesn't mean that we're meant to be together, Hendrix."

"Is it so bad that I want you in my life?"

I scoff. "It is when you try to force me to do it on your terms."

Silence falls between us. I feel his eyes on me.

"I'm sorry... I really am," he says and then lets out a sigh. "Is there any possibility..." He rakes his hands through his hair again. "That we can still be friends and then maybe see where that takes us?" he asks with a grin.

"Friends," I scoff. "Do you really think we can be friends?"

"We've been friends our whole lives. Why not?" he asks.

"Yeah, that was before... I don't think we can be just friends." I don't see us going back to where we were before we got together.

"Tell me this," he says. "Would you consider getting back with me?"

My heart rate quickens. I've thought about this countless times. Getting back together with him would be easy. Too easy. I look away from him.

"No, not right now." I'm unsure if my answer will ever change, but I'm also unsure if I'm ready for him to not be in my life. Even if it is just as a friend.

"I just royally fucked this up... *us* up," he says with regret in his tone.

I don't say anything for a few beats as he looks at me expectantly. "We both did," I shrug. "I don't mind trying to be friends. I stress *trying*. I can't promise that it will take us back to where we were or even somewhere new. I will admit now that me agreeing to be friends is for purely selfish reasons. I've missed you."

Letting go is a lot harder than it seems.

"I'm okay with that. I really did try to give you space, but then you posted that picture of you in my sweater, and I said fuck space."

I can't help but smile. "Funny how you get space and then don't want it."

He smiles. "You mean you haven't found a boyfriend yet?"

I scoff. "Oh yeah, I have three boyfriends now. I bounced right back." I roll my eyes with a grin on my face. "In all seriousness, I'm going to focus on getting settled here and not worry about relationships for a while. Any new girls for you?"

"Fuck no," he answers abruptly. "It's only you. Even though we aren't together. I only see myself with you."

Looking away from the camera, I pick at my sock. "If you find some pretty girl to change your life, don't stop on my account."

"Nah, I'm looking at her right now. Plus, I don't have time, nor do I care to chase after girls right now. My only focus is baseball... and you. As it's always been," he says seriously.

So much for a clean break up.

"What are the odds of me getting that sweater back?" he asks with a piqued eyebrow and a grin.

"Never," I reply, hugging it to my body.

Nodding with a smile, he says, "That's fair enough."

Hendrix and I talk for hours. It's as though we didn't break up at all, and it comforts yet terrifies me at the same time. Neither of us are making it easy to move on from the other. I wonder if there will ever be a point where we feel like we can live without the other. Right now, I feel as though we may never reach that point. Instead of degrading myself for still loving and wanting him in my life, I accept that this is where I am. And things can change at any given moment.

Sitting outside wrapped up in anxiety and a blanket, I sip my latte. It's six a.m., and today will be my first day adulting at my job. I have a private yoga session at nine a.m., and of course, I couldn't sleep because I thought of everything that could possibly go wrong. When I did fall asleep, I dreamt that I was late. Celeste assured me that everything will go smoothly and that I'm an amazing teacher. Yesterday, she had me guide her through a session, and she said I did amazing. I'll take her word for it because Celeste doesn't seem like someone who says things just to be nice. She says them because she means them.

After finishing my latte and aimlessly scrolling through social media for an hour, I decide to join West and Ava for breakfast. I haven't felt out of place since I've been here. They do everything they can to make me feel comfortable. I'm not the most talkative person, but Ava could strike up a conversation with a tree if she wanted to.

"Good morning," she says in a sing-song tone as I enter the kitchen.

"Morning."

"West had to leave early this morning to oversee some last-minute things at the new shop, so it's just us girls this morning." She smiles and sits down next to me at the kitchen island.

"Is the new shop far from here?" I ask as I grab a chocolate croissant from the tray in front of me.

"It's downtown. About a thirty-minute drive from us if traffic isn't terrible." She takes a sip of her coffee. "Are you ready for today?"

I sigh and put my croissant down on my plate. Suddenly I'm not hungry anymore. "I guess I am." I shrug. "I've thought of everything that could possibly go wrong."

"Now you've got to think of everything that could possibly go right," she quips and winks at me.

I blink at her, not even considering that anything could go right. "I suppose I could." I smile.

"Believe in yourself, babe! You are exactly where you need to be. You wouldn't be sitting here with me right now if you weren't." She gets up and puts her dishes in the sink.

Ava's right. I do spend a lot of time doubting myself and thinking about how there are people more deserving than I am. If I'm going to be teaching others though, I need to find some confidence.

"I saw your Instagram, by the way," she adds as she looks through her phone. "Did you take photography classes in high school or something?"

"No, why?"

"You have an eye for it. Your feed is gorgeous. I also saw all the pictures you put up in the apartment." She glances up from her phone. "Maybe you should take some classes," she suggests.

I study her. "Did my dad put you up to this?" I ask suspiciously.

Ava cackles. "No," she says, putting her hands up in front of her. "I promise he didn't. This is my suggestion."

"I never thought of it, to be completely honest. I just like to take pictures of things."

Even before Hendrix and I were a thing, I had a large following due to my travels and random posts of myself. I'm not an influencer by any means, but I do enjoy being able to share my pictures with others. But photography classes have never crossed my mind.

"Think about it. I've got to go. Remember, you've got this, and you deserve to be here." Giving my arm a reassuring squeeze, Ava smiles at me, and then grabs her bag as she heads out the door.

Glancing at my watch, I decide to head to the studio early so I can do a warmup flow by myself before my client arrives. I dig deep to find my confidence because Ava is right, I do deserve to be here.

I arrive at the studio an hour early and warm up. It isn't very far from my place. I still smile every time I say or think "my place." It feels good to be on my own.

Sitting at the front desk, I check my phone because the woman who is supposed to be here for the private session is running ten minutes late. Glancing up from my phone, I see a black Tesla SUV zip into the parking lot. Seconds later, a woman frantically gets out and comes running for the doors. I'm worried she may slam into them at the speed she's moving.

When she crashes into them head-on, she drops her bag, and I hear her scream, "Fuck!"

I decide to help her because she looks like she's had a hell of a morning. Jogging over to the door, I open it for her. As she finishes gathering the contents spilled from her bag, she blows her bangs out of her face with a huff and gives me an apologetic smile.

"Hi, I'm Sevyn. Sorry I'm late!" She extends her hand out to me.

I shake it with a smile. "Welcome, I'm Harlow."

"My twins thought it would be hilarious to hide my keys this morning. Then once I found my keys, they had hidden my purse and it... it really was just a mess," she admits, covering her face. "I understand if you don't have time to squeeze me in," she says in a rush.

All I can do is smile at her authenticity. Most people wouldn't admit to having a shit morning. They would pretend that everything is fine. "We have time. Don't worry about it."

"Really?"

"I'm positive. Plus, you look like you could use some relaxation."

She scoffs. "You have no idea."

My session with Sevyn goes perfectly, and afterwards we end up talking for a while and she tells me about her twins who are only two and a half. They sound like they keep her busy, but I can tell that they're her whole entire world. I tried to offer to babysit, but she told me she wouldn't bring that hell into my life. When she learned I'm new to Seattle, she insisted we exchange numbers so she could show me around. I've only known Sevyn a couple of hours, but I feel like she's an old friend and I can't wait to spend more time with her.

6

Harlow

"HOW ARE THINGS GOING, kiddo?" my dad asks as we video chat.

I shrug and sigh. "They're okay. I miss you, but I guess I'm settling in alright."

"You haven't even been there a month yet. It will take some getting used to." He reassures me with an encouraging smile.

"I have no friends here, Dad. Don't get me wrong, Ava and West have made me feel welcome, but it's not like we can hang out and be besties."

He chuckles. "You have to leave the house to make friends. Have you done that?"

I roll my eyes and grin. "No, I'm too –"

"Too stubborn to venture outside your comfort zone?"

"No, I just..." I try to come up with an excuse and can't think of one. "Fine, I guess you're right. But, in my defense, I've been going through a lot of changes lately."

He nods. "You have, and I'm proud of you. But you're going to have to push yourself to make friends. Work and home is a boring life to live."

"Oh, so I'm boring now?" I quirk an eyebrow.

"You know what I mean, Kiddo."

"I do," I chuckle. "I'll get out there eventually."

My dad's phone chimes. "Will's here to pick me up for golf. We'll catch up later?"

I smile. "Yeah, Dad. Love you. Have fun golfing."

"Love you, kiddo." He ends the call.

"Wow, my dad has more of life then I do," I mutter to myself.

He's right, as much as I hate to admit it. I haven't been here long, but not having friends here makes me homesick. I didn't realize how much time I spent with Marisa and Quinn until now. I'm not even sure where to go to make friends here. Do I even know how to make friends?

My phone chimes with a text, and I'm shocked to see Kyrell's name pop up on my screen. I met Kyrell in sixth grade, shortly after I lost my mom, when he became friends with Hendrix. He is just as close to me as he is to him because, before I met Marisa and Quinn, I was always with Hendrix and Kyrell.

Kyrell: *Hey Harls, I'm in Seattle for some business. Do you wanna link up?*

I haven't seen Kyrell in almost a year. He moved out to California shortly after he and Hendrix got back from Louisiana State University. He visited Texas frequently after he first moved and then he stopped. From what Hendrix has told me and from what I see on his social media, he's doing well for himself. He's working on opening his own dispensary.

Harlow: *I'd love to! Let me know when and I'll be there*.
Kyrell: *I'm a gentleman. I'll pick you up! Text me the address.*
Harlow: *Sure you are! What time will you be here?*

I text him the address, and he promptly texts me back.

Kyrell: 7 because I gotta make myself look presentable. Can't have you outshine me.

I leap off my bed. I'm excited to hang out with Kyrell because he knows how to have a good time. Maybe he'll be able to help me get over this homesick feeling that has had a grip on me the past few days.

⟨⟨✦⟩⟩

He arrives at exactly 7p.m. looking handsome as always in a simple white t-shirt, skinny jeans, and some Yeezys on his feet. He's got flowers in his hand and a smile on his face as he hugs me and hands me the flowers.

"Why the hell did you bring me flowers?" I ask with a raised eyebrow and a smile as I let him in.

"Why not? You're a girl. Don't you like flowers?" He enters and looks around my apartment, inspecting it.

I make my way to the kitchen to look for a vase while he settles on flipping through my record collection.

"That's presumptuous of you to think I like flowers just because I'm a girl."

Grinning, he asks, "Do you like them?"

"I love them," I admit as I set the vase now filled with roses on the center of my table.

"Then accept them as a gift and nothing more. Plus, I haven't seen you in a while," he says and looks at my pictures on the wall. "You know you're pretty good with the camera."

I grin as I go to my room to find my shoes. "You're the second person to say that this week. It's just something I enjoy. Nothing serious." I shrug as I slip some flats on.

"It could be." His eyes roam over me. "You look great, by the way."

"Thank you."

"I was serious about what I said all those years ago. I'm willing to get caught in an entanglement situation with you, whenever you're ready." He winks.

"Shut the hell up, Kyrell." I shove his arm.

Kyrell loves to joke with me. After Hendrix and I got together, he told me the exact same thing, after I tried to convince Hendrix that Kyrell wasn't attracted to me. He had to make it known that he was in fact attracted to me. A fight broke out between them over the comment.

He grins at me. "You do look great, though. Are you ready?"

I smile at his compliment and glance in the mirror. My kinky coils are pulled up into a half top knot bun, and I'm wearing a tight white, long sleeve crop top, with high-waisted skinny jeans and flats. I would wear heels, but I have no clue what Kyrell will get us into tonight, so I felt flats were the safest option.

"Yeah, I'm ready. Where are we going anyway?"

He shrugs, putting his arm out for me to hold. "No clue, but the night is young."

⋆⋅☆⋅⋆

Kyrell takes me to a gorgeous rooftop bar that overlooks Elliot Bay downtown.

"It's gorgeous here." I say. "Views like this make it hard for me to miss Texas."

"You miss that place?" he asks, wrinkling his nose.

I shrug. "It's where I was born and raised... hard not to miss it."

"Do you miss Texas, or do you miss Hendrix?"

"Both," I reply without hesitation. He doesn't say anything so I continue on. "I feel guilty for leaving my dad. I miss Quinn and Marisa. Weekly video chats aren't the same as spending physical time with them. And Hendrix... he annoys the hell out of me. He's arrogant and selfish, but for some stupid reason I'm still in love with him. I miss the familiarity of him. I'm just... homesick. I don't know. Maybe moving out here wasn't a good idea."

Kyrell rests his forearms on the table, leaning toward me. "Aren't you curious as to how your life will turn out here? It would be easy to go back home, back to him... back to all you've ever known. Sometimes comfort is what kills us. You said you wanted more, right? Maybe this move is your more. Stop doubting yourself."

"I do want more, but after the breakup, everything seemed at an all-time low for a few weeks. Then I went to Bali, got offered a new job, and then moved here. It was a series of highs. I was distracted from anything but the good. But now, I'm here alone, and I'm not sure I want to be alone."

"So... face your shit."

My eyes snap to his. "Excuse me?"

"Face your shit. You can't run from good thing to good thing, hoping it will erase the bad shit that happened. It happened. You're sitting at this table with me *because* it happened. Why would you want to go back to it?"

I let out a puff of air. "Damnit... you're right." I want to argue with him but there isn't anything I can say in protest. Going back home would be easy. "I guess I need to focus on my life here instead of focusing on what used to be."

"Exactly!" he exclaims. "Let yourself enjoy life here, and more importantly, let yourself enjoy the night with me."

"I can drink to that," I say as I raise my glass in the air to meet his.

⁂

After a fun night out with Kyrell that included eating, drinking, dancing, and sharing some joints, he drops me off at 2a.m. I'm surprised to see that the lights in the main house are still on. I know West and Ava stay up late, but this is late for them. I'd planned to make a trip through the kitchen to grab some snacks and food, but now I'm contemplating whether I should. I don't know what they're doing up this late, and I'm not sure that I want to know.

My stomach grumbles, and I decide that I better go through the kitchen after all. I open the door and tip-toe through the house, and as I near the kitchen, I hear them arguing in the living room.

"You can't take on more right now. I'm not willing to risk it," West says with a finality in his tone.

Ava scoffs. "Then tell me, what the hell are you going to do? You have no one to help you at the coffee shop now that Jewel decided she wanted to run off with her boyfriend."

"I'll figure it out!"

"How, please tell me how will you figure it out?" Ava demands. "I already see you so little now, and that stresses me out just as much as helping out as the coffee shop would. If you're working there, the other two locations, and the dispensary, please tell me when the hell am I going to see you?"

"Ava," West says with regret in his tone. "I know. I'm sorry. I just don't see how else this will work out if we're going to open on time."

I sneeze. I tried like hell to hold it in, but it escapes me. Their heads snap in my direction, and I look back at them like a deer in headlights.

I chuckle nervously. "Hi." I wave.

Ava smiles at me as if they weren't just in the middle of an argument. "Hey, girl! You look like you had fun." She smiles.

I know that I look a mess. I spilled a drink on myself and I'm wearing Kyrell's shirt that's too big for me. My eyeliner is smudged, and my hair is poofy from sweating on the dance floor. But, I did have a lot of fun.

"I did. Thanks," I say sheepishly. "Sorry to interrupt. I was just going to grab some snacks and get out of your way."

"No need to apologize," West assures me with a smile. "I get the muchies, too."

I cover my mouth and let out a snort. "Is it that obvious? Oh God, please don't tell my dad!"

"Yeah, it's very obvious," they say together.

"Your secret is safe with me, but your dad does know I own a dispensary. He pretends that I don't but..." West shrugs. "Maybe one day he'll learn to loosen his collar a bit."

I scoff. "Good luck with that! You guys aren't usually up this late," I say as I make my way to the kitchen to grab my snacks.

"West and I ran into a snag with the new coffee shop," Ava says as she plops onto the couch.

"I know, I heard," I say as I take a bite of a cupcake. Then my eyes widen. "Not that I was eavesdropping, I just –"

West puts up his hand with a smile. "Chill, Harlow, you're fine."

I swallow the piece of chocolate cupcake. "You know." I lick the frosting off my finger. "I could help."

"No, no. You need to focus on yourself right now," Ava interjects.

"Oh please, it's the least I could do. That way you and West can spend more time together." I look at them, hoping I haven't crossed the line.

"Ava's pregnant," West blurts out.

I blink and stare between Ava and West, not sure what to say. When she mentioned kids a few weeks ago, there was a sense of longing and sadness in her voice. I can only assume that they just found out.

Ava beams. "We just found out today. I wasn't feeling well and..." She shrugs. "Well anyway, I'm not that far along, and this is a dream come true for us both because it's been hard to conceive but... West is right, I really don't need the added stress right now."

"Then let me help. I mean, I don't know how to make coffee, but I'm capable of learning," I assure them.

"Are you sure?" West asks.

"I wouldn't offer if I wasn't," I say with a smile.

West's shoulders fall, and it looks like a huge weight has been lifted off his shoulders. "You are a lifesaver, Harlow. I need to step back and focus on Ava, but it's hard to do that when my employees decide to run off to Vegas with a biker named Big Joe."

I cackle. "Big Joe?"

West shakes his head. "I know, I know, but she's gone now. Anyway, if you want to help, I would appreciate it. It would only be temporary until I can find someone. Of course, I'll pay you, but I'm just so relieved that this worked out."

Ava gets up and hugs me. "Thank you. You have no idea how big of a help this is for us."

I hug her back. "No problem, guys." She releases me from the hug, and I pick up all my snacks. "I'm going to let you two be. Good night!"

"Thanks again, Harlow," West says as I walk out the door.

I wave a hand to let him know I heard and make my way to my apartment.

When I get inside, I collapse on my couch and open a bag of Cheetos. I pull out my phone and see that Kyrell has tagged me in some pictures. As I scroll through them, I see a steady progression of our night unfolding. The last one is of a shirtless Kyrell and me in his shirt with the caption: *wild night with the best*. I smile because Kyrell expects nothing from me other than to be myself. I believe that's why we always have a good time together.

He asked me about Hendrix tonight, and I told him everything. His reply to it all was that I deserve to be 100 percent happy, whether that's with or without him, and to not hold myself back for his sake. Kyrell knows how Hendrix can be and admitted to it being part of the reason they aren't as close as they once were. Of course, when Hendrix saw that Kyrell and I were together, he texted Kyrell multiple times. Kyrell decided to ignore him. It wasn't even about making him jealous. It was more of a celebration of us no longer being in his shadow.

7

Harlow

TALKING WITH SEVYN AFTER class, I glance at my watch and mumble, "Shit."

She gives me a puzzled look and asks, "Are you okay?"

"Yes, I'm going to be late to my other job though!" I roll up my mat.

"You have another job?" she asks.

"Yeah, I help my uncle out at his coffee shop part-time."

Sevyn groans. "I would love a coffee right now. Would you mind if I stop by later? The kids will be spending the weekend with Zane's parents." She tosses her head back dramatically and puts her hand over her heart. "Thank God!"

"You have the weekend alone with Zane and you want to come see me at a coffee shop?"

"Of course! Besides, Zane won't be home until later this evening, and he made plans for us. Until then, I'm free to do as I please. What's the name of the shop you work at?"

"Holy Shot, it's downtown."

"Oh, I know where that is! It just opened, didn't it?"

"It did. Just last week. It's worth stopping in. The vibe is warm and cozy," I mention as I get ready to head into the showers.

"Alright, I'll let you get ready and then see you in a few hours!" She slings her mat over her shoulder and waves.

The coffee shop has only been open for two weeks, and it's already insanely busy. I quickly understood why West and Ava needed help. His coffee houses are not only known for their coffee, but the entertainment they bring. Each evening, they have local artists come and perform music, comedy, poetry, or plays. It really is hard for me to call it a job when I enjoy it so much. I didn't think I would ever be a barista, but it turns out I'm a damn good one.

The afternoon lunch rush just died down, and I'm wiping down tables. Who knew that there would be a lunch rush for coffee? One thing that I've learned since starting here is that people fucking love their coffee. If there was an IV drip available for it, people would buy it.

I make my way back to the counter and hear the door open as someone enters. When I glance up, it's Sevyn, looking like she just stepped off the runway. She's dressed in a black jumpsuit with a Gucci belt cinched around her waist. Her deep red curls frame her face, and she carries a black clutch in her hand. She waves when she sees me. "I was worried I would miss you! I took a little longer than I anticipated to get ready." She twirls on the spot.

"You look drop dead gorgeous. Zane is going to eat you up!" I say.

"You weren't lying, this shop is a whole vibe," she remarks as she looks around.

The coffee shop has an industrial design with warm, rich colors throughout. There is a stage for performances, coffee tables in the center of the shop, and then plush chairs are scattered throughout. One of the walls has a floor-to-ceiling bookshelf that's stacked with a variety of books. Ava and West did a good job creating a space where you can relax and socialize.

"It really is. Did you want me to make you something?" I ask as I walk behind the counter and wash my hands.

Sevyn scrunches up her face as she studies the menu behind me. "Mmm... let me get the house blend, please."

"Alright, coming right up." I busy myself with making the shots. I'm listening to Sevyn talk when I look up, and the air is stolen from my lungs. A guy strides in, and every inch of his rich copper brown skin that I can see is adorned with tattoos. My eyes slowly rake up his hands and arms emblazoned with the most intricate ink. I imagine tracing each one with my fingertips. Ink covers the piece of chest exposed at the V-neck of his shirt that's pulled tautly over his broad shoulders. They continue to coil around his neck and abruptly stop at his sharp jawline. There are no tattoos on his face, and his lips are plump. They look soft enough to kiss. Our eyes lock onto one another; his are pensive and remind me of embers in a fire.

Sevyn continues talking to me, but I don't hear her. All noise is drowned out as we continue to look into one another's eyes. I tear my gaze away when the shot of coffee I hold spills over the sides of the shot glass and onto my finger. "Shit," I hiss, pulling my hand away.

"Are you okay?" Sevyn asks.

"I'm alright," I say while observing my fingers that are now beginning to turn red. "Just got a little distracted is all." The guy who is the source of my distraction chuckles, and heat creeps up my neck.

Sevyn turns her attention to him. "Well, well, well, nice of you to finally arrive."

I try not to stare between them, but he's hard not to look at. I wonder if they're related. His gaze moves to Sev, and I feel ridiculous for being disappointed his eyes are no longer on me.

"You act like you didn't just see me this past weekend." His voice is smooth and deep.

"Is it a crime for me to want to see my brother often?" Sevyn asks him. She never mentioned she had a brother.

"Why do you want to meet up at some hipster ass coffee shop anyway? All this bullshit tastes the same," he says.

Figures, he fits the whole asshole vibe. I may be taking more offense then necessary because it's my uncle's coffee shop, but I think this guy is probably just an asshole.

Sevyn raises her hand towards me like she's presenting me on a game show. "Harlow works here."

His brow furrows as his eyes rake over me. "And why does this matter?"

My eyes narrow, and I glare at him. I'm a *this* to him, not even a *she*. Well, fuck you too, then. If I hadn't blinked, I would have sworn I saw a smirk tugging at the corner of his lips.

"It matters because she is fucking amazing," Sevyn says matter-of-factly. I hand her order to her, and she takes a sip and closes her eyes. "Harlow, this is so good." She takes another sip and side-eyes her brother.

"This, regrettably, is my brother Acyn. He owns a tattoo shop a few blocks from here." She looks at me and beams. "Acyn, this is Harlow. She's my yoga instructor, but she works here to help out her uncle, so I thought I would come see her. And I'm glad I did because this coffee is fucking delicious." She hugs her cup between her hands.

I give him a half-smile because he behaves more pretentiously than the hipsters that frequent this shop, but I still try to practice good customer service. "Nice to meet you. Can I get you anything?"

"Eight-ounce Americano." It comes out of his mouth like a demand.

"Coming up." I force a smile, but it fades as soon as I turn around. I roll my eyes because he's a pleasure to look at... until he opened his mouth. He and Sevyn walk off and settle into armchairs near the window. The sun is just starting to set, and it's almost time for me to go home. I don't mind helping my uncle, but I feel exhausted on days I work both jobs.

I walk over to them and hand Acyn his coffee. He takes the coffee and observes it for a moment then puts the cup to his lips. As he sips, his ember eyes peer at me from over the rim of the cup.

"It's good, right?" Sevyn asks.

He takes another sip and then sets the cup back down on the saucer. "It tastes burned."

I cover my mouth with my hand and then reach for his cup. "I'm so sorry. I can-"

He puts his tattooed hand over mine to stop me from taking his cup, and I bite my lip because his touch feels electric.

"You're fine, I'll choke it down somehow," he says with a smirk.

I immediately remove my hand as though he burned me and glare at him. I'm two seconds away from calling him an asshole when Sevyn beats me to it.

"You're such an asshole, Acyn. Don't listen to him, Harlow." She gives me an apologetic smile. "He has a permanent dick stuck up his ass."

I try not to laugh, but it bubbles up in my throat and escapes me. His eyes narrow, but I see the glimmer in them.

"On that note, I'm going home. I'll see you next week, Sev." I wave at her. "Acyn, if you ever want another burned cup of coffee, you know where to find me." I flip my hair over my shoulder, turn on my heel, and walk away. I'll be damned if I let this guy ruin my day.

When I walk back through the shop to leave, I can feel his gaze on me, but I don't bother looking at him. He can choke on my burned coffee for all I care.

ACYN

I watch her walk out the door and round the corner. I smile into my cup of coffee as I finish it off.

"How long have you known her?" I try to sound casual because I don't want to give my sister any indication that I'm interested.

She puts a finger on her chin, and her eyes look up to the ceiling as she thinks. "Only a few weeks now. Do you think she's pretty?" She presses me with a smirk on her lips.

I have to watch what I say, or my sister will be setting up a date.

I keep a straight face and shrug. "She's alright."

I'm fucking lying. I couldn't take my eyes off of her. She couldn't keep her eyes off of me either... until I opened my mouth. I tend to have that effect on women. Some, the really thirsty ones, can look past it if they're looking for a quick fuck. If my judgement is correct, Harlow doesn't seem like she would be down for a quick fuck. She seems more like the type that wants to know what your sign is so she can see if your compatibility is written in the stars.

"Uh huh, I know you're a rolling stone, but it wouldn't hurt to make friends," Sevyn says. "She's new here anyway."

"Where is she from?"

"Texas. She just got her first apartment and—" she looks at me and then narrows her eyes. "Wait, why do you even care?"

"I don't... you just seemed obsessed with her, so I thought I'd ask. Is it a crime to ask questions?"

"No, but you were a bit of a dick to her. Clearly that coffee didn't taste bad, or you wouldn't have finished it."

"Or I just don't want to throw money away..."

She scoffs. "Like you have to worry about fucking money."

Sevyn's right, I don't have to worry about money. I own two tattoo shops, and I'm considering opening up a third. I started when I was eighteen and gave every ounce of energy I had to my art. Now at twenty-five, the hard work is finally paying off. I'm more successful than I could have ever imagined. I've been booked all year for the past three years and I'm adding celebrity clients. So yeah, a four-dollar cup of coffee is the least of my worries.

"Don't you have somewhere to be? I see you put on something other than yoga pants for once." I grin and wait for her to smack me.

She punches my arm. "You try having kids instead of freely dipping your dick into whatever flavor you feel like. Then we'll see how put together you are, asshole."

"I don't freely dip my dick... anymore. That was just a phase. I don't have time for that shit now," I admit while rubbing my arm. That lifestyle used to be exciting for me, but a warm body can only do so much for you. After a while you want more. Not that I'm actively looking. I'm perfectly fine with my own company.

Her phone chimes with a text, and she glances at it. "Zane is here. Are you coming by on Sunday for dinner?"

"Do I have a choice?"

With a sarcastic smile, she knocks my foot off the table it rests on as she walks past.

"No, you don't." She walks away before turning back around. "Be nice to Harlow, okay? I actually think you two could get along. Plus, she has no friends."

"Damn, I'm sure she really appreciates you putting her business out there like that. And if you're her only friend... she's really fucked." I smirk, and she flicks me off as she leaves to meet Zane.

8

Harlow

THE AFTERNOON SUN FILTERS through the trees as Ava and I walk through the forest behind the house.

"How are you settling in here?" Ava asks.

"It's starting to feel like home." I smile.

"Good! Are you making friends? I know it's hard to move from a place you've lived your whole life and start new somewhere else."

"Yeah, it is, but I think I'm doing alright. I've made some friends through teaching classes at the studio. We've hung out a few times, and I've enjoyed myself." Aside from Ava, I've met a few other people who have invited me out to do things. I was wrapped up in Hendrix for so long that I forgot what it's like to go out and have friends of my own.

"See, and you were worried." She nudges my arm, smiling.

"I've never kept a lot of friends anyway. I kind of made my boyfriend my life for two years, and I'm just rediscovering what friends are."

"I take it you're not dating anyone, then? I thought that maybe you and that boy you were with the other day were seeing each other."

I shake my head. "No, no Kyrell and I are just friends. I'm honestly not even interested in dating right now. Things are still complicated between my ex and I." I let out a sigh. "I want to focus on myself. I'm okay with being single."

Ava wraps her arm around me. "There's nothing wrong with being committed to yourself. When you're not focused on love, that's when it sweeps you up."

I tip my face up toward the sun's rays and let them warm my skin as we walk home. Love is the furthest thing from my mind. I'm not ready for another relationship. Hendrix and I still talk. After our phone call the first night I was here, we talked a lot. Then as we fell into our new routines—separately—the talks became less frequent.

I tried to tell myself that I was talking to him because I missed him, but honestly, he's also my security blanket. He has been there my whole life, and I can't deny that he knows me well. The problem with comfort is that it makes it easier to slip into routines. It makes it easier for us to become stagnant. I don't want to be stagnant, and that's what I felt like with him. That I wasn't growing and exploring.

I want the chance to know myself outside of being in a relationship. I want to fall in love with myself.

No, I *need* to fall in love with myself.

Walking into the yoga studio classroom, I start the music and then carefully weave my way through the students to the front of the class. Once I reach my mat, I sit cross-legged and rest my palms on my legs. Taking a few deep breaths, I begin the class.

"All you'll need for the next hour is yourself. Give thanks to yourself for being here today. Not only for making it to your mat, but more importantly, for showing up for yourself every single day. Starting each day anew even when you may not feel like it. The most important relationship we will ever cultivate is the one that we have with ourselves."

I look around the classroom and guide everyone to close their eyes. "Whenever you're feeling overwhelmed, whether it be here on your mat or out there in the world, remember you can come back to yourself." After guiding them, and myself, through a few rounds of breathing, I begin the class.

I've been working at Celeste's studio, Eunoia Yoga, for almost two months now. I remember being so nervous to start teaching classes because being in front of people, guiding them, makes me nervous. After the first few classes, I told Celeste that I wasn't sure if I was a good fit for a yoga instructor. She sucked her teeth and showed me the reviews that had been posted since the studio's opening:

"I took a class with Harlow. Her voice is soothing, and she makes every level of yogi feel welcomed."

"Harlow needs to record herself doing meditations. It was the most relaxing experience I've had."

"I feel like I actually belong to this studio. The instructor is so welcoming."

I couldn't help but grin because I didn't feel like I was doing a good job. Celeste told me that I need to stop doubting myself and trust that I know what I'm doing. She teases me that people only come here for me. I always brush off that remark, but it's hard to deny when my classes are fully booked as soon as the schedule is posted for the week. The proof is in the pudding, she says.

I'm gaining confidence in myself as a teacher. The reviews and Celeste's encouragement help, but I still have to find confidence within myself. People can tell you what you are all day, but you really have to believe it yourself for you to be able to embody it. I'm getting there.

For the next hour, I guide my students through their practice. I watch their stress, worries, and anxieties melt down onto their mat with their sweat. I'm grateful that I can play a small part in helping someone find peace. Even if it is only for a little while.

Once the class is over, I sit outside, waiting for my students as they trickle out of the class to offer them words of encouragement.

Sevyn comes walking through the door, her face flushed, wearing a grin. "Way to kick our asses in there."

The corners of my mouth turn up. "You must enjoy it if you're taking private and group lessons," I tease.

Her brow furrows with contemplation. "When you put it that way, I do sound a little crazy, don't I?"

"We all have a little crazy in us."

"Speaking of crazy, would you want to come over to my house today and meet my kids and husband?"

I'm both elated and let down that she invited me over. "I would love too, but I already committed to helping out at the coffee shop this afternoon." My shoulders sag. "I'm sorry."

"Don't be sorry. You're a busy woman. Trust me, there will be plenty of opportunities for you to come over." She slings her bag over her shoulder.

I grin. "Thanks. I'll see you later!" She waves as she heads towards the front doors. I would much rather spend the day with her than work at the coffee shop. West asked me this morning if I could help out. Well, he practically begged me to help out because another employee called in sick. Since my only plans for the day were to chill at home and sleep, I agreed.

I inhale deeply as I enter the coffee shop. I don't know that I will ever tire of the smell of freshly brewed coffee and warm pastries. A guitarist strums away on stage, and his smooth voice carries throughout the shop. Despite there being a line that nearly reaches the doors, the energy is calm and inviting.

Uncle West is behind the counter, making drinks and talking to customers. He's in his element. I can tell he really enjoys being here. When he sees me walk in, he smiles. "Hey! Thanks again for coming to help out."

I wave him off and smile. "Not a problem. What can I do to help?"

"We got a delivery order in from a shop a couple of blocks from here. Would you mind making the drinks and delivering them?"

It's a nice spring day so the chance to walk outside sounds perfect. "Yeah, let me set my things down and I'll get on it."

I wrap an apron around my waist and read over the delivery order that came in. There are a total of eight drinks, so I busy myself with making them because the order came in nearly half an hour ago. Once I finish making them all and secure them in a drink carrier, I tell West that I'm leaving and make my way to the address on the delivery receipt. I'm grateful the shop isn't too far because I'm already running late.

As I approach the shop, I stare up at the sign to make sure that I have the right address and then read the shop's name: Crown Ink. It's a sleek, modern tattoo shop. Definitely not what I envision as a tattoo shop. I think of seedy locations with neon signs, kind of like the one in Bali, but this shop is none of that.

I enter and walk into the reception area. A girl with electric blue hair and black, thick-rimmed glasses sits behind the counter. "Hi, welcome. Who do you have an appointment with?"

I'm too busy staring around the shop and don't immediately respond to her. "Do you have an appointment or do you want a consultation?" She smiles.

"Oh no I'm—" Before I can explain, my eyes fall on a familiar face.

ACYN

As I finish with my afternoon client and glance out my shop's windows, I do a double take because I realize that the girl my sister introduced me to is standing out there, staring at the sign. She's carrying the coffees I ordered—I glance at the clock on the wall—almost an hour ago. Not that I give a fuck about how long it took her to get here. I'm actually glad it took her longer because it would have gone cold while I finished up with my client. That doesn't stop me from wanting to give her shit about it. A smile pulls at my lips as I make my way to the lobby.

I hear her talking to Riley. Well, more so, Riley talking to her, because Harlow is too busy looking around the shop with curiosity to listen to what she has to say. I enjoy the view in the meantime. She has a willowy frame with legs for days and a nice ass. Her skin is a rich, velvety golden brown, and she has light brown kinky curly hair that's piled on top of her head in a bun. Her bright brown almond shaped eyes look like the sun shining through a glass of whiskey. Okay, so I may have studied her a little harder than I let on to my sister. Fucking sue me. It would be a sin to not appreciate that nice of a view.

"Oh, no I'm—" Her response to Riley stops mid-sentence when she turns around to examine the rest of the shop, and her gaze falls on me.

"Late," I finish her sentence for her.

She stands there with her lips slightly parted as if she isn't sure what to say.

Her full lips curve into a smile, and she looks around the shop again as she talks. "Yeah, sorry, it's busy at the shop, and I shouldn't even be working today, but my uncle needed me so I decided to work so..." Her voice trails off and she holds out the cup holder to me. "They should be hot..."

I don't immediately take them. I just let her stand there for a few seconds, holding them out to me while I continue to stare at her. She raises an eyebrow, still with a smile on her face, and I take them. Does she always smile this much?

"Is it burned?" I ask and try my best to keep the smile off of my face.

Her eyes narrow, and she crosses her arms over her chest. "I don't know, why don't you taste it and tell me since you're such a coffee connoisseur."

The smile I've kept at bay finally pulls at my lips. I look for my Americano and grab it. I turn my attention towards Riley. "Can you take these back for the rest of the crew?"

Riley gets up and looks between Harlow and I, clearly confused. I rarely make small talk with people. Especially someone who delivers coffee.

Harlow's eyes follow Riley as she leaves. Her smile is back on her face. "She's nice."

"That's because I pay her to be."

"Yeah, imagine customers having to deal with you first? Tragic." Her voice sounds like honey laced with venom.

This time, I give her a genuine smile, and she rolls her eyes.

"Well, I better get back to the shop. It's really busy right now."

I pique an eyebrow. "Aren't you curious as to whether the coffee is burned or not?"

She rests her hands on her hips. "I know it isn't, Acyn."

I'm shocked she remembered my name and that she calls me Acyn instead of Ace. Only family and a few close friends call me Acyn. To everyone else I'm Ace, the tattoo guy.

"You can call me Ace." She, bites her plush bottom lip, trying to a keep a smile off her face. "What's so funny?" I ask.

"Nothing... Ace," she says my nickname with a sarcastic tone and then chuckles. "I'll call you Acyn. It sounds better anyway."

I study her for a moment as she stands there and she shifts her weight to her other foot, waiting for me to say something back. Instead, I take a sip of the coffee she brought me and peer over the cup at her. When I'm done with my sip, which is fucking good, she raises her eyebrows waiting.

"It still tastes burned. Who–" But before I can finish my sentence, she closes the gap between us and reaches for my cup. She snatches it from my hand, and I brace to have hot coffee thrown on me. Instead, she raises the cup to her lips and takes a drink. She takes another drink and smacks her lips loudly at me.

"What the hell are you doing?" I ask her, confused because, one: she doesn't know me and she just drank from my cup, and two: she's smacking her lips at me like she's lost her fucking marbles.

She scrunches up her face as she continues to taste my coffee. "I'm just trying to see if I accidentally put a shot of asshole in there, and I think I fucking did." I raise my brows in disbelief, letting out a rumble of laughter.

Harlow hands it back to me. "Enjoy your burned coffee, asshole."

Before I can think of a comeback, she's heading out the door. On the way out, she looks over her shoulder at me with a smile.

Harlow

I hustle back to the shop knowing I took too long, talking shit with Acyn. Who the hell does he think he is anyway? That coffee wasn't burned in the slightest. It's almost as if it pains him to be a decent human being towards me. But maybe he's just like that with everyone. I don't know, but what I do know is that he isn't going to talk to me any type of way. I may be quiet but that doesn't mean I'm not willing to stand my ground.

Thankfully when I re-enter the shop, the crowd that was in earlier has died down. I find West behind the counter again.

"Did you find the shop okay?" he asks.

"Yeah, I did," I say, leaving out the part that the owner of the shop is an asshole.

"Good." He smiles. "I'm going to head out then... unless you want me to stay and you can go since you've been working all day?"

"No, go home to Ava. I'll be fine, just don't ask me for shit tomorrow."

"Fair enough." He chuckles. "Thanks for coming in."

"Yeah, yeah. See ya later." I wave him away.

Since the crowd has thinned, I decide to pull out my laptop and research photography courses. It's something that has been in the back of my mind since Ava mentioned it to me weeks ago. There's an abundance of courses available, so it really comes down to me choosing one. That's another reason why I haven't said no to any extra hours here at the shop;

I want to be able to pay for the photography courses. Although I know if I asked my dad, he wouldn't hesitate to help me.

But this is something that I want to do for myself. Since I've been "adulting", I've learned that things mean more to you when you're invest in them for yourself. I'll tell my dad once I've enrolled in a few classes. That way he can't try and pay for them. For the next few hours, I switch between my laptop and the counter, helping customers. The live entertainment that was here earlier is gone, and there's a steady trickle of people placing orders.

I glance at the clock and realize it's 9p.m. I wait for the last few customers to leave and then lock the door behind them. I turn up the music a little louder and start cleaning. It doesn't take me long because West, that work-a-holic, took care of most of it before he left.

I'm in the middle of wiping down the counter when I see someone walk past the front of the shop. When I glance up again, I see it's Acyn. He tries the door, and I stand there staring at him with a smile on my face. He points to the handle signaling for me to open it. I hold up a finger to tell him to wait a second. I quickly find a piece of paper and scribble on it. "We're fresh out of burned coffee."

I make my way around the counter and head towards the door, watching the smile on his face. Once I reach the door, I place the paper against the window so he can read it. I must admit that I find so much fucking joy as he leans down to read the paper and registers what it says. I then press my middle finger to the glass and give him a smile.

The smile that spreads across his face is an unexpected treat. "I'll see you around, Harlow." He gives me a two-finger salute and walks off into the night.

9

Harlow

Sevyn and I sit out on the trampoline while her kids bounce around us. I was going to stay in bed all day since it's Sunday and I have a full day off, but she said she had food and mimosas. Who am I to pass that up? Plus, I enjoy her company.

"Let me know if they're bothering you and I can send them inside with Zane."

I suck my teeth. "Girl, please, they're fine. Look at how happy they are." Her twins, Eli and Emery, zip around the trampoline in circles, giggling and chasing each other.

"When we first had them, Zane and I lost a lot of our friends. We were nineteen, and most of them were into the party lifestyle. He and I weren't. Well, we couldn't be because I got pregnant. We became focused on our family and education," Sevyn says. "You know that I work as a healthcare claim specialist, and Zane works in software development. We've created a nice life for ourselves and our kids... but I would be lying if I said I don't miss having real friends and being like most twenty-four year-olds. So, when I met you and we clicked, I hoped you wouldn't be a bitch about me being so young and having kids."

I tilt my head to the side. "So you're telling me that people you grew up with jumped ship once you started building a life?"

She nods.

"That's low of them, but... people who fade in and out of your life... they don't matter. The ones who do matter will stand by your side regardless of what you got going on."

She lets out a sigh. "You're right, but it's still difficult to make friends."

"I think making friends doesn't come as naturally as everyone makes it out to seem. Or maybe it does because we're friends now." I smile.

"Yeah, you're stuck with me," she says. "Are you sure you don't want to stay for dinner? Zane is making barbecue," she asks.

"Thank you for offering, but my aunt and uncle are expecting me. Besides, doesn't your whole family come over on Sunday?"

"They do, and now that I think of it, they're all running late per usual."

I laugh at her look of annoyance and hop off the trampoline. "Maybe another time then. Thanks for having me over. It was a lot of fun." She hops down off trampoline and gives me a hug.

"Tell Harlow goodbye, you two," she says to the twins.

"Byeeee," they say in unison. I give them a wave, and they giggle in response.

"I'll see you in class." Carrying my shoes in my hand, I let my toes sink into the lush green grass as I head to my car.

I had a nice afternoon with her adorable family. Sevyn and I are a year apart, but she's wise beyond her years. I wish I had my shit together like her. I don't think she realizes how badass she is. Not many people could create the life she has while raising two kids. She definitely needs to give herself more credit.

When I reach my car, a sleek, matte black Mercedes G-Wagon pulls up next to mine. The window rolls down, and a familiar smooth, deep voice calls my attention.

"Are you stalking me?"

Amused, I peer through the opened window at Acyn. "Don't flatter yourself. You're not that exciting."

He chuckles and gets out of his car. "I see you're not busy subjecting anyone to your terrible coffee making skills," he teases.

"Hahaha... you're hilarious," I say with a roll of my eyes as I climb into my car.

"Nice car. Did you restore it?" he says, referring to my Bronco.

I smile at him. "Thank you. My dad and I did."

He gives me a curious look as I start my car. "You're not staying for dinner?"

I slide my shades on. "No, I just came to see Sev and the kids. I'll see you around."

He nods. "Yeah, see you around. Maybe I'll stop by for another cup of shitty coffee."

I snort with laughter. "Go to hell." I put my car in reverse. "Watch your toes, I would hate to run them over."

He takes a few steps back with a grin on his face.

Between teaching group and private classes at the yoga studio and shifts at the coffee shop, I'm beat. I just finished my shift at the coffee shop, and instead of going home, I decide to a do a little more research on photography classes. I'm a naturally indecisive person who likes external validation, and that carries over into all areas of my life. I've read each class description at least a hundred times, but I've yet to pull the trigger on enrolling in one.

After the week I've had, the thought of adding one more thing to my already busy schedule makes me question my sanity. Before I can even take a class, I need to buy an actual camera. I've only ever used my phone, and if I want to be professional, I can't pull out my phone and expect people to pay me. If people already like my photos, the thought of what I could do with a real camera makes me excited.

I'm hunched over, staring at my computer screen, when the sound of a chair being dragged across the floor and someone clearing their throat interrupts my thoughts. When I look up, Acyn plops down on the seat in front of me. He has a smile on his face and cup of coffee in his hand.

"Uh, hi." I scan the room to see if maybe all the other tables are full, and they aren't. "Why are you sitting here?"

"Why not?" he asks with a shrug of his shoulders.

I straighten up. "I mean, I guess... I just... never mind." I don't understand why he's sitting with me when there are plenty of seats around me available.

"What are you working on?" he asks as he takes a sip of his coffee.

I sit back in my chair and cross my arms. "Are you really interested in what I'm doing, or are you just here to be annoying?"

Usually, if I'm working, Acyn will stop in for a drink and then proceed to tell me how terrible it tastes. I know he's full of shit, but that doesn't stop him from telling me all the improvements that could be made. Next time he does it, I'm telling him to get behind the counter and make it.

"Both," he says with a peaked eyebrow. Then he reaches for my laptop and spins it around to face him before I can close it.

"Excuse you." I reach for it, and he moves it off the table out of my reach. I don't have the energy to get up and snatch it back, so I sit back in my seat and wait for him to finish being nosy.

He scrolls for a good minute. "Are you into photography?"

"I mean... kind of. It's something I want to try and get better at. My aunt suggested I try it since my Instagram does so well."

He smirks. "Are you an influencer?"

"No, I just enjoy traveling, food, and an occasional picture of myself if the lighting is good. I've built up a decent following."

He nods and goes back to looking at the cameras. "Maybe you can come and take pictures at the studio. I've wanted to up our social media presence and update our website." I scoff, and his eyes snap to mine. "What's so funny?" he asks.

I set my elbow on the table and rest my chin on my hand. "Why, when you don't even like me? All you do is give me a hard time."

"I don't." He shrugs. "But that doesn't mean that I couldn't hire you to take nice pictures." He sets my laptop back on the table, and I snap it close.

"I don't get you, but if you're going to give me money to take pictures of your shitty tattoos, why not?"

"Why be nice when giving you shit is so much more fun?" he asks, trying to suppress a smile.

"So fun," I say sarcastically. My phone rings where it's sitting on the table. I see Hendrix's photo on my screen. I ignore it. I don't want to talk to him right now.

"You're not gonna answer that?"

I shake my head and silence my phone when it rings again. He's already calling me back. "Not when I'm engaged in this riveting conversation with you."

"Take a picture of me," he suggests, straightening up in his chair. He gives me a lopsided grin, waiting for me to take a picture.

A giggle escapes me. "What the hell is that?"

His smile fades. "What?"

"Is this supposed to be your," I form air quotes with my hands, "sexy look?"

He scoffs. "You can't handle a sexy look from me," he says, looking me up and down.

"You're so confident in yourself. I've seen better."

I'm lying through my fucking teeth. Acyn is a fine specimen of a man, but I won't give him any indication that I find him attractive. Instead, I snap pictures of him as he laughs at my remark. He's mid-laugh, and the light is filtering in through the windows, really making his tattoos stand out against his rich copper skin.

I slide my phone across the table when I'm satisfied with the pictures I've taken. "Don't swipe too far," I say with a wink.

"What the hell do you have on your phone?" he asks curiously.

I shrug and wait for him to look at the pictures while I pack up my things. I haven't taken any risqué pictures in a while, so if he scrolls all he will see are food and scenery pictures. But the look on his face is hilarious.

He scrolls cautiously and then a smile appears on his lips as he looks at the pictures I took of him. "You're surprisingly good at capturing people."

I snort. "Gee, thanks for the backhanded compliment." I snatch my phone out of his hand.

"I didn't mean – " He stops abruptly, reaching into his back pocket, pulling out his buzzing phone. "Just a second. It's my dad."

Acyn answers in Spanish, surprising me. Not only is this man tall, dark, curly haired, handsome, and covered in tattoos, but he speaks Spanish too? I don't need to understand what he's saying to know he's fluent with the way the words roll off his tongue. He's carrying on a conversation, but all his attention is on me. I look away, adjusting things in my bag to give myself something to do instead of stare at him. A few seconds later, he ends the call.

"You speak Spanish?" I blurt out.

"I do." He nods proudly. "Dad is from Dominican Republic. Mom is from here. Sevyn's never cursed or muttered menacingly under her breath in Spanish in front of you?"

"Not yet." I shake my head, zipping up my bag.

"Give her time. She will." He looks at my bag on my forearm. "You're leaving?"

"Yeah, it's been a long week, and I'm looking forward to becoming one with my bed."

He chuckles. "Alright, well can I have your Instagram? I was serious about you taking pictures for the shop."

I'm caught off guard. "Oh, yeah, okay. Ummm... if you give me your phone, I can just type it into your Instagram search."

He leans back in his chair, slides his phone out of his pocket, and hands it to me. I type in my handle and hand it back to him. "Enjoy being a stalker. I'll see you around."

Acyn gives me a two-finger salute. "See you around."

On my way back to my car, I contemplate uploading the picture of Acyn. It's a great picture. It also helps that he's good-looking. If I upload it though, Hendrix is going to have a shit fit. I have to constantly remind him that we aren't together, and we're both free to do as we please. Even though I'm not doing anything. I've told him a million times I'm not interested in a relationship right now with anyone, not just him.

I decide to upload the picture. What good is it being thousands of miles away from Hendrix if I still take him into consideration? It's not as though I've strung him along. I've been blatantly clear about where I'm right now, and he still thinks we're together. I chew on my thumbnail as my other thumb hovers over the check mark to upload.

I say, "Fuck it," and press it because I'm proud of the picture. I'm exhausted from taking Hendrix's feelings into consideration when we aren't even together. I leave my phone on silent because I know he's going to blow it up, and I don't want to hear it.

ACYN

I step into my boxers and let the towel around my waist fall to the floor. It's been a long day, and all I wanted was a hot shower and to fall in my bed. But, when I saw Harlow sitting at the coffee shop, I stopped in to talk to her. She doesn't give me the same attention that most women do. Not to be an arrogant son of a bitch, but I don't have to do much when it comes to women. They see the tattoos, the muscles, the nice clothes, the car, and it's a wrap. Not her, though; she's been annoyed with me since the moment she met me.

I find it entertaining and refreshing. I flop onto my bed and decide to finally look at her Instagram. Even though she thought I was joking about taking pictures for the shop, I wasn't. Nowadays you have to have a presence on social media in order to thrive. I've seen businesses miss out on potential customers because their social media presence was lacking. I navigate to her page and mumble, "Holy shit." When she said decent following, I thought she meant a few thousand followers... not almost a million followers.

Shit, maybe I can learn something from her. I also can't deny that she really does know how to take pictures. I wonder what she could do if she had a real camera and not just her phone. When I snatched her laptop from her, she was looking at cameras, so I assume that she doesn't have one. I scroll back to the top of her page and sit up when I see someone that looks familiar.

I click on it, and it's a picture of me with the caption: *annoying.* It really is a good picture, but the fact that she called me annoying is amusing. I'm even more surprised to see that the photo already has thousands of likes. The comments are "Who is he," "#thirsttrap", and lots of people asking if I'm a tattoo artist. The entrepreneur in me sees this as an opportunity to boost my business. Even though I'm not looking for clients, the other artists in my shop are just as good as me. I'm serious about my business and helping other artists.

I follow her and send her a DM.

Acyn: Hey it's me, annoying.

I scroll through her pictures and see she has photos with friends. There are a few photos that she has a with a guy that looks like a fuck boy. Something about his hair, clothes, and face annoys me. Judging from the comments, they were together at some point. I check the date, and their last photo together she posted was a few months ago. I do what any sane person does and follow the tag to his page. All his pictures are of Harlow, baseball, himself, and flashy cars. Scrolling past countless pictures of Harlow, I learn he's a professional baseball player for the Houston Astros.

He seems to be... obsessed with her. Clearly Harlow doesn't feel the same way. Reading the captions and his replies to comments, it's almost like he has a sense of entitlement to her. Exactly as I said... he's a fuck boy. I switch back to Harlow's page and start to scroll again when I get a DM from her:

Harlow: LMAO I was wondering if you would really check out my page or not.

Acyn: Why wouldn't I?

Harlow: Because you're you...

Acyn: To live up to my name, your pictures are alright. The best one is of me.

Harlow: I knew I just had to wait for the arrogance to drop in.

Acyn: LOL shouldn't you be one with your bed?

She sends me a picture of herself wrapped up like a fucking burrito in her bed. I decide since she responds in pictures, I will too. I send her a picture of me laying in my bed with my cat.

Harlow: Your picture would be perfect if you were out of it, and it was just your cat.

Laughing out loud, my cat leaps off the bed.

Acyn: LOL You talk about me but you're no better.

Harlow: I got to keep up with you and your onslaught of insults.

Acyn: I can't help it. It's a knee jerk reaction when it comes to you.

Harlow: Yeah, yeah... so really... what do you think of my page?

Acyn: I think you do have talent. I'm still serious about working with you.

Harlow: You should comment and tag your business page so I can pin it.

Acyn: Alright.

Maybe my sister was right... she and I could be friends. Not because of what she can do for me business-wise, but because I actually enjoy talking to her.

10

Harlow

I WAS RIGHT. HENDRIX lost his shit. I blocked all his calls and messages last night because I already knew the tantrum that was coming my way. After waking up and eating breakfast, I decide to answer his twentieth video call. I wish I were lying, but he really did call me twenty times.

"You're a hard person to reach." His jaw is tense; he looks like he's trying so hard not to fly off the handle.

"Yeah, I came home after work last night and went to sleep." I leave out the part where Acyn and I spent a few hours texting each other.

"Who's your friend with the tattoos?" He wastes no time getting to the root of his distress.

I can't help but roll my eyes. "Oh, for fucks sake, is this why you're on my FaceTime? Not even to see how I'm doing?"

"You seem to be doing alright if you're posting pictures of guys who look like they belong in prison."

"I didn't realize tattoos were a requirement for prison," I quip.

He shakes his head and rakes his fingers through his curls. "Are you fucking him?"

"Are you fucking kidding me right now? First of all, he would never want to fuck me, and last time I checked, I'm single and can be friends with whoever I damn well please."

"Is he gay?"

I scoff. "So, the only way he could not want to have sex with me is if he's gay?"

"You act like you're ugly, Harlow."

"You know what? When I see him next, I'll ask him if he wants to fuck me and let you know how it plays out."

His jaw flexes, and I can tell he's trying his best to not flip out on me. "Think of how this looks, Harlow. I mean people know Kyrell, but this guy... who the fuck is he?"

"I don't care how it looks, Hendrix, because I know how it is, and it isn't how you're making it seem."

He rakes his hands through his curls again and sighs. I don't say anything because there isn't anything left to say. After a moment he finally asks, "Would you tell me if you were seeing someone else?"

"I thought that you and I were friends, but you keep making me think that we would be better off not talking at all," I say. Maybe it was naïve of me to think that he and I could remain friends after being together for so long. I think that maybe there will always be a piece of me that wants him in my life even though I know that we would probably be better off parting ways.

"No, no, baby, don't say that," he begs.

"Look, I've got to go. I'm helping West at the coffee shop. I'll catch up with you when I can." I hang up on him and block his calls and messages... *again.*

Stepping onto my mat, I exhale, feeling as though it's the first time I've breathed all morning. The conversation with Hendrix did nothing for my mood. I'm grateful that I have some time on my mat this morning before heading into work. It's become rare for me to be a student here at the studio because I spend so much of my time teaching. While I do enjoy teaching, I miss being a student. When I'm teaching, I have to be mindful of everyone in my class, and I can't really focus on poses unless I'm just demonstrating for them to follow along.

By the end of the class, I do feel lighter. I'm still contemplating whether having Hendrix in my life is a good thing or not. We were friends before we ever had a relationship, but I think we've reached the point of no return for that now. I don't know why I can't simply let him go. It isn't as easy as people make it seem. Letting go takes a lot of time, indecisiveness, and fuck ups before you can officially walk away and feel done. I'm not there yet, and I guess that's okay, even though I'm wishing that I were.

Kyrell is in town and wants to meet up for lunch. Since I'm working at the coffee shop, I ask him to come see me during my lunch break. He knows West and Ava now because he and I have become best friends again since I've moved here. When he walks in, West greets him like they're lifelong friends. It makes me smile because I don't think there is a person that I've met that doesn't like Kyrell.

I shrug out of my apron, hang it up in the back, and go out front to meet him. "Hey." I give him a hug. "It's good to see you. We should eat outside."

"Yeah, sure, whatever you want, Harls." He turns his attention back to West. "We'll have to set up a time to talk more about the dispensary."

"Yes, definitely!" West agrees. "Enjoy your break."

We step outside, and I pick a table that's in direct sunlight.

"You know, you would think growing up in humid ass Texas that you would be tired of the sun," Kyrell says.

I turn my face towards the sun, squint my eyes closed, and smile. "Never will I ever tire of the sun. There's not enough of it here. And you have some nerve, living in California."

"Are you happy here despite the lack of sun?"

I chuckle. "Yeah, I am, actually. How about you? Are you enjoying California living?"

He gives me a huge grin. "I love it. Probably the best decision I made for myself. I actually just bought the space I want to open my dispensary."

I gape at him. "What? Really? Kyrell, this is amazing news! Why didn't you tell me sooner?"

"I didn't want to make a big deal."

"That's bullshit. You love a good party." I nudge his arm. "But... wow, your very own dispensary, huh? That's amazing! You're doing what you said you would years ago!"

After Kyrell came back home from Louisiana State University he told me that his dream was to start his own dispensary. He can make some amazing edibles and of course loves marijuana.

He bows in his seat. "Thank you, thank you! I tried calling Hendrix to tell him, but he was too hung up on you posting a picture of some guy to even congratulate me."

I drop my sub sandwich back onto the paper I just unwrapped it from and lean back in my chair. "Hung up? No, he was on a mission! Do you know how many times he called me after I posted it? Twenty fucking times!"

Kyrell smiles because he thinks it's hilarious when Hendrix gets his feathers ruffled. "You had to know that was going to happen, though."

I shrug and roll my eyes. "We aren't together anymore, Kyrell! He asked me to think about how it looks." I suck my teeth. "I don't give a fuck how it looks. It was an amazing picture. End of story."

He sighs, shaking his head. His shoulder-length locs fall into his eyes. "You know that you're going to have to be the one to cut things off, right? Because he never will. He truly believes that you two are meant to be together."

I take a bite out of my sandwich and chew on it. Am I ready to cut things off completely with Hendrix? Kyrell knows him just as well as I do, if not better. "It's complicated."

"I know. I'm not saying you have to cut him off right this second, but I'm letting you know that in his head, you're his endgame."

"Yeah, I—" I lose my train of thought because I see Acyn walking towards our table. "Speak of the devil."

"What?" Kyrell asks confused.

Acyn reaches our table. "Am I interrupting something?" he asks. I can tell he's trying to hide a smile.

I squint up at him, and he moves to block the sunlight from my eyes. "Thank you, and no, you're not. I'm just having lunch here with my friend Kyrell. Kyrell, this is Acyn, the guy from my Instagram."

Kyrell's face lights up. Oh shit, here we go. He stands to greet Acyn like he's the President of the United States. "Hey man, nice to meet you." Kyrell is shaking his hand vigorously, and I already know he's going to do something to really piss Hendrix off. He lives for it. It's all in good fun, Hendrix knows it, but he still lets it get to him.

"I'm the guy from Instagram now?" Acyn asks as he pulls up a chair to our table.

Yeah, sure join us for lunch. I take another bite of my sandwich as I stare at him.

"It's a long story," I say.

"Care to share?" Acyn asks.

"No, I don't. Kyrell and I already talked about it."

"I was checking out your page last night. I don't have any ink, but I'd love to get some. How can I get booked with you?" Kyrell asks and then gives me a wink.

I stare back at him wondering if he's being serious.

"I can see if I have any availability. I'm booked solid a year in advance, but I do make special accommodations for people... especially if they're friends with Harlow."

I almost choke on my sandwich as he says this because I'm not used to him being the slightest bit nice to me. He must have noticed because he chuckles.

"That would be great, man. I don't know if Harls told you, but I don't live here."

Acyn gives me a questioning look. "Harls?"

"It's a nickname I've had since I was a kid and it stuck." I shrug.

"And you talk about Ace."

I know Harls isn't the cutest nickname but it's what they call me. "Feel free to come up with a better one." I shrug, but when I think about it, I realize he'll probably come up with something atrocious. "Never mind, don't."

A smile spreads across his face. "Thought about it, didn't you?"

"It probably isn't the best idea," I continue eating my sandwich. I glance at the time on my phone and realize I only have ten minutes left of my break.

Acyn takes his card out of his wallet and hands it to Kyrell. "Call me when you're ready to get inked. I'll find a time. Send me what you're thinking of, and I'll see what I can come up with."

Kyrell looks at me. "C'mon Harls, what do you say? Should we get matching tats?" He wags his eyebrows at me.

"Ummm... as tempting as that sounds, I—"

"Do you have tattoos?" Acyn asks me.

I feel the heat creep up my neck because of my small butterfly tattoo on my hip. You wouldn't be able to see it unless I took off my panties. "I do." I nod and try to leave it at that. Of course, Kyrell can't leave it there.

"Bullshit! Where?" Kyrell asks, his eyes bright with excitement.

Both of them are staring at me, waiting for me to respond. This lunch just became so awkward. "It's a small butterfly but it's on my hip near my—" I point to my jeans and Kyrell's eyes widen with recognition.

Acyn's ember eyes are on me, glittering with curiosity. At least I think it's curiosity. I'm never sure with him.

"Really? When did you get that done?" Kyrell asks.

I smile. "While I was in Bali. Marisa, Quinn and I all got one."

"See, now you have to get one with me," Kyrell says matter-of-factly.

"I don't know about matching, but I'll go with you when you do get it done."

He claps his hands together. "Sweet!"

"Wait, that's if you have enough time for the both of us?" I ask Acyn.

"Yeah, let me know when, and I'll make it happen." He smiles at me.

I'm cleaning up the wrappings from my sandwich when West walks out. "Acyn DeConto! How have you been?"

I look between West and Acyn because I had no idea that they knew each other. Acyn gets up and gives West a dap. How in the hell do they know each other?

"I'm good. Just enjoying some conversation with Harlow and her friend." Acyn gives me a pearly white smile when he sees the confusion on my face.

"Well, I may as well invite you guys to the dinner we're having tomorrow," West says to Kyrell and Acyn. My eyes flit to West and then back to Acyn who is now looking at me with a raised eyebrow and a grin.

"If there's food, I'll be there," Kyrell says to West.

"Alright, I'll count you in." He looks over at Acyn, "What about you? I have to ask because Ava likes to know how many people are coming so she can do all her planning stuff."

Acyn is looking at me. "Yeah, I'll go." His annoying, lopsided grin is still on his face.

I can't help but sigh with exasperation because I know he's only agreeing because it annoys me. "You don't even like me," I say to him.

Acyn leans forward, resting his forearms on the table. "Who says I'm going for you?"

West and Kyrell are looking between Acyn and I. I feel the heat creep up my neck again. "Oh, okay," I say with a shrug, "I'll just see my way out of this little bromance conversation y'all have going on." Getting up, I throw my trash away as they try to stifle their laughter.

"Oh, c'mon, Harls, don't be like that," Kyrell says.

I wave them off. "I have to get back inside anyway. I'll see you tomorrow."

They go back to talking, but I can't hear what they're saying as the door closes behind me. I forgot about the dinner West and Ava are having tomorrow. It's in honor of West opening up the newest coffee shop. They had a celebration on the first day it opened, but Ava wants to do something more intimate for him. I love how they celebrate each other and have built each other up in their relationship. I can only hope that one day I find a love like that. One where I can grow and don't feel like I have to erase myself for their benefit.

11

Acyn

I ARRIVE AT THE party fashionably late. Social events really aren't my thing, but I'm trying to put myself out there more. Even if that means I'll have to be uncomfortable for a few hours. I may own tattoo shops, but you can honestly never have enough connections. In the short time I've known West, I've learned that he is very well-connected, which isn't surprising given the fact that he has three successful business. As men of color, owning our own successful and thriving businesses is a big fucking deal.

I make my way to their backyard, and everyone is gathered around listening to music, talking, and eating. The vibe is right. I always worry about events dragging and being boring, but I can already tell that this will be anything but that. There are servers walking around with drinks and appetizers. I see that West is at the grill chatting with guests while Ava walks around conversing. They're a power couple if I ever did see one.

There's a guest house further in the back of their yard. That must be where Harlow lives. As I'm looking at the house, she comes out the front door wearing a short red sundress that hits her mid-thigh. She's laughing, as always, pulling Kyrell along behind her. Her hair is different; it's in waist-length twists that are adorned with gold hair jewelry.

She and Kyrell make their way towards where I'm standing. Her eyes observe the crowd of people and then they meet mine. She weaves and dances her way through the crowd which causes me to smile. When she reaches me, I'm startled when she gives me a hug. I let my creep tendencies shine bright and smell her subtly sweet, spicy perfume. She smells good, so no regrets.

"You made it. I didn't think you'd come. This doesn't seem like your scene," she says as Kyrell gives me a dap.

"It typically isn't, but West is different. So, I thought I would make an effort."

She smiles. "Yeah, he and Ava sure know how to throw a party."

Know how to throw a party is an understatement. Their backyard looks like something you would see on TV.

"Have you eaten?" she asks. "Kyrell and I were just going to get something to eat. I know you're not here for me." She smirks. "But do you care to join us?"

I chuckle. "Yeah, I'll join you guys."

We make our way through the crowd of people, Harlow leading the way. She reaches West. "Look who came," she says as she points to me.

West and I exchange greetings. "Thanks for coming. I hope you're hungry. I just finished some burgers, ribs, and hot dogs. Let me know if there's anything else you would like," he says.

"Nah man, that's more than enough to satisfy my appetite," I say as I eye the table that's filled with food. I wasn't hungry when I arrived, but looking at all this food, I'm going to eat like a king tonight.

"Enjoy," West says with a smile. "I'll catch up with you later."

We all fill our plates with a variety of foods and then make our way to sit down on some chairs that are away from the crowd. I'm about to take a bite of my ribs when I hear a moan that catches my attention in more ways than one. When I look up, Harlow has her eyes shut, and she's chewing her food... and *moaning*. I can't help but stare at her.

She opens her eyes and gives me a dazed look. "This is sooo good!" she exclaims.

I've never in my life heard someone moan like that while eating food. My mind wanders as I wonder how she would sound on top of – I stop the thought before I can finish it. I'm still watching her eat because she looks like she's experiencing ecstasy and it's hard to look away. Kyrell is busy eating and doesn't seem to notice it. He must be used to this. I'm sure as fuck not, and neither is my dick apparently.

Her eyes flutter open. "Have you tasted it yet?" she asks.

I snap out of it and look down at my ribs that are apparently just as good as sex. "Uhhh, no, I haven't." I take a bite and I almost want to moan too. I've never had ribs like this that are so tender they melt in your mouth. "Damn, these are good."

She licks her fingers as she looks at me. "I told you."

I have to tell my dick to calm the fuck down. I don't know what's going on right now, but we're just eating food, and she has somehow turned it into a whole different experience.

Thankfully, the conversation shifts to shows to watch and she stops moaning. Not that I would complain if she started up again, but it makes it hard for me to eat. When we've cleared our plates, Harlow takes them and tosses them in the trash. The she collapses onto the couch with a satisfied look on her face. "West sure can cook."

The sound of her moaning is on repeat in my head. "He sure can." A thought occurs to me, and I have to ask, "You don't call him Uncle?"

She shakes her head with a smile on her lips. "No. He said he's too young to be an uncle, so I dropped it."

"He does look young to be an uncle. That's why I asked."

She shrugs. "Black doesn't crack either. My dad is forty-three and looks like a more polished version of West."

Kyrell cuts in. "Does anyone care to smoke with me?" He holds the joint in front of Harlow, and her eyes light up, which surprises me. I haven't spent a lot of time with her, and when I do see her, she's at work. I enjoy seeing this carefree side of her.

She reaches for it. "The perks of living on the west coast. Care to join?" she asks. "I understand if you want to mingle or don't smoke."

"I'll join. I don't care for small talk or mingling."

"Let me grab some blankets from my place to sit on. I'll meet you guys under the willow trees."

When she's gone, I turn to Kyrell as we walk towards the trees. "How long have you known Harlow?"

"Harls and I have known each other since sixth grade. She's like a sister to me."

I wasn't looking for an answer on their relationship status, but I can't help the small bit of relief I feel when he says that. "That's a long time."

"Yeah, she's amazing. Are you and her friends or...?"

"I would say we're acquaintances more than anything. This is the first time I've actually spent time with her outside of the coffee shop."

"Careful." He nudges my arm and smirks. "You'll want her around all the time. She has a magnetic personality and is one of the few genuine people that I know."

He says it jokingly, but I can tell that he's serious. Since I've met her, I find myself stopping in the shop whenever she's working. She's different to me because she's the first woman I've built a friendship with. Well... we mainly pick at each other, but that's more than what I usually have with women.

She catches up with us with blankets draped over her shoulders. Once we're standing under the shade of the willow tree, she lays the blankets out on the ground. She sits down and lays her head on Kyrell's knee. Their relationship is different. At first, I thought that maybe they were sleeping together, not that that's any of my business, but after talking to him, it's clear that they don't see each other that way.

I lay down on the blanket and try to remember the last time I hung out with people that weren't family in this way. Most people I know want to party and live a faster paced life than I care for. I've always been a bit of loner, and I keep my circle of friends small. I try to hang out with my best friends when I can, but we all have a lot going on. That becomes even more difficult when we don't live in the same area.

Kyrell's phone chimes with a text. "Hey Harls, I gotta go. I'm going to meet up with a lady friend before I head back to LA."

"Lady friend?!"

"Yeah, what else am I supposed to call her?"

"Gee, I don't know, her name maybe?" Harlow giggles.

Kyrell stares up at the dancing willow tree. "If I could remember what the fuck it is, I would."

Harlow and I give him a look of incredulity, shaking our heads. I thought I was bad when it came to relationships with women. Kyrell clearly has me beat.

"I'm keeping your weed," she proclaims, giving him a hug. "Text me when you get home, okay?"

"Sure, Mom." He winks at her, then turns his attention to me. "It was nice to get to know you. I'll text you some ideas for the tattoos for the next time I'm in town."

"Yeah, you too, man. That sounds good to me. See you around."

Harlow twirls back around after watching him go. "You're welcome to stay if you want. I don't know if you have plans with a lady friend, too."

I chuckle. "Nah, no lady friends for me."

She sits up on her elbows and gives me a curious look. "You have no lady friends at all?"

I lay back down next to her. "Nope. Why does that seem hard for you to believe? Am I that good-looking that it's unbelievable I'm not interested in entertaining women?"

Harlow falls into a fit of laughter. It's contagious. Once you hear it, you kind of want to make her laugh again and again just to get lost in the sound. It's melodic and genuine. Sometimes when people laugh, it's forced or out of nervousness, but with her, she finds the joy in whatever you tell her.

Once she catches her breath, she focuses her brown eyes on me. "You're alright." She raises the joint to her lips with a smirk on her face and inhales. She exhales, passing the joint to me. "Had a bad experience?"

The willow branches sway with the warm breeze, and I wonder if I should give her the watered-down reason or real reason. She doesn't seem to water herself down for me, so I decide to be honest.

"I want more," I say plainly.

Her head turns towards me, and her eyes give me a searching look. "More?"

"Yeah, more... I want a real relationship. Not some shallow hook-up shit. But that seems to be all that's available, or they want hook ups and money. I need for there to be some depth and not have it all be superficial. I have money? Cool. I have nice cars and clothes? Cool. But at the end of the day, all that shit doesn't matter. I want someone I can vibe with on every level. So, until then... I'm fine being solo. I'll know when I know."

I'm surprised about how honest I'm being with her. Maybe it's the weed or maybe I just feel comfortable with her. I don't know.

She lets out a sigh. "I know what you mean. About wanting more and not settling for someone who you don't really vibe with just for the sake of not being alone. That's why I refused my ex's proposal."

Her confession alarms me, and I sit up to get a better look at her. "You refused his proposal?"

"I did." She gives me a half-smile and then looks away from me. "We've known each other our whole lives... but I still felt like I couldn't be myself with him. I felt like our relationship was more of an expectation than anything. If I had said yes, I would've had to erase myself to be with him. Everything was about him and his career. Everything. And he expected me to follow along... so I said no. I guess we're somewhat friends now... I don't know." She shrugs.

I want to applaud her for saying no, but I can also see the sadness in her eyes. "Do you think you two will get back together?"

"No," she says without hesitation. "I just want to focus on myself and what I want to do... and make some friends. Since I was so wrapped up in him for two years, I didn't really have a lot of friends. I still don't." She cringes, breaking eye contact, adjusting the bracelets hugging her wrists. "Annndd that makes me sound like a loser."

"It's okay. I already knew you were. Sevyn told me you have no friends," I say.

She bolts upright with wide eyes. "She did?"

"Yeah, she said to be nice to you because you have no friends." Harlow cracks up. "I told her not to put your business out there like that, but you know Sevyn."

"I can't believe she told you that. I'm going to tell her something when I see her next. Please don't be my friend out of pity."

"I don't do anything out of pity, and Sevyn means well... in her own way. I think I would consider you a friend now... I think."

She gives me an incredulous look and puts her hand across her chest. "Acyn DeConto, is it possible you don't hate me after all?"

"It's possible." I shrug. "It's not like you have anyone else anyway."

Harlow shoves my arm, catching me off guard, and it causes me to topple over. She snorts with laughter as she collapses on top of me. Sitting up, she pulls me by my shirt, making me sit up with her.

"C'mon, we have to take a picture to immortalize this moment. You're admitting to being my friend and now everyone must know. Plus, it's golden hour." I can't help but smile because she looks truly happy about this. "Here." She shoves her phone at me. "Your arms are longer than mine. So, you take it and don't fuck it up."

"No pressure."

She gets as close as she possibly can without sitting on my lap. Her temple is pressed to my cheek and we both smile at the camera, but it doesn't seem right, so I tickle her, and she erupts with laughter. I snap as many pictures as I can while she's giving me a genuine smile.

"You jerk!" She squeaks. I hold her phone out to her. She glares at me and snatches it from my hand. I lay down with a satisfied smile on my face because between the alcohol and weed, the buzz is kicking in.

Harlow swipes through the pictures on her phone. "These are pretty good, Acyn."

"I know. There isn't anything I can't do," I say smugly.

She smacks my chest and then rests her head on me, flipping her twists into my face.

"You just had to flip your hair in my face?"

She giggles. "Okay, which one? I think this one." Her finger points to one where my arm is wrapped around her as she leans into me, her hand gripping the collar of my shirt while she laughs uncontrollably, and I look at the camera smiling.

"I like that one."

"Me, too."

She busies herself with uploading it. It's nearly dusk, but the party is still going strong. I almost don't want to go home, and I'm not sure I can move at this point. I don't know what the fuck kind of weed Kyrell brought, but I feel like I can lay here with her for days. My phone vibrates in my pocket, and I pull it out to see a notification that Harlow has tagged me in a post. I click on it and see the picture she chose with the caption: *Immortalizing Memories.*

I learned two things tonight. First, Harlow is comfortable enough with me to be herself which makes me feel good because I think she spends a lot of time second guessing herself. The second thing I learned is that Kyrell is one hundred percent right.

She is magnetic.

12

Harlow

ACYN AND I REJOINED the party after the sun had set. We ate, because munchies, lost count of our drinks, danced, and had the most fun I'd had in a while. I could easily say that the weed or alcohol made me more comfortable with him, but the truth is that I've never felt uncomfortable with Acyn. Sure, he can be a bit of an ass, but I've always felt like I can be myself with him.

We fall onto one of the couches underneath a canopy decorated in twinkle lights.

"I think I should go home now. What time is it?" he asks.

I reach for my phone, and it takes my eyes a moment to focus on the time. "I think it's... almost 3a.m."

"You think?" he asks, chuckling.

"I am properly intoxicated. Don't judge me," I say.

He puts his hands up in defense. "Aye, you'll receive no judgement from me because I was right alongside you. But if it's almost three... I should really go." I watch him and already know he isn't going to make it. He stands up for about five seconds and then falls back down on top of me.

With all of his body weight on me — he isn't light, but he smells so good — I try to help him sit up right. My voice is muffled because his back is pressed against my mouth. "Um, as your new friend, I cannot allow you to drive home. You're welcome to stay at my place, or you can stay in one of the guest bedrooms in West and Ava's house."

He's still lying on top of me. "I think you're right. So far, you're a good friend."

"Okay, can you be a good friend and get off of me? It's getting hard to breathe."

"Oh shit, sorry. I was comfortable."

I shove him off of me with as much force as I can muster, and he finally moves. "Okay, so where are you staying? With me or in a guest bedroom?"

"I'll stay with you," he says and for some reason it makes me smile. He also doesn't have a choice. I wouldn't let him leave even if he wanted to.

"Alright, up! We've got to make it to my place. I need some water and my bed." This time he makes it to his feet and holds his hand out to me. I grab it and feel the electricity I felt the first day I met him. He wraps his arm around my neck, and I wrap my arm around his waist as we walk towards my place.

I head for the kitchen to get water because I feel like I just walked through the desert. I offer him a glass, and we down them quickly. Once he's done, he looks around my place with interest.

"This is very... you," he says as he looks back at me with a lopsided grin. "Do you like sunflowers or something?"

I have sunflowers in vases on both my coffee and kitchen table. "Yeah, they're my favorite flower."

"That fits you, too."

"Why do you say that?"

He puts his hand in his pocket as he looks at the pictures on my wall. "You light shit up."

"Wow... a compliment." I curtsy. "Thank you."

He grins. "Yeah, yeah, don't get used to it. I'll be back to insults tomorrow."

"Wouldn't expect anything less. Do you want the bed or the couch?"

He turns towards me with his brows furrowed. "What kind of man would I be if I let you sleep on the couch?"

I cross my arms. "Oh, now you're a gentleman?"

"Yes, but only on Saturdays at 3a.m." He winks.

I chuckle. "I'm going to go change. I don't have any clothes for you... unless you want a t-shirt. I think I have one big enough for you."

"Oh, I'm good. I sleep in my boxers anyway," he says as he flips through my record collection. I gaze at him a moment and try to ignore the butterflies in my stomach about seeing him almost naked. Friends or not... he is GQ material.

I nod. "Of course you do."

He chuckles as I walk to my bedroom to change. I rummage through my drawers, looking for a t-shirt to put on when I hear UB40's *Red, Red Wine* playing from my record player. I smile because I remember dancing to this song with my mom. I head back out to the living room to see that Acyn has made himself at home as he digs through my fridge.

"Where did you get your records from?" He stands upright and turns around with a container of leftover pasta. Unbelievable.

"They were my mom's." I sit down at the table and watch him move around my kitchen. Instead of asking me where things are at, he opens drawers and stops only when he finds a fork.

"Were? She didn't want them anymore? That's a nice collection of vinyl." He sits down at the kitchen table with me and digs into the pasta.

I watch him eat a few bites and hug my knees to my chest. "Yeah... she died."

He stops mid-bite with a mouth full of pasta. "Shit, I am so sorry. I didn't mean to be a downer. You don't have to talk about it. We can talk about something else." The look in his eyes isn't one of pity but one of care.

"It's okay," I shrug. "I can tell you or we can talk about something else."

"Yeah, you can tell me."

I grapple with my emotions. I could easily keep the bandage on the wound as I've done for the past eleven years, or I can bare it and see what happens.

"My mom..." A smile tugs at my lips as an image of her appears in my head. "My mom was vibrant and full of life. She was our sun. Everyone always says I'm her spitting image. If you put our photos next to one another at similar ages, it's hard to tell us apart." Acyn gives me a warm smile.

"She died when I was twelve." My palms start to sweat. I barely know him. Why the hell am I sitting here on the verge of spilling my guts? He doesn't say a word. I squeeze my arms tighter around my legs as he waits for me to continue. He's not looking at me expectantly or sympathetically. He's simply sitting next to me in this moment. Holding the space for me to let it out.

"On Friday nights we would get a pizza and watch a movie together. I looked forward to Fridays. I'm sure I was one of the few kids who actually enjoyed spending time with their parents and admitted it." I smile and Acyn chuckles. "My dad would usually pick up the pizza on his way home from work, but that particular Friday he had off. My mom worked as a curator for a museum and had Fridays off. Since my dad was glued to some game on TV, my mom said she would go pick up the pizza. She invited me to go along, and of course I said yes because it sounded more fun than watching a game I knew nothing about."

"She..." Tears sting my eyes. My heart thumps in my chest but again Acyn says nothing and simply holds the space for me to continue on. "She and I went to pick up the pizza. I remember we were talking about what movie we were going to watch when we got home. And then everything happened so fast..." A tear escapes and I wipe it away. "A car hit my mom's side. I saw it coming but there was nothing I could do but scream. I remember screaming for her and then everything went black."

"Hours later, I woke up thrashing and screaming for her in the hospital. I had a concussion and a broken arm." I show him the scar near my elbow of where the bone pierced my skin when it cracked. "My dad grabbed me, and it took me a couple of seconds to realize it was him. When I calmed back down, I noticed he was sobbing. I asked him why he was crying, and he didn't immediately respond. I got an unsettling feeling that it had something to do with my mom. I asked him again and he... he told me that she didn't make it."

I let out a shaky breath, "I didn't believe him. I thought there was a mistake. I wanted to believe there was a mistake. It was just an accident. People walk away from accidents all the time. The longer my dad kept sobbing, the more real it became that my mom was gone. We were struck by a drunk driver. My mom was killed instantly..."

I let silence fall between us for a moment as my eyes find his.

"For a long time after she died, I wished it was my side that got hit." I wait for him to protest, but he doesn't. "So many people told me that I should be grateful to be alive or that it's a miracle I'm alive... at that time it didn't seem like that. It felt like a curse or some sick joke to be in the same car with my mother who was killed and walk away with minor injuries.

For a long time after she died, everything was a blur. I remember bits and pieces. Trying to desperately function with my mom gone... forever."

"My dad blamed himself for a long time because he wished it were him who picked up the pizza that day. I wished it were my side of the car that got hit. It was a rough few years after she passed. It's still hard but..." I exhale. "After a while I realized my mom wouldn't want me to live in misery. So I try to honor her as much as I can in all that I do. I have way more good days then bad days now..."

Tears stream down my face. I'm startled when Acyn's rough hands wipe them away. My eyes meet his, and he pulls me into a hug, wrapping his brawny arms around me. I don't pull away. I allow myself to melt into him and cry. We stay like this for what feels like forever. I'm sure it's only a few minutes but it feels like longer.

My ear is pressed to his chest, and I feel the deep vibrations of his voice. "All I can say is that your mom would be proud of who you are now. I also feel like a jackass for trying to leave while under the influence."

"Two compliments in one day? I don't know what to do with myself, Acyn." I hug him back. "You didn't know. Don't feel bad. Thank you... for listening to me."

"I may be full of myself, but I am a good listener."

I chuckle. He scoops me up in his arms.

"Um, are you insane? What if we both fall?"

"Then I will use you as cushion," he says with a smile. "Where is your bed?"

I point to my bedroom. Once we're near my bed, he tosses me onto it. "What the fuck was that?"

"It makes up for the two compliments I gave you," he says with a smirk.

And then he fucking strips. He grabs the hem of his shirt and peels it up. I feel I should turn away, but I can't. My presumption of every inch of him being covered in tattoos is correct. His abs are embellished with tattoos that wind around to his back and disappear beneath the band of his boxers. I feel like I'm in the desert again.

Then as if that isn't enough, he slides his pants off, his V on full display, and I watch him step out of them. Standing in front of me in just boxers and tattoos, he folds his clothes and sets them on the chair at my vanity. I quickly pretend to be more interested in crawling under the covers then ogling him, but then he leaves the room. I lay back against my pillow with a sigh and wonder what the fuck is wrong with me.

Acyn reappears moments later with a blanket and stage dives onto the bed next to me. "What the hell is wrong with you?" I shout as he sprawls out and almost pushes me off the bed. "Clearly your gentlemanly gestures have a short lifespan."

"Your bed looks more comfortable than the couch. I think I made the right choice," he says with a smug smile.

I climb out of bed to turn off the light, and my shirt rides up, exposing my ass cheeks. I turn back around as I try to pull it down and catch Acyn quickly look away and smile at the ceiling. Once I turn off the light, I crawl back in bed and snuggle up with my pillow.

We both lie still in the dark. "Tonight was fun," Acyn says.

"Yeah, it was."

He chuckles, "Even without seeing your face, I can tell you're smiling."

"I am. I'm glad you came."

He grabs my hand and holds it while placing it on his chest interlaced with his. I don't know what to do or say, so I don't do or say anything because my hand in his feels... *nice*. He rubs my hand with his other. It calms me, and I start to feel drowsy.

"Night, Acyn," I say sleepily.

"Night, Harlow."

ACYN

I roll over and open an eye as I slowly start to remember where I am. I look over towards Harlow's side and she isn't there. The smell of bacon makes my mouth water. Of course she's a morning person. If I don't have any clients, I sleep in until my cat meows at me like he's dying because he needs food. Even then, getting out of bed is trivial.

I climb out of her bed and follow the scent of bacon to the kitchen. When I round the corner, I see her lip syncing and dancing. She gives it her fucking all as she winds her hips, flips her hair, and rubs her hand over her body. My eyes are fixed on her hand as she rubs it over her breasts, down her torso, past the hem of her shirt, and I follow it back up her thigh as it rubs over her ass. Do friends get morning wood? In my defense, I just wanted some bacon and ended up with a show.

I decide to stop being a creep and let her know I'm here. "Morning, Sunshine."

She whips around with her hand over her heart. "How long have you been standing there?"

"Long enough to enjoy your flash dance," I say with a smirk. *Why lie?*

Her eyes widen and then she shifts her gaze downwards. "Oh... uh... I'm not used to people being here and I really can't not move when I love a song." She goes back to cooking.

"Hey, this is your place. I'm just a guest. Do what you want, and I'll enjoy the show."

"Shut up," she says while shaking her head with a grin.

"Please tell me your cooking is better than your coffee making."

She glares at me. "You know, I don't have to feed you. You can just watch me eat."

"What about southern hospitality?" I honestly wouldn't put it past her to make me watch her eat. She's a sweetheart, but I can tell that there's a side to her that you don't want to cross. Something about the quiet ones.

"That doesn't apply to you. But you're lucky today because I've already made your food." Turning off the stove, she removes the pan and makes her way to the table that's set with two place settings. "I hope you like orange juice."

"Sounds good, Sunshine. Thank you."

I'm honestly shocked that she even cooked me breakfast. When I'm in the company of women, it's mostly for dick and then they, or I, dash. There was no dick involved last night. It wasn't even on my mind. Okay, I'm fuckin' lyin'. When her t-shirt rode up and exposed her ass last night, I thought about it. But it wasn't a motive. I really just wanted to be in her space. I also didn't want to leave her alone after she told me about her mom. So I opted for the bed. I have never built a *real* relationship with a woman. I've never cared to because I already knew what it was.

"What did you call me?" Her voice cuts through my thoughts. I glance at her and there is a hint of a smile on her lips.

"Sunshine. It suits you and, quite frankly, is better than Harls." I shrug unapologetically.

She nods, considering the name. "I was expecting something much worse than Sunshine coming from you."

"Have some faith in me." I wink.

We're mid-conversation when there's a knock at her door. Her hand slaps over her mouth as she stares at me with wide eyes.

"What?" The look on her face has me worried.

"I forgot your sister was coming over today!" Harlow looks panicked, and I can't help but laugh because what a fucking sight this is. She jumps up and dashes to her room. "I've got to find pants, and you need to get dressed." Hopping on one foot as she tries to pull her pants on, she says, "Hurry, Acyn she's going to think that you and I—"

"Slept together?" I look at her with amusement. I have no plans of putting clothes on. She tries shoving me out of my seat, but I sit as solid as a tree trunk with a smirk on my face. Eventually she gives up and whisper yells at me.

"Yes! Put your fucking clothes on."

My sister knocks again, and Harlow's phone rings. I go back to eating. "I'm comfortable."

"Acyn!" she scream-whispers and her eyes narrow. "You fucking twat! Oh my god!"

She runs her hands over her face and looks between me, her ringing phone, and the door. I continue eating my omelet with a grin on my face. Harlow slowly walks towards the door and only opens it a sliver.

"Hey, Sevyn." Her tone is a little too high and enthusiastic.

"Were you slee—"

I tried my best to stifle a laugh, but fail.

"Wait a minute, I know that fucking laugh!"

Sevyn pushes past Harlow and sees me sitting at the table. She then stands there, gaping between Harlow and I. Harlow looks like she wants to die. Her head is tilted towards the ceiling and her hands cover her face. I on the other hand am extremely amused.

"Are you two... sleeping together?" Sevyn asks, still looking between Harlow and me.

"Sevyn, I can explain-" Harlow begins but I don't let her finish.

"We did sleep together."

"Acyn! Why are you lying to her?" Harlow yells.

I shrug. "I'm not, Sunshine. Did we or did we not sleep together?" I drink my orange juice as I gaze at her, waiting for her to answer the question.

Her hands are on the side of her head, and she looks at war with herself because, technically, we did sleep together. "I mean, yes, we did, but—"

Sevyn gasps. "You guys did sleep together? How long has this been going on?"

Harlow puts her hands up in front of her in protest. "No, we didn't... we didn't actually sleep together. I mean we slept together but – I'm making this worse! Acyn, tell her!"

I give her a clueless expression and shrug. She gives me a murderous look, and it makes me chuckle. I could easily explain, but I enjoy watching Harlow struggle with getting the words out.

Then, Sevyn squeals and hugs Harlow. "Oh, my God! Why didn't you guys tell me? This makes me so happy because maybe you'll become my sister-in-law!" She looks like she's about to burst with happiness. "Can you imagine if we became—"

Harlow pulls away and her brows are pinched. "You're not mad?"

"Hell no! This benefits me, not just Acyn. Forget about Acyn. This is a dream come true for me."

Harlow grabs my sister's face and looks her in the eyes. "Sevyn, Acyn and I didn't sleep together as in have sex. We just shared my bed. We're not together. We're just friends. I couldn't let him drive home in his intoxicated state, and he wanted to sleep in my bed. But nothing happened."

Sevyn looks as though someone just told her the most devastating news. "You both suck. I was so happy for you two for a moment."

Harlow looks at me with a puzzled expression. I shake my head and shrug. "Sevyn doesn't care. As you can see, she would be elated if you and I got together."

Harlow grabs her chest and looks completely relieved. "I cannot stand you, Acyn."

I chuckle as I clear our plates. "You love me, Sunshine. Even if you don't want to admit it."

She gives me the middle finger and a glare. "I'm going to go get ready. Are we still going shopping today?"

"Yes, I'll need a pick-me-up since you two just crushed my dreams," Sevyn says.

Harlow doesn't give her a response as she heads towards the bathroom. Sevyn turns her attention to me. I pretend to not notice her staring at me because I already know what she's going to ask me. "Do you like her?"

I scrub my hand over my face. "Here you go on your bullshit."

She shrugs defensively. "It's just a simple question. Do you like her?"

"I enjoyed spending time with her. We're friends. Can that be enough? Or do I need to buy a ring right now?"

"Touchy, touchy." A grin pulls at her lips.

"Neither of us are looking for a romantic relationship. Stop trying to play matchmaker."

"Alright, alright I'll leave it alone but if you two do end up –"

"Sevyn, drop it!"

Her mouth snaps shut mid-sentence. I rarely get short with people, especially my sister, but she knows how to push my buttons. Why can't a man and a woman simply enjoy one another's company? I don't understand this automatic relationship thing because we spent one night together as friends. It's exhausting and probably the reason why the few friends I do have that are women are fellow tattoo artists. It's all strictly business.

"Sorry," she mumbles without looking at me.

"It's fine."

I head to the bedroom to get dressed. I grab my t-shirt and pull it over my head. When I look up again, Harlow stands in front of me wrapped up in a robe. I can find my friend attractive, right?

She grins. "Leaving so soon?"

I grab for my pants so that I can form a thought and give her a response. I clear my throat. "Yeah, I don't want to impose on your shopping trip with Sevyn."

She disappears into her closet and then tosses her robe she was just wearing onto her bed. My mind immediately thinks of her naked but then her voice cuts through my thoughts. "You don't want to come with us?"

I shake my head, attempting to shake the thoughts I just had out of it. "Nah, I'm good, Sunshine."

She reappears from the closet, wearing clothes. "Some friend you are," she teases.

"Sounds like you like having me around."

"Mm, you're alright." She looks at me in the mirror as she applies her face moisturizer. "I feel like if I give you a compliment, it's going to go to your already big head."

I put my hand over my heart. "That's how you feel?"

"Only speaking facts." She walks towards me and holds out her hand. "Let me see your phone so I can add my number to it so you can text me. Sometimes I turn off my IG notifications."

I pull my phone from my pocket, unlock it, and place it in her palm.

"Oh my God! How cute are we?" she asks, referring to my phone's background picture.

I changed it from me and my cat to the one we took yesterday under the willow tree.

"Just add your number. You don't have to ooh and aww. It will be back to a picture of me and my cat soon enough."

"No, leave it. I won't say another word."

I side-eye her.

"Aweeee, but Acyn look at us," she says.

I snatch my phone back from her, letting out a falsely annoyed sigh. "Are you done?"

She purses her lips, pretending to lock them. "Yes, text me so I have yours and don't think you're a creep. Wait... already too late for that."

"I'm second guessing this friendship." I shoot her a text and also quickly change her name from Harls to Sunshine in my phone and then lock it. "Alright, I better get going."

"See you around." She wraps her arms around me, and I kiss the top of her head.

"Later, Sunshine."

13

Harlow

MY LIFE WENT FROM being pretty mundane to full on Technicolor in a short time. If someone would have told me six months ago that I would be *thriving* in Seattle – living on my own – I would have called their bluff. I haven't been here long, and it already feels like home to me. I worried that I wouldn't be able to get settled after feeling unsettled for so long.

It also helps that I've been fortunate enough to cultivate a family of friends. West and Ava are wonderful, but I know firsthand how limiting it can be to keep your circle a little too close knit. I've really had to push myself, like my dad suggested, to make new friends. The most unlikely person has been my ace. No pun intended. Acyn and I have become really close since the night we spent together.

Harlow: Do you want to go camera shopping with me? Sevyn is busy.
Acyn: Sounds boring but count me in, Sunshine.
Harlow: I'll pick you up after I'm done.

I signed up for two six-week photography classes that start soon. Acyn told me to stop being indecisive and pick some because I can always take more in the future if I want but I need to start somewhere. He also added, since I'm a hands-on learner, that I should look for work as a photography assistant. I hadn't considered that and mentioned it to Ava, who had a photographer friend willing to take me on a few shoots with her. I'm excited because that means I'll be able to get some hands-on experience while building my portfolio.

My schedule right now is pretty full between the yoga studio and coffee shop. I was hesitant to add on another commitment because I already feel like I'm spreading myself thin. But, if I don't start now, then when will I start? I'm tired of waiting for things to happen when I can make things happen instead.

⁙

Later that evening, I sit in Acyn's car, playing DJ while he gives me shit about my music selection. Harry Styles serenades us while Acyn looks like it pains him to listen.

"Tell me he can't sing!" I dance in my seat while he tries to hold back a smile.

"I'm actually surprised he can sing," he admits.

"Aha!" I point my finger at him. "See, you like his music."

"Whoa, whoa." He holds up his hand in protest. "I didn't say that. I said he can sing. That doesn't mean I want to listen to his album on repeat."

"Would it kill you to admit you like something I like?"

He gives me a sidelong glance. "I don't want to find out."

I turn the music up a little louder to annoy him. He shakes his head and pretends he doesn't notice. I jam the rest of the way to the store, even catching Acyn drumming his thumbs against the steering wheel a few times.

When we arrive, I'm faced with a million choices. There are a lot of cameras on display with very little variances between them. We spend an hour looking due to my indecisiveness. Acyn patiently leans against a counter in the aisle, watching me re-read each info card over and over... and over again.

He bends down next to me, with his hands on his knees, while I read one of the info cards. "Which one is your least favorite?"

I immediately point to the one I'm in front of.

"Okay," he says, nudging me. "Then there's no need to read the info card again. Which one do you like?"

I walk a little further down the row of cameras and point to another one.

"Alright." He grabs one of the scanner cards. "Now, which one do you love?"

I move further down the row. "This one." I chew my thumbnail while staring at it.

"Why are you wasting your time reading the other ones then if you know you love this one?"

"Because," I look up at him as he stands next to me. "It's out of my budget." Even though I'm a single person and work two jobs, I still have bills. I pay rent to West & Ava, pay for my own food, gas, paid for classes – that weren't cheap – and everything else that I need in between. I have the money, but if I were to buy it, things would be tight for a little while. And I don't like that feeling.

Acyn cups his chin in his hand, with his other arm folded against his abdomen, as he stares at the camera I love. "You know I could hel – "

I place my fingers over his mouth. "No, Acyn. Thank you... really. But no. I can buy the one I like and save for the one I love." I smile at him. While I'm grateful that he's willing to help me, there is no reason why I *need* the more expensive camera. The one I like will get me started and that's all I need – a start.

"Alright, just an offer, Sunshine." He holds the scanner card for my camera of choice up in front of my face. "Are you ready then?" he asks, waving the card in front of my face.

"Yes." I take the card from his hand.

He does a dramatic sigh and looks up at the ceiling. "Thank fuck for that!"

I shove him playfully and laugh. "You said you wanted to come with me."

"I did, and like I said, it was boring."

I ignore his remarks and head for the checkout. Once they hand me the camera, I turn to Acyn with the biggest grin on my face. "Look, I have a camera!"

He gives me a smile that matches my own.

ACYN

She's always happy, but in this moment, she is *ecstatic*. It's hard not to feel as excited as she is because it radiates off of her.

"Hold on, I'll take a picture." I hold up my phone and snap a picture of her beaming and hugging her camera. "Okay, can we get out of here now?"

She takes my phone as I hold it out to her, looking at the picture. "Yeah, you grouch."

"I'm not grouchy. I'm just hungry. Do you want to come and eat at my place?" I ask as I open my car door for her.

She slides in and gives me a look of surprise. "You're inviting me over?"

"Don't make me regret it, Sunshine. It isn't a big deal. You're just coming to my place for food and to meet my cat."

I can tell she's trying to contain a squeal. She closes her eyes and breathes to calm herself, smiling all the while. "Yeah, sure." She shrugs. "Whatever. Sounds good."

I chuckle to myself because she's trying so hard to not make it a big deal, when for her, it is. I guess it is for me, too. I haven't had a woman, aside from my sister and mom, at my place in a long time.

"Calm down, Sunshine. It's just my place and dinner." I shut her door and slide behind the wheel.

"You know how to cook? Or am I going to get food poisoning after this meal?" She looks at me with a raised brow and a hint of a smile.

"How else would I eat while living alone, smartass?"

She chuckles. "I don't know, but I'm about to find out."

"Regretting my invitation."

Covering her mouth, she stifles a laugh. "Alright, I'll stop."

I quickly connect my phone to the Bluetooth because I'm not going to be forced to listen to Harry Styles for the thirty-minute drive to my place. The guy can sing, but I'd rather listen to something a little more my tempo. When I glance over at her, she's texting someone that she seems annoyed with by how fast she's typing and rolling her eyes... *repeatedly*.

"Let me guess. The ex."

She sucks her teeth and does an imitation of what I assume is his voice. "'You two are sure spending a lot of time together.' And? So what?"

I really don't understand how this guy still has a hold on her when they aren't even together. I've also never been in a long-term relationship, so I'm definitely missing something. It's always obvious when she's talking to him because her usual bright and bubbly attitude disappears.

"I mean, I have no words of advice other than fuck him." Really though, fuck him. He seems like a needy asshole. Although I'm sure he thinks I'm an asshole for simply spending time with her.

She looks at me and sighs. "You're right. Fuck him." She tosses her phone in her bag and messes around with her camera that she just took out of the box. "It has a little bit of charge. I'm going to charge this at your place so I can try and snap some pictures of you and your cat." Her smile is back. She looks out the window. "How far is your house?"

"About fifteen more minutes. I used to live in the city in a tiny ass apartment with insane rent. Then my sister convinced me to buy a house outside of town, and honestly, it's the best decision I've ever made."

"Wow, twenty-five and you have your own house and businesses? Acyn, how are you single?" she asks with a grin.

I do have my shit together for my age. A lot of people assume I don't given my appearance, but I have been working for this life that I have now since before I moved out of my parents' house. I got my first job when I was sixteen – pushing carts – and I've been working consistently since then.

"Are you admitting that I'm a catch?" I give her a lopsided grin.

"Mmm..." She closes her eyes and lays her head back against the seat. "You are. You'll make some woman very happy one day. Not just because of what you can offer but because of who you are." When she opens her eyes, she looks at me with a smile on her face and then looks out the window. "You live in a nice neighborhood."

Her words knock me off kilter. I let them wash over me like an unexpected wave. She's a lot like the ocean, you know. Unpredictable and beautiful.

I clear my throat. "Uh, thanks. I tried to think of the future when I bought this house and not just right now." I park in my garage and turn to her. "I hope you like steak."

Just inside, my cat waits for me, per usual, and meows like I'm cruel for leaving him home alone all day. His meows stop once he realizes I have someone new. "Harlow, meet my cat, Six-Two-Six."

Her eyes glitter with excitement. "Did you really name your cat Six-Two-Six after Stitch from Lilo & Stitch?"

"Yeah... my niece and nephew were really into it at the time I got him and I thought it was cool so..."

She finally lets out the squeal she had been holding in since the store parking lot. "Eee that's the cutest thing ever! He is so soft. Oh my God, I'm going to steal him." And like the traitor Six-Two-Six is, he rubs against her legs. He loves the attention. Apparently, me providing him with ridiculous amounts of food, love, and a place to live is now subpar. She picks him up and he snuggles into her neck. Yeah, eat it up buddy. "It's so cozy here... I was expecting..."

"A bachelor pad?" I ask her as he looks around.

"Yeah." She grins as she holds and pets Six-Two-Six who now purrs in her arms.

"Nah, I went through that phase before I bought this house." I chuckle. "C'mon you can sit with me in the kitchen or feel free to stream something in the living room."

"Oh no, I'm going to watch you cook. I love cooking, too. Plus, I need to make sure you don't poison my food," she teases.

Six-Two-Six only jumps down from Harlow's arms when I put food in his bowl.

"Do you want to come take pictures at the studio next week?" I ask her as I wash my hands.

"Next week?" Her voice sounds higher than usual. "Don't you want me to practice?"

"I know you're capable, so what's the hesitation?"

She chews on her thumbnail which I know she does when she's nervous or unsure. "What if you hate them?"

"Then I'll tell you, but I doubt I will."

She doesn't say anything for a few breaths while she watches me prepare the steak. "Yeah, I can."

"See... was that so hard?" I put the pan on the stove.

"No," she chuckles. "Now feed me."

"Aye, aye captain."

While I prepare the food, Harlow snaps pictures with her new camera, until it dies, and then switches to her phone. I've never met someone who has such a well-documented life. The majority of the pictures she takes don't make it to her social media. They're hanging all over the walls at her place. I wonder if she's always been like this or if losing her mom had something to do with it. I haven't lost anyone close to me but I imagine it makes you hold onto every happy moment a little tighter.

⟨⊱❀⊰⟩

After we've eaten, Harlow and I sit outside on my back porch, listening to the rain fall. I've become comfortable living alone, but it's nice having her here tonight. Even Six-Two-Six seems happy to have someone around other than me. She sits snuggled up in the crook of my arm, wrapped in a blanket, with her head resting on my shoulder.

"Thanks for dinner tonight. It was delicious."

She'd distracted me with her moaning – yet again. I can't act like I didn't feel some satisfaction that my food got that reaction out of her. "Told you I can cook."

"Who taught you to cook?"

"My mom gave me the basic knowledge and love for it."

"Ah, my mom loved to cook too. Do your parents come over to your house or just Sevyn's?"

"They come to my house, too. Sevyn and I swap Sundays. Now that it's summer though, they'll be traveling a lot. Visiting my other siblings and doing whatever it is that retired people do." She chuckles. "How's your dad?" I ask.

"He's good but misses me. I may go home for my birthday. I haven't decided yet."

"When is your birthday?"

"September twenty-second. What about yours?"

"I just celebrated mine in February, on the twelfth."

"Awe, a little Valentine's baby. That's cute."

"I guess." I check the time on my phone, and it's almost eleven. "You can let me know when you want me to take you home." I've gotten so used to having her around. I've spent a few more nights at her house but it wasn't intentional, we just fell asleep watching shows.

"Are you kicking me out?"

"No, you can stay if you want." I try to sound indifferent when I'm just hoping she'll stay.

"I'll stay... for Six-Two-Six."

"Oh, just fuck me, huh? Stay for my cat?"

"I am also unbelievably comfortable, and the thought of getting up to have you drive me home sounds unappealing," she says, yawning. She readjusts so now her head rests on my lap.

Sitting here, listening to the rain, and feeling her body weight on me is relaxing. When I first met Harlow, I didn't expect her to become someone that I would grow attached to. I have my guy friends that I do things with, but it's not like we're going to snuggle up on the couch together listening to the rain. She brings a different kind of energy to my life that I didn't know I needed.

"Do you want to go inside and watch something?"

There's no response. I look down at her and see that she has fallen asleep. I gently slide her head off my lap and get up so that I can carry her inside. When I lift her, she doesn't even stir. Six-Two-Six watches me with a puzzled expression, wondering where the hell I'm taking his pillow. I could put her on the couch, but it's not the most comfortable place to sleep. I've fallen asleep there enough to know that she'll wake up with aches and pains. I pass the living room and head for my room instead. I lay her down gently on my bed and cover her with some blankets. She loves her fucking blankets. Even if it's warm, she wants to be wrapped in a blanket.

I lie there, listening to her soft snores and drifting off to sleep, when she turns over and her hand lands on my chest. I interlace my fingers with hers. She lets out a sigh and her breathing slows again, and I fall asleep wondering how I became so attached to her in such a short period of time.

14

Harlow

WITH THE ADDITION OF the photography classes – to my already busy schedule – I'm feeling it both physically and mentally. I overslept and woke up with a headache from the depths of hell. I'm flitting from room to room, looking for my clothes because I'm supposed to work at the yoga studio for two hours, the coffee shop for eight hours, and then zip over to my photography class for two hours. The shifts aren't long, but they wear me out because I'm on my feet, moving the whole entire time. Even in my photography class, I'm not just sitting down and taking notes. I'm active – *all day long*.

West did offer to cut back my hours at the coffee shop, but I told him not to worry about it because I don't mind working at the coffee shop.

Okay, if I'm being honest, I enjoy working at the coffee shop because Acyn works a few blocks away. I've been so busy these past couple of weeks that the shop is the only place we get to see each other. At the end of the day, I'm utterly exhausted. We still see each other in the evenings sometimes, but I'm not really fun to be around when I'm falling asleep as soon as I slow down.

He hasn't complained and assures me that it's fine, but I still feel bad. Hendrix is still bothered by our relationship – of course. I keep telling him that Acyn and I are just friends. I didn't tell him that we sleep together frequently. There is no way he could wrap his mind around

that without thinking that we're having sex. It's just Netflix and Chill...
without the chill.

Nothing, aside from hand holding, has happened between Acyn and
I. Friends hold hands, right? It's not like I'm secretly pining for him.
Except for when he smiles a certain way, or says some smartass remark, or
does something sweet for me – like making me dinner – a feeling blooms
within me that's beyond friendship.

I hustle out my door to my car and I get a text from Acyn.

Acyn: *Morning, Sunshine! Are we still on for pics tonight?*

I smack my hand to my forehead because I forgot I agreed to take
pictures today.

Harlow: Of course, what time should I be there?
Acyn: 5 should be good.
Harlow: K, see you then! Stop by for shitty coffee.
Acyn: I wouldn't miss it.

He still won't admit that my coffee is good. Ass.

⁂

By the end of my yoga class, I feel feverish. I brush it off because I did just
teach back-to-back classes in a 100-degree room. I down a bottle of water
and take a cool shower. I hope that I'll feel better by the time I reach the
coffee shop. Except I don't. Even West notices.

"You don't look so good, Kid." He calls me Kid now, because my dad calls me Kiddo, and they refer to me as "the kid" when they talk.

"I don't feel good... at all."

He looks at me with a furrowed brow. "You know, I can handle it today. You've been doing a lot. Maybe a day off will do you some good."

I don't want to agree, but the look he gives me lets me know that I have no say in the matter. "Yeah, you're probably right. Don't burn the place down without me," I say over my shoulder as I walk out the doors I just came through.

Once I'm home, I have to run to the bathroom because I feel like I need to throw up. As soon I see the toilet, I pull back the lid and puke. Once everything that I ate for breakfast is out of my stomach, I lean back against the tub. I feel so drained, like I can't get up. I'd rather be in my bed than lying on the bathroom floor even though the cold feels good on my hot skin. After a few moments of rest, I get up, and the nausea hits me again. I puke and sit back down on the floor.

When I feel like maybe I can get up, I try again. I make it to my feet; the nausea is there, but I'm able to steady myself with the help of the bathroom sink, and I make my way to my bed. Thankfully, it isn't far. I flop onto it and let sleep win.

ACYN

I glance at the clock; it's five-fifteen, and Harlow still isn't here. I sent her a text earlier to let her know a tattoo I was doing was taking a little longer than expected, so her shitty coffee would have to wait. There was no response from her, but I didn't trip because I know people go ape shit over coffee around noon.

It isn't like her to not show up for something, especially something that deals with photography. After I finish with my last client of the day, I walk over to the shop, confused when I don't see her there. I do see West and make my way over to him.

"Hey, West. Have you seen Harlow?"

"Yeah, I sent her home because she looked terrible."

"Terrible, how?"

"I think she came down with something. I had Ava check on her because she didn't respond to my text, and she said Harlow's knocked out."

"Oh, okay. Thanks, man. I'll see you around."

He raises his hands up. "What, no coffee? Is mine not good enough for you?"

I chuckle. "Nah, it's been a long day. Next time." I'm not about to admit to him that he doesn't provide me with the same company as Harlow.

"Understood. See you around, man."

I give him a two-finger salute and head out the door.

Once in my car, I drum my fingers on the steering wheel, trying to decide if I should go home or go see Harlow. If she's sleeping, I don't want to startle her, but... I also don't want her to be alone. Or maybe... I don't want to be alone. If we don't physically chill with each other in the evenings, we're FaceTiming. It's become our routine, and now I don't know what to do without it.

I think for a few more minutes about what to do. Starting my car, I decide that I'll go and see her. I make a quick stop by the store to grab the ingredients for my mom's chicken noodle soup. When I walk to the checkout, some sunflowers catch my eye, so I buy those too because I know she loves them.

All the lights are off at her place. I'm sure I look like a level ten stalker creeping into her place at night. Hopefully, she doesn't freak out. I put the ingredients and flowers down in the kitchen before I head towards her room to see if she's still sleeping. When I open the door, she's sound asleep. I sit on the edge of her bed, pressing my palm to her forehead. West was right; she's burning up. She groans and her eyes slowly open.

"Acyn?" she asks groggily.

"Yeah, Sunshine. You're burning up."

"I feel like shit. You shouldn't be here. I've been puking, and I don't want to get you sick."

"Eh, I'm strong as an ox. I'll be fine," I say as I stroke her hair.

She opens her mouth to say something, but abruptly stops as she scrambles off the bed, dashing into the bathroom. Seconds later, I hear retching followed by puking. I follow her into the bathroom, but she tries to protest.

"No –" She retches and pukes again.

I crouch down next to her, pulling her hair back. She tries to push me away, but she just rests her hand on my chest after she realizes I'm not moving and goes back to puking. She flushes the toilet and leans back against the tub, wiping her mouth.

"You don't have to help me," she says weakly.

"I know I don't have to, but what if I want to?"

Her eyes are watery from puking as she looks at me. I can tell she wants to make a smartass remark but doesn't have the energy for it. She closes her eyes and smiles. "Fine, welcome to my puke show."

I chuckle and sit next to her. "Front row seats, how did I luck out?"

She rests her head on my shoulder. "You said you wanted it. Can't back out now."

"I'm not. I'll be here for whatever you need."

"Good." She snakes her fingers through mine. "My whole body hurts. I want to take a hot shower."

"Can you stand to take a shower?" I look at her as she rests on my shoulder. Her eyes are closed, and she looks like she could fall asleep right here.

"Probably not."

"How about a bath?"

"I guess that works, too," she says.

"I got you."

She moves her head off my shoulder as I get up to turn the bathtub faucet on. I look around the tub and see that she has a collection of bath products. I choose one and squeeze it into the water. The scent of lavender quickly fills the bathroom. I sit back down next to her and she rests her head on my shoulder. I bring my hand up to her cheek and gently rub my thumb along her cheek bone. We sit like this while water and bubbles fill the tub.

I check over my shoulder to see that it's filled. "Sunshine, you can get in the bath now."

She slowly slides to an upright position. "Thank you."

"Uh... I'm not trying to be a creep, but can you get your clothes off?" I observe her as she sits there with her eyes closed. Her color is dull and not as luminous as it usually is.

"If you want to see me naked, you just have to ask," she says with a mischievous smile and peels her shirt over her head. I quickly turn away and find interests in other things in the bathroom. "Don't look, creep."

I chuckle and watch her clothes as she tosses them near my feet. T-shirt, socks, jeans, bra, and then her panties. I hear her step into the water and let out a sigh as she lowers herself into the tub. "Okay, I'm in."

I swallow and turn back around. She's covered in bubbles up to her neck and she looks comfortable. I still feel awkward looking at her. I rub the back of my neck while looking at the floor. "Uh... I can just wait out there now that you're safely in the bathtub. You won't fall asleep, will you?"

She shakes her head.

"Okay, I'll leave the door open a bit. Just yell if you need me."

Stepping out of the bathroom, I head towards the kitchen to put the stuff I brought for chicken noodle soup away and to find a vase for the sunflowers. I run out to my car to grab my phone so that I can text Sevyn to stop by my place and feed Six-Two-Six.

Acyn: Hey, would you have time to feed 626?
Sev: Where are you?
Acyn: Helping a friend.
Sev: Would that friend happen to be a girl named Harlow?
Acyn: Can you feed him or not?
Sev: Sure, tell Harlow I said Hi.

I shake my head. I love and hate her at the same damn time. I'm closer with her than my other two siblings. I'm the only boy in my family. I have two older sisters and then there is me. Sevyn is the youngest. For whatever reason, she latched on to me as a baby, and we've been close ever since. I don't tell her anything about Harlow's and my relationship though, and I can tell it annoys her. There really isn't anything to tell her anyway, plus I figured Harlow would tell her. She hasn't either though – Harlow is a lot like me in that she keeps certain things private.

I go into her room to strip her sheets and put new ones on because when I arrived, she was drenched in sweat. There's a picture of her and me on her nightstand that wasn't there the last time I was here. I smile and then my attention is drawn to her phone that vibrates next to the picture. The name Hendrix appears across the screen with an eye roll emoji after it. It stops ringing and then starts up again. Goddamn, bruh, let her fucking breathe. I thought he was supposed to be a professional athlete, so I don't know where he finds the time to blow up her phone. He must sit on the bench a lot.

I turn my attention back to searching for sheets. I look through her drawers but find nothing but clothes and... two vibrators. I slam that drawer shut as soon as my brain registered what I saw. I also curse myself for my dick responding to seeing those. I just watched her puke, but when you can't remember the last time you've been with someone... it doesn't take much for your mind to take you there. I went from dipping my dick, as Sevyn says, into everything to *nothing*. I've become well acquainted with my hand since then.

I push those thoughts out of my mind and eventually find sheets stacked in the top of her closet. When I'm done making her bed, I look up, and she's standing there in her robe, watching me make her bed.

Her mouth is curved into a smile as she leans against the door frame. "You're so...domestic, Acyn." She looks a little brighter than she did before her bath.

"We've already established I'm a catch," I say with a wink as I fluff up her pillows and pull back the blankets. "It's ready when you are. Do you want water or anything?"

She holds her hand up as she walks towards her dresser. I avert my eyes because I know what's in there now, and I can't unsee it. "No, I just want to lay in bed."

I glance at her as she pulls her panties up her legs and I turn back around. "Uh, maybe I should go. That way you can get some rest," I say, rubbing my neck.

"I like having you here. You're not a bother at all," she says as she crawls into bed and buries herself under the covers.

"Alright, I'll stay, but let me shower first and throw my clothes in the wash."

She covers her face. "Did I get puke on you?"

"It's not a big deal, Sunshine. You're sick."

"This is embarrassing." Her eyes are wide as she stares at me through the slits of her fingers. "I'm sorry you – "

"People get sick, and they puke. It's life." I shrug. It really isn't that big of deal to me. She has no reason to be embarrassed. "I'll be back."

I quickly shower, throw my clothes in the washer along with hers, and return back to the room to find that she's already dozing off again. Well, I thought she was.

She raises a finger, pointing to her closet, "There's some of your stuff you've left here over the past few weeks. If I didn't know any better, I would think you're moving in."

After the first few times of unintentionally staying over, the staying over became intentional.

"Thanks." I disappear into her closet, surprised to find that she has given me a designated section. I'm not sure how I missed this when I was looking for sheets earlier. I put on a pair of boxers and a white t-shirt. Instead of doing my usual stage dive – that annoys the shit out of her –

onto the bed, I decide to slide in next to her instead. She hugs my arm and rests her cheek on my shoulder.

"Thank you for taking care of me. Only my mom, dad, or my best friend back home have cared for me like this. It means a lot to me that you stayed... even though I puked on you."

I give her a reassuring smile. "Let the puke go. I'm not even thinking about it, so neither should you." I can't help but wonder how someone she was with for two years didn't take care of her if she wasn't feeling well. "Your... boyfriend didn't take care of you?"

"Hendrix? No..." she scoffs. "The few times I was sick he wouldn't come near me. He said he couldn't be sick because of training. Had to be in tip-top shape." She sighs, and I already know it was followed by an eyeroll without seeing her face.

"You did a lot for him though... didn't you?"

"More than I care to admit. He was... is very self-absorbed. It's always been all about him and how his future will be. I had to fit in where I could with him."

I knit my eyebrows because I struggle to understand how a dude like that had Harlow by his side... and he fucked it up. I decide to drop it because I really don't care to know anything about him. "You should get some rest, Sunshine."

"Yeah," she says with a yawn. "You're right."

It doesn't take her long to fall asleep.

15

Harlow

I TRY TO OPEN my eyes, but they're still heavy with sleep. Once I open them and focus, I glance at my clock and see it's a little past one in the afternoon. Instead of getting up and scrambling out of bed like I usually do, I lay here a little longer. I've been running for so long, and I think it finally caught up with me yesterday. My nausea has subsided but my body still aches and my throat is killing me. No doubt from all the vomiting I did yesterday. My stomach rumbles, but I'm scared to eat. When I look at my nightstand, there's a glass of water there with a note next to it.

> Hey Sunshine,
> I had to work.
> Hopefully you're feeling better.
> There's soup in the fridge.
> Ace

I smile and put the note back on my nightstand. I must have been exhausted if I slept through him cooking. Taking a small sip of water, I wait to see how my stomach responds. It doesn't hurt or make me nauseous, so I gulp down the rest of it. My stomach protests again, reminding me that I need food and not just water.

I enter the kitchen which looks as though it hasn't been touched. Except for the vase of sunflowers on the counter. There goes those blooming feelings again. I open the fridge to find the soup he made me, and it's still somewhat warm. He must not have left that long ago.

I warm it up to piping hot and settle on my couch to eat it. When the first spoonful of soup hits my tongue, I close my eyes and moan. It soothes my throat and tastes delicious. I've never had soup this good before. I'm going to have to steal his recipe.

I quickly finish the bowl and warm up a second. While I wait for it to heat up on the stove, I find my phone. Of course, I have the usual missed calls from Hendrix – no surprise there. I also missed a few calls from my dad. I call him back and he picks up in two rings.

"How are you feeling, Kiddo? West told me that you weren't feeling well. Sorry I'm not there to take care of you."

I remove my soup from the stove and pour it in my bowl. "I'm fine Dad. I feel a lot better today."

He hesitates for a few seconds and then sighs. "Harlow, I think maybe you're doing a little too much. You essentially have three jobs."

I knew this was coming. He isn't wrong, but I don't want to think about slowing down right now. "People get sick, Dad."

"They do, but you also know that you have a lot on your plate right now. There's nothing wrong with stepping back from something."

To appease him, I agree. "You're right, Dad. I'll think about it."

I hear the smile in his voice. "Good. I still worry about you even though I'm not physically there."

I chuckle and take a spoon of my soup. "I know, Dad. I wouldn't expect anything else from you. My friend was kind enough to come over and help me out. He made me the most delicious chicken soup."

"Is this that Acyn fellow?"

"Yeah, can you believe he can cook?" I ask him as I almost gulp down the rest of the soup.

"I'm glad you have someone there with you. He sounds like a good guy."

"He is," I say with a smile.

"I'm going to let you get some rest, Kiddo. I just wanted to check in on you. I have an appointment and a meeting to get to."

"An appointment? How are *you* feeling?"

He chuckles. "Just a checkup. I love you, and I'll check in with you later today."

"Love you, Dad. Talk to you later."

I end the call and contemplate another bowl of soup. A yawn escapes me, and my bed seems more appealing than another bowl of soup. I make my way back to my room and bury myself beneath the covers, feeling satiated.

I clear Hendrix's texts and calls from my notifications, and I type a message to Acyn.

Harlow: Thank you for the soup. It made me feel better.

A few minutes later, I get a reply.

Acyn: You're awake. Good. I'll be done here in a couple of hours.
I'll stop by after.
Harlow: Aww, you're sweet.
Acyn: Stop that shit. I'm doing what any decent person would do.

I know that was a subtle shot at Hendrix. He rarely says anything about him, but if he does, he usually isn't impressed. I often find myself wondering what the hell I was so impressed by all those years. Even before we got together. I don't have an answer and I may never have one. I let the thought go instead.

Harlow: *I'm gonna sleep. I'll see you when you get here.*
Acyn: *Rest up, Sunshine.*

I slide my phone under my pillow and get comfortable. It doesn't take long for me to find sleep.

When I wake up again, it's 4p.m. I haven't slept like this since I was in high school. I clearly took naps for granted. Acyn still isn't home. I correct my thoughts. He isn't *back* yet. I have to correct myself a lot because I often tell him, "Let's go home."

He always replies, "Which one?" He messes it up just as much as I do. We've blurred a few lines, but neither one of us can find a fuck to give.

Feeling feverish again, I take a shower and then settle in front of the TV. I feel better than yesterday, but I'm still not a hundred percent. I hate to even think it, but I feel like I'm coming down with a cold. My dad was right, though, I have been stretching myself as far as I can go and then some. Ava and West haven't dared come in my place. I don't blame them. Since Ava is pregnant, neither of them need to get whatever cold from hell that I have.

I text Acyn and ask him to pick some medicine up on his way back over here. I check my e-mails, and my photography instructor assured me that most of the stuff I can do at home which helped me relax a little bit more.

My head snaps to the door when it opens, and Acyn walks through, carrying grocery bags, flowers, and a duffel bag. "Moving in?" I ask with a smile tugging at my lips.

"Just an extended sleepover," he says with a smile as he kicks the door shut behind him. "I was ahead of you and picked up some medicine when I stopped at the store. Eli and Emery have happily volunteered to care for Six-Two-Six. I may not have a cat after this. So, you owe me a new cat."

"Six-Two-Six must not love you." I tease.

"His loyalty is very shaky, if you didn't notice." He sets all the stuff he was carrying down in the kitchen. "How are you feeling?" he asks as he sits next to me on the couch and snatches the remote out of my hand.

"Jerk. If I had my strength I would – "

"You would what, Sunshine? Puke on me?" There's a smirk on his face that I would love to smack off, but I refrain.

I sit there with my mouth slightly open, glaring at him, while he grins back at me. "I'm sick and this is how you treat me?"

"I asked you how you are."

"I honestly think I'm getting a cold. My body really isn't having it right now."

"It's telling you to slow the fuck down," he says as he looks at me. I ignore him and get up from the couch to go rummage through the bags he brought. He follows me. "I'm taking next week off of work."

I gape at him. "Not for me, I hope!"

"No, I had already planned to take a week off during this time months ago."

I'm instantly relieved when he says that. As much as I enjoy his company, I don't want him jeopardizing his work for me.

"What do you have planned?"

"I'm going to the Oregon Coast for the week. I rent a house there and just chill. It's simple but the views are... I think you would like it."

I still as I pour some medicine into the measuring cup. "Me? What does this have to do with me?"

"I wanted to invite you to go with me. After seeing how sick you've gotten, I think that a little time away could be good for you."

"Acyn, I don't want to intrude on your solitude if you've already had this planned for months." I stare at the small cup of blue liquid and make a face. I hate the taste of cold medicine. I have to mentally hype myself up to down it.

"I wouldn't invite you if I felt you would be intruding."

I down the disgusting medicine, chasing it with a cup of water. "You really want me to go with you?" I wipe my mouth with the back of my hand.

"Yeah."

I nod. "I would have to talk to Celeste and see if she'll be alright for a week. She already told me to take some time off. I don't think West would mind either. In fact, he and Ava would probably be happy to get my sickly ass out of here."

"You're a walking germ."

"You were so sweet just a few hours ago... when you weren't here."

"I have to keep the balance, Sunshine." He smiles brightly.

"Uh huh." I put the new bouquet of sunflowers he brought into a vase. "Thanks for the flowers, asshole."

Setting them on the coffee table, I take a picture of them because they're too pretty not to. I upload it with a caption that reads: *when he's an ass but brings your favorite flowers*, followed by the hashtag #acetheass. I hear his phone chime in the kitchen where he's busy cooking something again.

He lets out a rumble of laughter as soon as he sees it. "I'm Ace the Ass now?"

"If the shoe fits." I lie down on the couch so that I can watch cooking shows. A little while later, Acyn appears in front of me, holding out a hot bowl of something. When I look in the bowl, I see it's teriyaki with white rice.

"If I had known getting sick would cause you to become my own personal chef, I would have gotten sick sooner."

He chuckles with his mouth full of food as he sits down next to me. "Eat," is all he says.

I don't say a word as I eat because it's that good. Food is definitely a love language.

After we devour our bowls of teriyaki – that taste better than the restaurants' – I lie with my head resting on Acyn's lap while we watch cold case shows. I had never really watched them until I let him pick something one night and now I'm hooked.

Even though the bottles of cold medicine say "non-drowsy" they always make me sleepy. The cold medicine mixed with a full stomach – I didn't stand a chance. My eyes grow heavy and become harder to keep open. I hear Acyn talk to me but he sounds far away.

I hear him say, "Sleep, Sunshine. I'll be here." And then I drift back off to sleep.

After a few days of consistent rest and Acyn's cooking, I feel like myself again. This past week would have been hell if he weren't around to keep me company and care of me. I didn't have to ask him for a thing. He just did it. It was nice to be taken care of. Today is the first day that I've felt up to do anything aside from laying down or sleeping. It's Friday morning, and I still have to talk to Celeste about taking next week off to join Acyn on his trip.

I'm nervous to ask Celeste for a week off. West agreed without hesitation, but I feel like I'm abandoning Celeste even though she has never made me feel that way. I call her, chewing on my thumbnail, and wait for her to pick up.

"Harlow, darling, how are you?"

"I'm feeling better, Celeste. Thank you."

"Good, good I was worried about you. Everything okay?" she asks.

"Um, I wanted to ask you something... I was wondering if I could take this week off? Everyone keeps telling me that maybe I need to slow down. I think I agree. Even if it is reluctantly..." I don't know why I'm holding my breath. I guess I feel like I owe Celeste something because I wouldn't be in Seattle if it weren't for her.

"Of course, you can! We'll manage without you just fine," she reassures me and I let out the breath I was holding. "Anytime you need something Harlow – just ask. Your health, in every aspect, is more important than anything."

"Thank you. That means a lot to me."

"Where are you heading off to this week?"

"My friend is taking me to the Oregon Coast. I've never been."

"Oh, you will love it. It's beautiful. Well, I don't want to keep you for too long. Enjoy your time off. I'll talk to you when you get back."

"Thanks, Celeste. I'll see you soon."

I end the call and let out a few breaths. I haven't been working for Celeste long but she has been nothing but good to me. Now that everything is setup for me to go away, the excitement settles in.

I shoot Acyn a text.

Harlow: All set!
Acyn: I knew she wasn't going to say no. Pack your shit.
Harlow: I'll have my 3 bags ready for Monday morning.
Acyn: 3?! What could you possibly be taking?!
Harlow: Everything I could possibly need, duh.
Acyn: It's a week, not a month.

I chuckle at the eye roll emoji. I'm rubbing off on him. He rarely ever uses emojis but now, when he texts me, he'll throw them in here and there.

Harlow: I'll try and narrow down my outfit options.
Harlow: Are you stopping by tonight?

I've gotten used to him being around. I see him more than I see Sevyn. We still talk constantly, but I didn't think that Acyn and I would end up being closer then she and I are. She doesn't seem the least bit bothered by it, though.

My attention is drawn to the door when a knock resounds from the other side. I glance through the window near the door and see someone holding a box filled with red roses. Cautiously opening the door, I peek around it.

"Good afternoon, are you Harlow Shaw?"

"Uh...yes..." I'm sure my face looks as confused as I sound.

"I have a flower delivery from Hendrix Moore." Oh, for fuck's sake. I cover my face with my hands. "If you could sign here, and I will go get the rest."

"The rest?"

He gives me an apologetic smile which has me worried. "Um, yes, there are twelve more boxes."

Handing me the first box of roses, I read the side of the box, which says Venus Et Fleur. I've seen these all over Instagram. While they're pretty, what the hell am I going to do with twelve boxes of them?

It goes without saying that Hendrix was really bothered by Acyn's bouquet of sunflowers. Apparently, he now feels the need to flex. The more I think about it, the angrier I become. The delivery guy finishes carrying all the boxes into my living room, which is now covered in roses.

"Thanks," I say as I slam the door behind him.

I find a note attached to one of the boxes.

I'll give you everything and more, if you'd let me.

I scoff and rip it in half. Why the hell does he have to do shit like this? My phone rings from my back pocket. Staring angrily at the roses, I don't bother looking at who it is.

"Did you get my delivery?"

"Yeah." My tone is clipped.

"You don't sound as happy as I was hoping you would."

"What the hell am I going to do with twelve boxes filled with roses?" I wave my hand around like he can see me.

"I just thought it was a nice gesture. Since you've been sick... and I miss you."

I laugh bitterly. "No, these roses are a pissing contest."

He's silent for a beat, letting out a sigh. "Do you know how fucking hard it is to see some guy you've only known for a few months get to spend all this time with you?"

"Hendrix, c'mon!" I groan. "Acyn and I are just friends."

"It's funny because that's what you used to say about us."

The retort that was forming dies on my tongue, because he isn't wrong.

"But when I said it, I meant it right? This whole relationship, or whatever the hell it is between us, has become so damn exhausting!" I enunciate every word. "I can't do shit without you having some opinion that nobody fucking asked for, about what I'm doing or who I'm with. Even when I'm with Kyrell, you have a damn problem!"

"I just want to be with you, Harlow. Do the past two years mean absolutely nothing to you?"

"No, no. You want me to follow you around. To be there for you but... you don't really want me. You just want what I can provide for you. Which is funny, because you should know how that feels better than anyone, yet you fail to see it."

"Harlow, I lo – "

"I'm going away for a week." I cut him off. "I think it's best *you* take some time to figure out what the hell *you're* doing because this..." I point an angry finger at the roses. "Isn't it."

He doesn't say anything for a couple of breaths. "Are you fucking him?" I can tell he's trying to keep his voice steady.

I squeeze my eyes shut, gritting my teeth, and ball my hand into a fist. "I'm going away for a week. I think it's best you and I don't talk for a while. We have distance between us but not enough space. I can't keep doing this back and forth with you. I'm exhausted. This is exhausting."

"Harlow, I'm sorry, I – "

"Save it, Hendrix. We're past the point of apologies." The tears threaten to fall. I feel stupid for crying but I'm so angry.

His voice is low. "Is he going with you?" I can hear his anger threatening to boil over.

"Yes! Yes! Acyn is going to fucking be with me. There isn't anything you can do about it." I know I sound like a petulant child but I am over him. *This.* Whatever the fuck it is. "And for the record... I like sunflowers, not roses." I hang up the phone.

He doesn't call me back like he normally does. I know he's fuming just as badly as I am right now. I look around at all the roses and then I lose it. I tear them apart. Box by box, petal by petal, I unleash all the anger and annoyance that has been steadily building within me.

Tears stream down my face, my chest heaves, my hands shake as I stare at my living room floor that's littered with petals and torn boxes. A *fake* gesture of caring. I wipe the tears from my face and sit on the couch until my breathing becomes steady again.

It's dark now, but I trudge outside to the fire pit and grab the lighter and some kindling. Once it's lit, I tromp back into my living room and grab all the remnants of my meltdown and drag them out to the flames. I toss it all in and watch it burn.

Thank God West and Ava aren't home so that I can self-destruct in peace. I grab another handful of the destroyed roses and stomp back outside when I run directly into someone. Looking up, it's Acyn's eyes I see, matching the flames in intensity.

His brows knit together. "Sunshine, what's wrong?"

"Nothing," I say as I push past him and make my way back towards the fire.

I toss another armful in. Acyn stands there looking at me. I feel bad for snapping at him but I'm finding it hard to calm down. I make a few more trips until I finally get all the *trash* off of my living room floor, I sit outside by the fire and stare at it. Moments later, Acyn comes and sits down next to me. He doesn't say anything. We sit in silence, watching the blazing flames. Acyn pulls me towards him and I let him. He still doesn't say anything, but he holds me tight enough so that I know he's got me.

"He... He didn't propose out of love or because he envisioned a life with me. He was afraid of losing me. If I had said yes, then he knew he would have me by his side. A perfect example is a delivery guy showing up with thousands of dollars' worth of roses. He told me it was a gesture of love and caring but... I know it's bullshit. He's doing it because he's threatened by you. You got me the sunflowers because... you know me. He got me all these unnecessary burning roses to make himself feel better. Like he wasn't losing me. So... I destroyed them. As I tore through them, I just got angrier and angrier. Because..." My voice trails off. "Sorry, I'm rambling." I sit up. "You don't want to hear this." I hug my knees to my chest.

"You got angrier because?" he coaxes me.

I rest my temple on my knee and look at him. "Because... I still care. I feel stupid for caring about someone who so blatantly doesn't really care about me."

Acyn pulls me back into his arms. "You realize you're human, right? We can't just switch off emotions. You two were together for a long time. Over time you'll care a little less, until you realize that you don't care about him anymore at all. To get there... that's going to take time. I think you're being too hard on yourself, Sunshine. That's my job."

Smiling, I wrap my arms around his middle. "What would I do without you?"

"Starve and have no friends."

Laughter tumbles from my lips. "I wish Sevyn never told you that. It's sadly true, though."

16

Harlow

ACYN AND I SETTLE on the beach. There's a light mist along with a subtle breeze, but it doesn't stop me from fully enjoying where we are. I stare around in awe at the breathtaking views of the Oregon Coast. The beaches and lush greenery is unlike anything that I've ever seen. It's colder than the beaches I'm used to, but it has been nice to slow down in such a beautiful place. I didn't realize how badly I needed a break until I noticed that I haven't felt anxious or stressed since we arrived here.

I take a sip of my hot chocolate, wrap my blanket around me a little tighter, and watch the waves. Acyn is busy lighting a joint. He takes a hit and then passes it to me. I inhale and close my eyes, listening to the wind, the seagulls, and feel at peace as I open my eyes and exhale.

"Thank you for bringing me here."

"No need to thank me, Sunshine." He lays back on the blanket and stares at the darkening sky. "It's nice to have you here."

I chuckle. "Even though I've made you stop a million times to take pictures."

"I've accepted that you're annoying," he says as he side-eyes me. I playfully swat his leg in retaliation.

"I tried to stay home but *someone* insisted on me taking a break."

"For your own good," he says matter-of-factly. "Have you considered not taking on so much once we're back home?"

"I have, but I don't know where to start." On the way here, he and I talked about my busy schedule and the possibility of me cutting back.

"I'm not trying to press you into making a choice, but when something affects your overall health, it isn't worth it."

"I know, but you also know how I make choices." He learned firsthand. We stopped at some little gift shop and it took me almost twenty minutes to pick out a postcard to send to my dad. He insisted that I'm the only person still sending postcards.

"Okay, so we'll play a game of hate, like, and love. What do you hate?"

I finish my cup of hot chocolate and lay down next to him so I can gaze at the stars appearing in the sky. "Honestly... I hate teaching."

"Really?" he asks as he props himself up on his elbow next to me. "I thought you loved teaching?"

I shrug. "I did... but I miss being a student. The private classes I don't mind, but teaching is exhausting. I can take classes whenever I want, but I really don't want to take one after a day in the studio... no matter how much I love yoga."

"That's understandable." He nods. "Now..." He takes another pull on the joint and exhales. "What do you like?"

"The coffee shop," I say without hesitation. "I didn't think I would like working there, but I look forward to my shifts. Yeah, people can be assholes about coffee– " I give him side eye and he winks at me " –but I still enjoy the people and the place."

"So, you like assholes is what you're saying?"

"If I'm sitting here with you, then yes, I must like assholes."

He lays back down next to me, with a smile on his face. "Alright, so then what do you love, Sunshine?"

"Photography." I exhale after taking a hit. "I love photography. I would love to have my own photography business."

He smiles. "You have your answers, then."

I sigh and rub my hands over my face. "It isn't that easy, though. I can't just quit on Celeste. She's the reason I'm even here."

Acyn sits up and looks at me. "Stop acting like you owe everybody something. You don't owe anyone anything. The only person you owe something to is yourself. It's okay to walk away from something that isn't working for you."

I gaze up at the stars. He's right. I appreciate all Celeste has done for me, for believing in me, but I can't continue on simply because I feel bad. That's how I ended up dragging things on for so long with Hendrix.

"I want to be you when I grow up, Acyn."

He chuckles. "You're pretty badass. You just need to believe it."

There go those blooming feelings again. I smile. "Thank you. I'm starting to."

"Would you be down to meet my friends... tomorrow?"

I sit up to face him. "You want me to meet your friends?"

He quirks an eyebrow. "Yeah... why do you sound so surprised?"

"I... don't know." I shrug. "I didn't expect it."

"Why not? We spend a lot of time together. I can tolerate you, so why wouldn't I think my friends could, too?"

Scoffing, I gape at him. "Tolerate me? Is it such a burden to be around me."

"Sometimes I do question –" I smack his arm and he cowers away from me. "I'm just kidding. Honestly, life was pretty fucking boring until you came along. You've grown on me... like a fungus."

I suck my teeth. "You're the king of backhanded compliments. I'm afraid of what your friends will be like."

"I would say they're nicer than me, but they're my friends so that's probably a lie. Asher and Greyson are good people though. I would trust them with my life if it came down to it."

A grin spreads across my face. Acyn keeps to himself for the most part, so the fact he has friends he's that close with makes me happy. "I'd love to meet them. I'm surprised anyone would want to be your friend."

Before I can react, he grabs me and throws me over his shoulder. I shriek with laughter. "I'm going to throw you in the ocean!"

"Acyn! I will murder you if you throw me into that frigid ass water!" I yell as I latch onto his torso because he's got me all the way fucked up. It's dark and who knows what the hell is lurking in the water.

"I'd love to see you try, Sunshine." He keeps walking towards the water.

"Acyn!" I yell as if that's going to do anything. He's holding my legs too tightly for me to get off of his shoulder. I decide to do what any person in danger would: *I bite him.*

He yells— it's really almost a growl— and we tumble to the ground. Laughing uncontrollably, I struggle to breathe. Acyn is looking at me with wild eyes and in total disbelief.

"What the fuck are you? A piranha?" he asks.

"I did what I had to do!" I shout, scrambling backwards.

"Bet," he says, grabbing my ankle, pulling me towards him, and picks me up *again*. Except now, he's holding me in front of him with my arms secured tightly in his. I scream at the top of my fucking lungs as he plunges both of us into the icy cold water of the Pacific Ocean.

As we crash into the surf, I gasp. It shocks my system and steals my breath. I resurface, coughing, sputtering, and grabbing around for Acyn like a mad woman as waves continue to wash over me. I hear him laughing beside me and I lunge for him, but I miss and dive straight back into the water. He's taunting me with laughter now. I want to wring his fucking neck, but I'm so numb that my ability to move isn't the same.

Instead, I make my way back to the dry sand and strip off my clothes with shaky hands. Once he realizes what I'm doing, his laughter stops, and he just watches me. I don't think he can see much. Oh, well. If he can, I have a plan. I reach my panties, peel them off, and launch them directly at his face. They hit him with a wet *smack*. I grab my blankets and wrap them around me. His ember eyes are still fixed on me. The moonlight must be brighter than I thought. I walk towards the house.

"Good luck getting inside, fucker," I scream.

I run like hell because I can hear him struggling to get out of the water to catch up with me, but I have too much of a lead and make it into the house before he does. I lock the door seconds before he reaches it. I give him the middle finger and head for a hot bath.

Serves his ass right.

ACYN

Harlow lets me back inside *after* she takes a shower and uses *all* the hot water. Thankfully, she loves blankets and always has them at the ready. I was able to grab some from the car and wait like a locked-out puppy until she let me in.

She has a smug look on her face as she opens the door. When she started stripping on the beach, I felt like I had plunged into the icy water all over again. Every ounce of air I had left me. I held my breath the entire time I watched her peel off her clothes layer by layer.

I thought she would stop once she reached her bra and panties. She didn't. Everything about her is fucking perfect. Then she threw her panties in my face. I easily could have come from that alone, but I snapped out of it as soon as I heard her shouting. She got me. I think it may have been worth it, though.

The image of her bathed in moonlight – *naked* – will forever be seared into my memory. My dick immediately reacts as soon as I think about it. I know we're friends, but it still doesn't stop me from rubbing one... or two out in the shower. It's been a long fucking while since I've been with anyone, and being around her is a constant reminder.

The next morning, she doesn't say anything as I walk into the kitchen. I can feel her eyes on my back. I'm sure they would shoot laser beams if she were capable. I turn around to face her as I lean against the kitchen counter, then smile at her as I slowly slurp my coffee. She hates when I do that, so I know I'm not helping my case, but I find some satisfaction in annoying her. Harlow rolls her eyes, heading toward the back door.

I follow her outside to the porch and plop down next to her on the bench. She lets out an annoyed sigh as she turns her back to me.

"Sunshine, are you going to be mad at me all day?"

She shrugs in response. I've pissed her off plenty of times, but never to the point where she won't utter a single word to me. I'll take insults over silence.

"Do you still want to hang out with me and my friends today?" I hope I didn't ruin the possibility of her meeting Greyson and Asher, because I've been looking forward to it. I usually don't give a fuck whose feelings I hurt, but her not talking to me is making me feel some type of way.

She stands, leaving me alone as she heads inside. Her hand rests on the handle of the door as she turns back around, flashing me a smile. "Had you worried, didn't I?"

Usually, I'm a good reader of bullshit, but in this moment, I realize I would do anything for her.

I shake my head, smiling, as I wipe my hand over my face. "You're a fucking headache."

"Shouldn't have thrown me in the Pacific and I wouldn't have to be." She shrugs, smiling smugly. "Now excuse me while I go get ready."

Once she's gone, I walk across the deck and rest my forearms on the railing as I look out at the coast with one question on my mind. Are we blurring the line between friendship and... *more*?

⁂

I watch Harlow as she talks with Asher, Greyson, and his girlfriend, Selene. We spent the afternoon on a boat crabbing, and then we came back to the beach house to eat and hang out. Night has already fallen and surprisingly, neither Grey nor Ash have managed to embarrass me. I think they're too shocked by the fact I introduced them to a woman. They're probably not wanting to do anything that would scare her off.

Any women they have met in the past were by accident. Even then, I never bothered introducing them by name. Both of them already knew what the situation was. But this is different. I wasn't even sure about inviting Harlow in the first place. Not because I didn't want her here, but because I didn't think she would come with me.

Harlow looks over at me and smiles as she talks with Selene about yoga. They've already made plans to meetup once we get back home. Greyson lives in Seattle but works as a pilot, so he's gone a lot. And Ash lives in LA, working as an architect, so we all try to get together when we can. This is the first time in a while that we've all been able to do so.

"Do you want to go find something on Netflix?" Selene asks Harlow.

"Sure." Harlow stands, wrapping her blanket around her shoulders. "It's about the time Acyn starts throwing people in the ocean anyway." She grins over her shoulder at me as she walks into the house with Selene.

"He did what?" Selene asks.

Harlow doesn't hesitate to talk as much shit about me as she can.

I smile and shake my head as they walk away and into the house.

Greyson turns to look at me once they're in the house. "Man, I never thought I would see the day that you actually introduced us to someone. I like her."

"Yeah, when you said you weren't doing the whole hook up thing anymore, I thought you were full of shit," Asher adds.

"When have I said something and not meant it?"

"That's true." Greyson nods. "You're one of the few whose word is bond."

"We're just friends anyway. We like spending time together," I say with a shrug.

Asher snorts. "You're not just a friend to her, bruh."

My brows knit together. "What do you mean?"

"She looks at you a certain way," Greyson says.

"Damn, I didn't realize you two were so observant," I say with a chuckle. "She may look at me with annoyance or anger... but I don't know what look you two are seeing?"

"Nah, she looks at you like you're... everything," Asher says.

I look at Greyson, who nods as if he agrees.

"Why aren't you two together?" Greyson asks.

"Neither of us are looking for a relationship. We're just hanging out and keeping each other company. Plus, she just got out of a long-term relationship and has voiced that she isn't ready for another relationship yet. So, I'm respecting that," I say.

That's the main reason why I'm okay just being friends with Harlow. I know she needs the space to figure herself out. I can appreciate and respect that. Most people hop from person to person, hoping they'll find what the previous was lacking in the next.

"That's honorable of you," Asher says with a smirk. "How's your dick hangin'?"

"It's hangin' just fine," I say, punching his arm.

"You know, Selene and I were friends for a while before we ever knocked boots." He thinks for a moment. "Okay, *Selene* made us wait before anything happened."

"Sounds about right." Asher mutters.

"But–" He raises his hands up. "–Hear me out. There is something about the prolonged anticipation that makes the first time something out of this world."

"Yeah, it's called pent up frustration, Grey," Asher says and I crack up.

Greyson shrugs. "You may be right, but what I'm trying to fucking say is, smashing at first sight isn't all it's cracked up to be."

"Well shit, it looks like I'm the last man standing," Asher says with a grin. "More women for me. I was getting kind of tired of all of them seeing your tats and you getting all the play, Ace. I'll have to thank Harlow for taking you off the field. Does she have any friends, though?"

"You're not tired of chasing women?" I ask, feeling exhausted at the thought.

"Not when they're chasing me, bruh." A smile spreads across his face.

The three of us continue to talk into the night. When we get into the house, both Selene and Harlow are knocked out. I carry Harlow to her room and tuck her into her bed. I get up to leave, but she grabs my hand.

"Stay," she says. So, I do.

17

Harlow

MY STOMACH IS IN knots and my palms are sweaty.

I wait for Celeste to get done with her class so that I can give her my two weeks' notice. This isn't a decision I made lightly. It was on my mind all week while at the coast. Acyn's words stuck with me. Staying in a situation because I feel like I owe someone something isn't going to get me anywhere.

I can appreciate what someone has done for me, but that doesn't mean I owe them something in return. I'm learning to have the courage to change my mind, whether it be about proposals or jobs – if they aren't serving me – I can move on without permission.

"Harlow," Celeste says as she kisses my cheek. "So good to see you healthy and well. How was Oregon?"

"It was beautiful." I force a smile even though my heart is racing.

"Peaceful, isn't? A nice place to reset." She leads us to her office. "Water?"

I clear my throat. "I'm fine, thank you." My voice is almost a squeak. Get a grip, Harlow.

Celeste sits down in her chair and smiles at me. "What did you want to speak with me about?"

Straight to the point. I wring my hands together as I stare down at them. "Celeste... I love working here at the studio with you. I've learned so much in such a short time." I force myself to look at her. "But right now, I just have too much on my plate. I thought I would find joy in teaching because I love yoga, but... I've realized that isn't the case. I miss being a student and yoga being medicine for me instead of a job. I decided that it's best for me to resign from my teaching position." I almost apologize, but I swallow it instead because I'm not sorry about doing what's best for me.

Celeste leans back in her chair with a smile. "I knew it was only a matter of time before you were off to bigger and better things."

I let out a puff of air. "You're not... upset?"

"No, why would I be upset when you're being honest and doing what you want?"

My shoulders fall with relief. I'm glad that she sees it that way instead of me abandoning her. "I'm trying. I just feel bad for leaving since this job is what brought me here."

"Maybe that's all that was meant to happen," she says with a shrug. "Just because the job brought you here doesn't mean that you're tied to it. Life unfolds in interesting ways. If you hadn't moved here, would you have discovered your passion for photography?"

I knit my brows, considering her words. Ava is the one who said that I should try photography. "Honestly, probably not."

"See, you didn't move here just for a job. You moved here for yourself."

She smiles, and the knots in my stomach unravel. "Thank you, Celeste."

"Now, I wanted to ask you if you would be able to take photos for the studio's website and social media pages?"

"Of course I can," I say without hesitation. "I'd love to do that."

"Great!" she smiles. "I have some ideas of places where we can take the photos. Of course, I do want some here at the studio, but I also think some outdoors would be wonderful, too. What do you think?"

Over the next hour, we discuss what vision and vibe she has in mind for the photos. This meeting went better than I had anticipated. I didn't think that I would walk away with a new project. Life truly does unfold in interesting ways.

I sit in Acyn's shop, sipping on an iced latte, waiting for him to finish up with a client. I didn't tell him that I was going to talk to Celeste today because I wasn't sure whether I was going to follow through with it or not. Now that I have, I'm excited to tell him the news.

I watch him work on his client's tattoo. He's hunched over with his tattoo machine buzzing away; he's completely in his element. His client is talking up a storm and somehow Acyn is able to carry on a conversation without missing a beat. Tattooing is like breathing for him. He could do it in his sleep. I admire the love and passion he has for his work.

I grab my bag and pull out my camera to capture a few shots of him.

"Would you mind if I take some pictures?" I ask his client.

"Not at all. But be sure to get my good side," he says, playfully.

"Of course," I say with a chuckle as I adjust my aperture and shutter speed on my camera.

Acyn doesn't even look up from what he's doing once I start taking pictures. He's so used to me doing this when he's with me that it doesn't even faze him.

I take plenty of shots from different angles as he works. Acyn looks pensive most of the time, but as I watch him through my lens, he looks relaxed and happy. Watching him makes me smile.

Riding my wave of inspiration, I wander around the shop taking pictures of things. There's a wall that's covered in art from floor to ceiling and another lined with intricate, framed, tattoo drawings from Acyn and the other tattoo artist.

I head outside to take pictures of the shop's sign and the exterior. I'm not sure what Acyn wants for pictures, but hopefully he likes what I'm taking. I'm in the middle of a picture when the guy who was just sitting with Acyn steps outside. I snap some more pictures of him standing in front of the shop, showing off his tattoo before he leaves. It's hard to look at Acyn's work and not want a tattoo for yourself. I would already have another one if I hadn't promised Kyrell we could get one together. He's already booked our appointment, but he won't be back in town until after my birthday. I find Acyn cleaning up when I go back inside to sit down and look at the pictures. I can't wait to get these on my computer to edit them; I'm super proud of how they came out.

"Did you get some good shots?"

"Yeah." I sit on the bench near the window. "I think you'll like them." Acyn sits beside me, putting his head next to mine as I scroll through the pictures.

"These are really good," he says as I turn my head to look at him, not realizing how close we are. If I just move a little closer, we would be kissing. He notices too because I watch his eyes flit to my lips and linger there for a moment, as if he's contemplating closing the distance. I almost close my eyes when he pulls away, rubbing the back of his neck. He clears his throat while I try to ignore the butterflies that flutter in my stomach.

"Um, would you want to come to my house this Sunday?"

"For your family dinner?" I ask as the butterflies start to dance again.

"You make it sound so formal." He chuckles. "It really is just dinner with my parents plus Sevyn, Zane, and the twins."

Sevyn has invited me before when it was her week to host, but I've always said no because I didn't want to intrude. Now that Acyn is inviting me, I want to say yes because it's him. I love Sevyn, don't get me wrong, but Acyn and I have developed a close friendship since we've been hanging out regularly.

I nod and smile. "Yeah, I'll go."

"Good, you can help me cook."

I scoff, letting my mouth fall open. "Why do I feel like I got swindled?"

"Because you did," he says with a smug smile. "You can choose what we eat if that makes you feel better."

"Wow, here I was thinking you invited me out of the goodness of your heart and you really just want cooking help."

"You're always welcome wherever I am. C'mon," he says, holding his hand out to me. "Let's go catch a movie at the park or something. I don't want to be inside."

I've never been to a movie in the park before. Needless to say, I'm excited that Acyn brought us here. People are scattered around, sitting on blankets and lawn chairs. He must have had this planned because he had a blanket and sweaters in his car. It's not cold anymore, but with the setting sun, the air will be chilly soon. We pick a spot underneath a tree and then order nachos, popcorn, and soda.

"Do you come here a lot?" I ask as we settle down on the blanket.

"Yeah, with Sevyn and the kids. It's better than the movie theater because they can run around."

Acyn really enjoys spending time with Sevyn and her family, even though he acts like she annoys him. He doesn't mention his other siblings much. From what he's told me, they're older and moved away to start their own lives before he could develop relationships with them. Since he and Sevyn are only a little over a year apart, they've always been close. I also don't think Sevyn would ever allow them not to be. Family is everything to them.

"I talked to Celeste today." I intended to tell him earlier but got distracted by our "almost" kiss.

"You did?" He pauses with a chip halfway to his mouth. "How did that go? Did she tell you that you couldn't quit because you owe her your life?"

I playfully push him. "No, you jerk. She said she was proud of me for doing what's best for me. Plus, she asked if I could do some photography for her studios. You know she owns the one here and in LA."

"What? That's amazing news!" He exclaims. "See, now you have room to do stuff like that and not feel stressed about it."

"I know. I'm excited. Thanks for giving me the push."

"Nah, all I did was verbalize what you've been thinking. This is all you, Sunshine."

I beam at him. We quiet down as the movie starts. I look at him with surprise when the opening credits for "The Goonies" start. He doesn't say a word, he just gives me a smile and goes back to watching the movie. It's one of my all-time favorites. I mentioned it to him once in passing when we were scrolling through Netflix one night. On the way to the coast, he surprised me with a stop in Astoria and took me to the house where the movie was filmed.

My eyes are on the screen, but my mind is on him. I think about all the time we've spent together and how comfortable I've become with him.

Not the mundane kind of comfortable, where you fall into a routine and then shit goes stale. It's the kind of comfort where I can be myself while giving me room to grow and evolve.

I rest my head on his shoulder, and he wraps his arm around me, pulling me closer to him as we rest against the tree trunk.

18

Harlow

ACYN PICKS ME UP to go to the store to get the ingredients I need to make my mom's spaghetti. I've only had to cook a handful of times since Acyn and I have been hanging out, so I don't mind making the meal tonight. I just hope his parents like it. I chew my thumbnail as I think of everything that could go wrong. I should have met them months ago. What if Sevyn's told them about me and how I haven't wanted to stay for family dinner? What if they don't like me?

"Are you nervous?" Acyn pulls me from my spiraling thoughts.

"No," I lie as if I weren't just thinking of everything that could go wrong.

"Then why are you chewing on your thumbnail?"

I immediately stop and shove my hand under my thigh. Which is no use because my knee starts bouncing. I don't know why I'm so damn nervous to meet them. I was actually excited until my mind started wandering.

"Because... because I'm nervous."

I can tell he's trying his best not to laugh. "Why?"

I know I'm being ridiculous but once I start thinking about something it's hard to stop. "I'm just nervous." I shrug. "We spend a lot of time together, so I care what your parents think. What if they hate my food? What if they hate me? What if –"

"Chill, Sunshine. It really isn't as serious as you're making it seem. My dad is a lot like me." He pauses, considering what he just said and adds, "Okay, that was meant to bring you comfort but I can see how that could possibly cause more anxiety."

Covering my mouth, I stifle a laugh. Our first encounter wasn't exactly friendly.

"What I'm trying to say is, that you have nothing to worry about," he says.

After laughing, I feel better. I resolve that it isn't my job to make them like me. Either they will or they won't, and there isn't anything I can do about it. Not just with them but with anyone. It becomes exhausting trying to appeal to people. When you start being yourself, you attract people who you naturally vibe with. I mean, look at Acyn and I.

⁂

I feed Acyn a forkful of spaghetti once it's done. His parents should be arriving any moment with Sevyn and her family. The expression on his face says it all as he savors the bite I just gave him. He closes his eyes as he chews it slowly. I lick my lips as I watch him and smile when he opens his eyes like I wasn't just thinking of other ways to see that expression.

"Why have you been hiding this recipe from me this whole time?"

"I haven't," I giggle. "I usually only save it for when I feel like going all out because it takes a while to cook."

"That's so good." He grabs the fork to take another bite, and I snatch it out of his hand.

"No, I've seen the way you eat and this will be gone in minutes if I let you have another bite. So you'll just have to wait." I move the dish of spaghetti to the table, which is already set for everyone. I turn back around and narrow my eyes at him. "Touch it and die. I have to go change before they all get here." He raises his hands up in defense as I back out of the dining room pointing my finger at him.

I go to his room and change into a flirty, off the shoulder, powder blue romper I brought with me a few weeks ago when I couldn't decide on an outfit. I slip on white platform espadrille sandals which accentuate my long legs. I quickly apply some mascara, gloss, and give myself one last glance in the mirror before heading back out to the dining room.

"Sevyn said…" He stops mid-sentence as I enter the room, which causes me to look up from trying to fasten my bracelet. His eyes are trailing up my legs, over my body, and then his gaze meets mine. The fire that I saw in them when we first met is there again. I've noticed it more lately, which causes me to feel tingly, like I have butterflies coursing through my veins.

He swallows. "Uh… fuck… I just lost my train of thought. Let me help you with that," he says, closing the distance between us. He brings his hands to my wrist. His touch is gentle as he fastens my bracelet. My skin feels electric as his fingertips brush against the skin of my wrist. He gently sweeps his thumb across my quickening pulse. I don't dare move because I'm enjoying his close proximity. His only move is to get closer to me… and then, his doorbell rings.

I blink and look into his eyes. "That's them."

"Yeah… you look beautiful, Sunshine." His voice is deeper than usual, and it resonates in places that haven't been spoken to in a while. "Better go let them in," he says as he reluctantly tears his eyes from mine to go get the door.

I place my hand on my stomach once he's out of sight, trying to steady myself after that exchange. Even the simplest of touches from him have my body at full attention. The tingles start again when I imagine what it would be like to be fully consumed by the fire in his eyes.

That thought is doused out when Sevyn walks into the dining room. Her eyes give me the up and down. "Okay, but I need to know who gave you permission to look this fine?" she asks.

"Who says I need permission?" I twirl on the spot to give her a 360 view and then give her a hug as we laugh together.

"I'll never understand how Ace spends all his time with you without devouring you."

"Sev, it's none of your business what other grown people do," Zane says as he stands next to her.

I smile and give him a quick hug. "I don't know why you try. She's going to say whatever she wants to say."

Zane opens his mouth to respond, but the twins zoom, running full speed toward me.

I pick up Emery, who gives me a hug, as Eli latches onto my leg.

"I think they may have missed you," Sevyn smiles.

"And I missed them. How did you two grow so much in such a short amount of time?" They both giggle while they try to convince me one is bigger than the other.

Acyn appears seconds later with his mom on his arm. His dad is on his other side with his arm draped over Acyn's shoulders. I can see now that he looks like his dad and Sevyn is a spitting image of their mom. Emery plays with the necklaces layered on my neck, and Eli went off to pester Six-Two-Six. I smile at Acyn as I watch him with his parents and then he makes his way over to me. *Breathe, Harlow. Breathe.*

"Mom, Dad, this is my friend Harlow. Harlow, I would like you to meet my parents. Gloria and Rafael." Both of them beam at me, and my anxiety instantly melts away.

I hold Emery in one arm and hold my hand out to his mom first. She bypasses my hand, pulling me into a hug.

"A pleasure to meet you," Gloria says.

His dad pulls me into a hug next. "Our kids have told us so much about you," he says with a hint of a Spanish accent. "It's a pleasure to finally meet you," he says.

"Thank you, nice to meet you, too." I smile, filled with a warm, fuzzy feeling. I can see why Acyn and Sevyn are such good people. They have two amazing parents. I don't need to talk with them for hours to know that they love their children unconditionally. It's apparent in the way they look at them with such pride and joy.

"Let's eat," Acyn announces. He places his hand on the small of my back, as we walk to the dining room table, and whispers so only I can hear. "See, Sunshine, they adore you."

A smile tugs at my lips as he pulls the chair out for me. I try to sit Emery next to me, but she refuses to leave my lap. Sevyn tries to get after her but I assure her she's fine and my clothes are washable. Acyn sits next to me instead, and Emery stays seated on my lap, giving Sevyn a smug smile.

"She loves you." Sevyn says as she serves herself. "You would think you're her mother the way she stays attached to you when you're around."

"She knows who her mama is. Don't you Emery?" She points to Sevyn with a grin. "See, I'm just a stand in."

Laughter ripples around the table. One day, I hope to start a family. I'm not in any rush, but whenever I'm around the twins, it's hard to not think of my future kids.

Everyone serves themselves, and I feed myself and Emery. She's managed to only drop a few pieces of spaghetti on my thigh. Acyn has been all too willing to help me clean it up which makes me giggle.

"Acyn, this meal is so good. How come you've never made it before?" his mom asks.

"It wasn't me," Acyn says. "It's Harlow's recipe. She cooked everything today."

Sevyn chimes in. "Harlow, you realize you're spoiling my brother, right? He's taking full advantage of this friendship."

His mom points her fork at me. "You must come to our house and teach me how to make this, okay?"

I nod and smile. "My pleasure. Let me know when and I'll be there." I didn't think I would feel this welcomed into their family. I glance at Acyn as he talks with his dad and Zane. An overwhelming sense of belonging washes over me as I realize Acyn feels like home to me.

Later on in the evening, we all sit on the back porch listening to music, chatting, and watching Eli and Emery chase Six-Two-Six. I listen to Acyn as he seamlessly switches from speaking in Spanish to English as he talks with his mom and dad. I try my best not to stare at him because he sounds so sexy to me. Goodness, I'm losing it. I need to sort out these feelings before I end up really blurring the already fine line of our friendship.

"Alright my loves, we have to go," Gloria says. "We have an early flight to the Dominican Republic tomorrow and you know how hard it is to get your father out the door on time." She kisses Acyn goodbye and then gives me a hug. "You're a beautiful young woman, and I'm happy that my kids have you in their lives."

I hug her a little tighter for two reasons. The first being that I imagine this is what it would feel like to hug my mom if she were here. The second is, she has no idea how happy I am to have Sevyn and Acyn in my life. His dad gives me a hug as well. "I can see why Acyn enjoys spending all his free time with you."

I glance over my shoulder at Acyn, who I'm shocked to see is looking anywhere but at me as he rubs his hand along the back of his neck. He smirks and shakes his head as his dad embraces him.

Since his parents and Sevyn's family all came in one car, everyone is gone at once. As soon as we wave them off and close the door, Acyn grabs me and twirls me around. I let out a squeal. "Told you they would love you. Worried for no damn reason."

We settle on the couch after he sets me down. "I love your parents. Makes me miss my dad. I didn't know you sing my praises to them so much, though," I say with a cocky grin as I flip my hair over my shoulder.

His rare shyness returns as he scrubs his hand over his face. "I was really hoping my dad wouldn't say some embarrassing shit. Of course he saves it for the last minute as they're walking out the door." He slides my shoes off my feet and drapes my legs over his.

"It's cute. I've never seen you embarrassed before. I'm going to catalog this in my brain to bring up when I can't think of a comeback fast enough."

He lets out a rumble of laughter. "I knew this was coming," he says. "Do you want me to take you home? Or are you staying here?"

Since we work in such close proximity to one another now that I left the yoga studio, we've been riding with each other to and from work. It's becoming more difficult to know where one of us begins and the other ends. I've never had a friendship this deep before. I'm not sure if we're crossing the line into something more or if we're still in friend territory.

I pet Six-Two-Six as he makes himself comfortable in my lap. I question myself, wondering if I'm getting lost in Acyn like I once lost myself in Hendrix. I want a relationship where I can still be my own separate being with hopes, dreams, and desires. Since I've met Acyn, he's only ever pushed me to do things for the benefit of myself. He's let me know that I always have a choice and that I don't owe anyone anything, him included.

"I have to be at the shop to open tomorrow. I don't want you to have to wake up that early just to take me to work." I asked West for the opening shifts because I knew no one else really wanted them. Most of his employees are college kids who stay up late and hate the morning shifts. I don't mind because it means that I get off at two in the afternoon and have the rest of the day to myself.

"I don't know why you act like you're an inconvenience," Acyn says.

"It's not about inconvenience, it's about being courteous and knowing that you aren't a morning person."

"I'm not but... I don't mind. How about this, do you want to stay and watch a horror movie with me?"

"Now you know if we watch a scary movie, I'm not going to want to be alone so I will just sit my ass right here."

"No hesitation for that choice."

"Yeah, well I don't wanna be murdered in my sleep now, do I? At the very least I can use you as a shield."

He lets out a belt of laughter, knowing I usually stay up all night after watching a scary movie. Every noise is a possible murderer or spirit lurking in the shadows waiting to kill me. Okay, I may be a bit dramatic, but I really struggle with scary movies. Acyn loves them though so I try to watch as much as I can. That usually means holding onto him for dear life and staring through the slits of my fingers, though.

"I would never let anything happen to you anyway."

I know his words are true. He's never given me a reason to ever doubt anything he does or says. I've noticed that if Acyn says something, he fucking means it. His words make me feel warm and tingly.

"Pick out a movie while I go steal your clothes."

I didn't plan on changing, but I will now because I don't want to take things further with him. It's becoming more difficult to stay on the friend side of things without dipping my toes into the possibility of more. Hendrix, even though we haven't talked for a few weeks now, is still in the back of my mind. I wish I could snuff out that flame, but I also don't want to push anything with Acyn right now. I value our friendship... relationship too much. I wouldn't want to jeopardize it by acting on feelings of desire.

Desire... is it just desire? No, if we were playing our game of hate, like, and love, I would be teetering on the edge of like. Ready to freefall into love.

19

Harlow

I INHALE FRESH AIR as I resurface from beneath the water of the pool. The sun is glistening off my body as I climb onto the pool's edge to sit. It feels so good to be back in the water. It's one of my favorite summer pastimes. I peek over my shoulder at Acyn who is trying to pretend he wasn't just staring at me. I've caught him staring more than once. I can't blame him. This bikini isn't much more than a few pieces of fabric barely doing their job held together by some string.

I arrived back home yesterday after a few days in LA, taking photos for Celeste's studio. When I first met her, I got the notion that she could and would make a lot happen for me, and she has made so much happen for me in a short amount of time. More than I could have ever expected. I've gotten new photography clients after she revamped her website and social media pages with my photos. I'm slowly building a clientele. Of course, she assures me that I put in all the hard work to get my name out there, but I'm still grateful for her help along the way.

This is the first time I've been able to indulge in Ava and West's pool in a few weeks. I've been busy, a good busy, between working at Holy Shot and doing photoshoots. I purposely took a few days off to slow down because I would prefer to not have a repeat of wearing myself into the ground. It's hard not to do that when you're doing something that you love. Acyn helps remind me that I can't do it all and I won't miss opportunities that are meant for me.

When he asked me what I wanted to do today, all I could think about is hanging out by the pool and listening to music. He may be regretting agreeing to that now because I'm one of the few people who loves being in the heat of the sun. I get up from the pool's ledge and saunter over to where he's sitting. He has shades on, but I can tell he's looking at me.

I sit next to him as he gives me a grin. "You know, pictures last longer."

"How old are you?"

"You're looking at me like I owe you something. I thought I would give you an easy solution," I say sassily.

"I'm staring because it's hotter than the devil's asshole, yet you don't seem the least bit fazed."

I snatch his shades, sliding them onto my face. "I'm from Texas. A little 90-degree heatwave ain't gonna stop me." I search around for my phone, eventually finding it tucked underneath my towel. "Let me take some pictures of us and then we can go inside, you crybaby." He chuckles, and I lean against his chest, getting comfortable, while I open my camera. "Look sexy. I know that's hard for you."

He smiles brilliantly in response to my dig at him. "Fuck you, Sunshine. I look sexy all the time."

I open my mouth to throw out a smartass comment, but my phone rings and my dad's picture appears on the screen. I smile and answer it.

"Hey, Dad!" Acyn puts his arm around my shoulders and scrolls through his phone.

"Hey, Kiddo and Acyn," my dad says with a wave.

Acyn gives him a two-finger salute. "Mr. Shaw, always a pleasure."

My dad has become used to Acyn being with me when he calls. He and Acyn even talk about me as if I'm not in the room. I think if they ever met, they would get along well. "What are you kids up to?"

Acyn answers before I can. "Dying in the heat."

I snort with laughter. "You're such a baby. We're enjoying the sun and pool, Dad. How have you been?"

"Good, just wanted to call to check on my favorite daughter." He chuckles. This is a running joke between the two of us.

I roll my eyes, trying to be annoyed, but it always brings a smile to my face. "I'm your only child, Dad."

"I know and what a lucky man I am. I also wanted to ask– well, more like Charlotte has been hounding me – are you coming home for your birthday?"

My face falls because, if Charlotte is asking, that means she's planning on throwing a party for Hendrix and me *together*. "Um, I want to, but I don't know about the party, Dad." I really do want to see him, but he has no clue about how things are going between Hendrix and me. There's nothing going between us. He'll send me occasional texts to check in, but I don't always respond. It's for the best, honestly. I feel freer than I've felt in a long time.

"It's up to you, Kiddo. I'll just be happy to have you home."

I don't want to spoil the party. Even though my dad says Charlotte has been hounding him, I know he looks forward to my yearly birthday party. It's a tradition that my mom started with Charlotte.

"Yeah, Dad, I'll be there." I force a smile because I'm not sure whether I'm going home for myself, my dad, or in memory of my mom.

"Great! I'll tell Charlotte. I'm so happy to see you in a few weeks. I'll let you get back to baking in the sun. Love you."

"Love you, Dad." I toss my phone aside, letting out a sigh.

"Why are you bullshitting?" Acyn asks.

I turn to look at him. "What do you mean?"

"Why are you agreeing to shit you clearly don't want to do?"

I don't really want to go home. It isn't home for me anymore, but I do want to see my dad. He looked so happy about the party and seeing me that it was hard to say no.

"It's... I don't know." I shrug. "It's something my mom and Hendrix's mom started when we were babies... it's tradition."

"I'm going to support your choice, but also know you can stop saying yes to shit you hate at any given time," Acyn says.

I know he's right. "Do you want to go with me?" I think my question catches him off guard because his phone slips from his hand a little. "You can meet my dad and my friends back home." I've told Marisa and Quinn all about Acyn, and they're dying to meet him.

"I would have to check my schedule and see if I could even take time off then. It's September twenty-second, right?"

"Yeah, it's no big deal if you can't come. It's kind of short notice with it being a little less than a month away." I do want him to come, but I also don't want him rearranging things for work on my behalf, even though I know he would if I asked him to. That's one thing I love about our friendship; we spend a lot of time together but we're still our own people.

"I'll see what I got going on," he says. "But for fuck's sake, can we go inside where we aren't burning in this fucking heat?"

"Alright, alright. I've got my sun fix. Let's go inside... weakling."

He gathers all our stuff. "What do you want for your birthday?"

I shrug, "Nothing really." Acyn could get me a cotton ball and I would be excited. All that would matter is that it came from him.

ACYN

I lean against the front desk of my shop as I scroll through my phone. "Riley, can you tell me what my schedule is like around of the twenty-second of next month."

She gives me a confused look. "Are you going somewhere?"

"I'm thinking about it. I need to know how busy my schedule is first." I want to tell her to clear my schedule, but I haven't missed an appointment with a client since I opened Crown Ink six years ago. People book me months in advance for a reason.

"You have one client for a small tattoo the morning of the twenty-first, the twenty-second is a back tattoo, and the twenty-third you have nothing because it's a Saturday."

"Damn." There's no way I could swing that. Even though I know Harlow won't be disappointed, I am.

"Where did you want to go?"

"It's my friend's birthday." I don't give Riley much information because she's a chatterbox. While everyone in the shop knows Harlow, they also know that I like to keep my personal life private. That doesn't seem to ever stop Riley from trying to get more.

"A friend, huh?" she asks, giving me a side long glance. "What are you getting said friend?" Her eyes glitter with excitement.

"Uh, nothing. My friend said they didn't want anything."

She scrunches her face up. "You believe that? If this is the friend I think you're referring to, you better get her something."

I give her a blank expression. "She said she didn't want anything..."

"Yeah so...?" She says with a shrug. "She can say she doesn't want anything, but what she really means is she's leaving it up to you to figure it out. She expects you to get her *something*."

I knit my eyebrows together. "That's not what she said, though."

"Jesus, Ace, are you truly this dense? She probably said that because you two are close, but I bet you anything she'll be disappointed if you don't get her something or do something for her."

I open my mouth to say something, but then close it. Fuck. She's right... especially now that I'm not able to go to Texas with her. Harlow usually says what she means with me but... I think Riley may be right about this one. If I don't get her anything, she might assume I don't care. The only women I've ever bought stuff for are my mom and sisters. They've never hesitated to tell me what they want.

"What the hell do I get her?" I'm mostly talking to myself, but Riley answers anyway.

"You don't necessarily have to get her something. You can do something with her." She gives me a wink.

I scrub my hands over my face. "Riley... that's not the type of relationship we have."

"Oh, I just thought since you two spend so much time together that..." She cringes and shuts her mouth.

Even if our relationship were like that, I wouldn't tell her. It's none of her business. I also know she tends to gossip, and I don't want her telling everyone we're sleeping together.

"Thanks for the help." I grumble, returning to my work area.

I spend the rest of the day trying to figure out what the hell to get Harlow for her birthday. While driving home, I get an idea that makes me drum my hands on the steering wheel with excitement. Maybe Riley was onto something. Harlow may have said she didn't want anything, but that doesn't mean I can't do something with her.

I grab my computer as soon as I get home to see if the idea I have in my head can happen. I'm not sure if it's the right season for what I have in mind.

It says that it is. I pick up Six-Two-Six who has been meowing at my feet for food while I googled my idea. "I think your human pillow is going to love this," I say excitedly.

I decide not to tell her. I'll just make sure to ask her about her schedule for next week so I know what day to do it. I'm not sure who will be more excited, me or her.

It's the day of Harlow's birthday surprise. I told her that we have plans this afternoon and to wear something nice. Of course, she took offense to me telling her to wear something nice and accused me of politely calling her a bum. I would find her beautiful even if she were wearing a trash bag.

As soon as I step into her place, she's asking me twenty-one questions because my typical sneakers, jeans, and t-shirt are gone. I went for a dressier look and wore a white button up shirt with nice slacks and a pair of dress shoes.

"Acyn! You look... very handsome." She bites her bottom lip and gives me a hug. "I've never seen you dress up before." Her eyes roam over me as she pulls away.

"You look stunning, as always." I'm starting to like summer, since she's always either in bikinis that barely cover anything or sundresses that hug every single curve. She has legs for days that I would love – alright, maybe now isn't the time to think of that.

"Thank you." She curtsies which causes me to chuckle.

"There is one thing..." I say.

"What?"

I pull a yellow, satin blindfold from my pocket. "I'm going to need you to wear this."

"A...blindfold?" She tilts her head to the side, staring at it skeptically. "Am I going to end up on Cold Case?" she teases.

I knew the blindfold would give her pause. "No, I just don't want you to see where we're going. Do you trust me?"

"With my life." She turns around, waiting for me to tie it on her.

"Can you see?" I ask her once it's tied.

"No."

"Good, because I was flipping you off."

She tries to swat me, but misses. "Jerk."

"Alright, grab my arm so you don't bite the dust." Harlow loops her arm through mine.

"Wait, wait. Take a picture." She pulls on my arm.

"Right, right. Pictures." I've learned the basics of taking pictures because somehow, I've become her personal photographer. "Are you going to pose or am I just going to take them?" She gives me a cheesy grin. I chuckle and take a few pictures so she can choose her favorite. "Alright, are you ready now?"

"Yes!"

Harlow hasn't stopped smiling since I picked her up nearly thirty minutes ago. I haven't either if I'm being honest. I hope she's this excited when she sees where we are. I pull into the parking lot. "Alright, we're here."

She lets out a squeal that I'm sure she was holding in. "Can I take off the blindfold yet?"

"No, not yet. Let's walk a little further and then you can."

I place her arm on my hand and lead the way.

20

Harlow

I GRASP ACYN'S ARM as he leads me to wherever we're going. We're not in the city because it's quiet. I feel the crunch of gravel beneath my feet and then the softness of dirt. I don't think where he's taking me is indoors. We walk for a few more minutes, then he stops.

"Ready, Sunshine?" he asks, standing behind me.

"Yes!" I clasp my hands together with excitement.

"You already know that I'm not going to be there with you in Texas for your birthday. You also said that you didn't want me to get you anything. However, you didn't say that I couldn't do something with you." He unties the blindfold and says, "Happy birthday, Sunshine."

It takes my eyes a moment to adjust, but when they do, I blink in disbelief. We're standing in the center of a sunflower field. The warm glow of the afternoon sun illuminates the golden yellow leaves. I look at Acyn and then back at the sunflowers because I feel like I'm in a dream. I get closer to one standing in front of me, and it's so much taller than I am. I reach up to touch it to be sure that I'm not dreaming; this is all so surreal.

"Do you like it?" he asks.

There's a lump in my throat and tears prick my eyes. "I love it, Acyn." I stand on my tiptoes and kiss him on the cheek.

He wraps his arms around me. "I've had this planned for weeks. That's why I kept asking you about your schedule because I wanted to be sure that we got here before golden hour. I knew you would want to take pictures."

I don't want to let him go. "This is the sweetest and most thoughtful thing anyone has ever done for me. Thank you." I give him one last squeeze and then reluctantly let him go.

"Never need to thank me, Sunshine. I brought some stuff for a picnic, too."

I notice that there's a picnic basket sitting next to his feet.

My God, and they say chivalry is dead. "Acyn... I'm... I feel like I'm dreaming. This is the best birthday present ever."

"Shall we?" he asks with a grin.

He thought of everything. There's champagne, fruits, and a charcuterie board filled with bread, meats, cheeses, and jams. Everything is perfect. Even him.

"This is a day I will never forget," I announce as I stuff my face with food and sip champagne.

He chuckles. "Good. I was worried that it was a stupid idea."

"What?! Why?"

"I guess because it isn't a physical gift," he says, shrugging. "But I knew that I wanted to do something special for you. Especially since I'm not going to be there for your birthday."

He was more disappointed than I was when he told me he couldn't take the time off to fly home with me. I'd already suspected that would be the case, but I can tell he still feels bad.

"Acyn, this–" I wave my hand around the sunflower field. " –Will *always* top any birthday party. Trust me, I already know I'm going to get a bunch of meaningless bullshit gifts." I look down at the bubbles rising in my glass of champagne. "You know me so much better in the short time I've known you than people who have known me my whole life." I look into his ember eyes. "Stop feeling bad for not being able to be there. This is amazing."

He gazes at me as if searching for a lie on my face. When he doesn't see it, he nods. "Alright. I'll stop mentioning it... maybe."

I roll my eyes, grabbing his hand. "It's almost golden hour. I want to get some pictures."

Acyn snaps pictures of me amongst the sunflowers. I must admit that he has become quite the photographer. It wasn't my intention, but I'm not surprised because I'm always asking him to take pictures of me doing something. As we walk through the field, I spot some people and ask them if they can take a picture of us. Before we leave, Acyn buys me a huge bouquet of sunflowers that has various other flowers mixed in with it. It's gorgeous. I can't wait to get it home and in a vase.

I rest my head against the window of his car as we drive back to my place. "What would I do without you, Acyn?"

"I ask myself the same question about you." He keeps his eyes on the road as he grabs my hand to hold it.

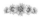

"So, are you two together yet?" Quinn asks during our early-morning video chat we have every week over coffee.

I scramble to find my ear buds because Acyn is still sleeping and my volume is all the way up on my phone.

"Keep it down," I hiss.

"Oh my God!" Marisa exclaims. "Is he sleeping over again? How do you keep your hands to yourself?"

I rest my head in my hands. "Had I known this was going to be an interrogation, I wouldn't have answered the call."

"Marisa does have a point though." Quinn narrows her eyes at me. "How?"

To be honest, I'm questioning my own self-control at this point. Especially after my birthday surprise. I'm seeing him in a whole new light. My fingertips are slipping off the ledge of *like*. One by one. "Because I don't want to ruin what we have now."

"Please don't tell me you're still hung up on Hendrix," Quinn says.

They know everything that has gone down between us. My contact with him has still been minimal. He lives his life, and I live mine. I know that he still keeps tabs on me on social media because he's always the first to view my stories and like my photos. Even the ones with Acyn in them. I think by liking them he's trying to show some maturity.

"I don't think I feel the same way for him that I used to. I guess I'll know more when I see him next week. That's if he's even there." I think Acyn was right. With time, you realize people who were once your world matter a little less to you each day.

Marisa cackles. "Like he would miss an opportunity to see you. I bet his bags are packed right now, waiting at the door."

I shake my head at her ridiculousness. "I cannot stand you two. Can we talk about something else?"

Acyn appears behind me in the camera, and it makes me jump. He, of course, thinks it's hilarious. I swat at him. "Ass."

Both Quinn and Marisa are begging in my ear to see him. I flip the camera around. "Say hello to your little fan club."

"Hi," he says in his low, gravelly, sexy morning voice. Acyn doesn't seem to care that he's only wearing boxers and neither do we.

"Morning," Marisa and Quinn say dreamily.

I roll my eyes and turn my attention back to them while Acyn busies himself in the kitchen. "Alright, I've gotta go."

"That man is a God. I think I saw his morning salute," Quinn says.

The heat of embarrassment creeps up my neck. I cover my face with my hand, thankful I have ear buds in and he can't hear what my thirsty friends are saying.

"Yeah, yeah, yeah, I gotta go. I'll see you two soon." Rolling my eyes, I wave at them.

They both giggle. "Bye, babe! See ya!"

I wasn't initially thrilled to go back home, but after talking to the girls, it's hard not to be excited to see them. I've contemplated asking Hendrix when he'll be arriving back in Galveston. It's going to be weird to be around him and not be friends or lovers anymore. I'm more worried about still feeling something for him. It's easy to ignore someone when they aren't physically in your space. I've wondered if maybe there is still a part of me that hopes he and I could work things out.

After we broke up, that was my hope. That we could somehow find our way back to each other. For the first few weeks in Seattle, he was my life jacket. Helping me feel secure in a new place by holding onto something familiar. But I found my footing, and then our relationship became exhausting because he was treating me as if we were still together. As if he had a say in what I did and didn't do. Slowly, the hope of working things out faded. I didn't want to put forth the effort for a friendship with him. Let alone a romantic relationship.

But then... Acyn happened.

21

Harlow

"Sunshine, you realize we have to be at the airport... now," Acyn calls from the other room as I scramble around my place, trying to gather the last of my things for my trip. I've accepted that I'm perpetually late. Acyn has not. Bless him for trying his best to get my ass out the door on time for things.

"I know, I know. I'm coming, I'm commiinnnggggg," I yell as I find the flats I tore my room apart for. I throw open my already stuffed suitcase and cram them in on the side.

"You know you're only going to be gone four days...," he says, eyeing my three bags.

"Yes, but... who knows what will happen. I had to have enough outfits to choose from. You know how I am." I sit on my suitcase as I zip it up.

"Wouldn't it be logical to take less instead, then? Take less and suddenly you don't have so many choices," he says with a smirk.

"Are you going to help me with my bags or are you just going to give me lessons on decision making? This is who I am as a person, babe. Take it or leave it." I go in my closet and take one last glance through my clothes to make sure I'm not forgetting anything. Acyn follows me, picks me up, and places me back in front of my bags. I don't even fight because I already know I'm being unreasonable.

He places his hands on my shoulders and brings his eyes down to mine. "Breathe."

I narrow my eyes, ready to say something, but he raises an eyebrow, so I close them and do as he says.

"You cannot take your entire closet with you. You're going for four days. Put your shoes on or you'll miss your flight."

I open my eyes and stare into his. "Fine," I huff. "But if I'm missing something –"

"You can say 'I told you so' when you get back. It's not like you can't buy something while you're there."

I raise my hands. "Alright, alright. Let's go."

Acyn looks up at the ceiling and lets out an exasperated sigh as if he's thanking the heavens.

He loads all my bags into his G-Wagon, and I hop into the front seat to scroll through IG.

My heart rate picks up when Hendrix is first on my feed with a picture of him in his parents' backyard with the caption: *Home to celebrate my twenty-fourth.* I chew on my thumbnail because I don't know why I was hopeful that his baseball schedule wouldn't allow him to be there. Charlotte is throwing the party. Professional baseball player or not, she would expect him home regardless of what he has going on.

Acyn gets in and swats my thumb out of my mouth.

I blink, gaping at him. "I can't stand you."

The corners of his mouth tip up as he starts his car. "You love me and my bullshit."

"Yeah, yeah." I wave my hand dismissively, facing my phone's camera toward him, recording for my IG stories. "Acyn, are you going to miss me?"

He scrunches up his face and sucks his teeth. "Can one miss someone as annoying as you?"

"Stunt for the gram." I nod my head, chuckling. "I feel you."

We pull to a stop at a light, and he looks directly at me. "I'll always miss you when you're not with me."

Butterflies are coursing through my veins now, and I'm grinning like an idiot. I'm thankful when the light turns green so he has to focus on the road.

When we get to the airport, I'm cutting it close like Acyn said I would be. "I told you we should have left earlier," he says.

"Are your observations going to help me get there faster?" I ask as we practically run towards check in, knowing I still have to make it through security.

He chuckles. "No, but it's fun to tell you I told you so." I ignore him and hand the agent all the stuff she asks for to check in. Once my bags are checked, Acyn walks with me to the security line.

I wrap my arms around him when we get to the point he can't go past. "Wish you could come with me, but I'll see you when I get back."

He hugs me back. "I'll be here. Enjoy time with your dad and friends. Call or text when you can."

Standing on my tippy toes I give him a kiss on the cheek. He smiles, waving me off.

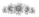

I feel like I can't breathe when I step off the plane. I forgot how thick the humidity is in Texas. My clothes cling to me as I wipe the sheen of sweat from my forehead. "Ah, the great state of Texas," I mutter to myself.

My excitement grows as I near baggage claim. I can't wait to see my dad. It's been months, and I really miss his hugs. As I near, I see him waiting with a smile on his face. I can't contain the smile on my face, walking as fast as I can without running because my carry-on is pretty heavy.

"Harlow," he says, giving me a bear hug. "It's so good to see you, Kiddo."

I cling to him. I missed his hugs, his voice... everything. This is the longest I've been away from him. "I've missed you, Dad."

"Missed you, too. I'm happy you finally came home to see your old man."

I give him one last squeeze before pulling away. "You know you can come see me anytime you want, right?"

"I know, I just like to give you a hard time." He nudges my arm, and we wait for my bags to appear. When we get my three bags of luggage, he gives me a look of incredulity. "Three bags? Really?"

I put my hand up, stopping further questions. "Look, Acyn already laid into me about it. I know it's over the top, but I also like options." I grab two of the suitcases. "Are we going home or are you going to judge me, too?"

"Still dramatic, I see." He chuckles and leads the way to his car.

An hour later, we're pulling up to the home where I was born and raised, and I'm feeling nostalgic. Growing up, I didn't think I would ever move away. Especially after my mom passed, the thought of leaving terrified me. At that time, I couldn't have imagined moving and leaving my dad alone. When you lose someone it makes you acutely aware of how fleeting time is. When we consider time, it's for appointments, birthdays, milestones, celebrations, et cetera. We don't consider time being a series of moments we will eventually miss.

"Nothing's changed," my dad says as he pulls into the driveway.

I've been away for half a year. Staring at the front door, it feels like an eternity. I think about how much I've changed since I walked out that door six months ago. I inhale the familiar scent of this house. It instantly makes me feel at ease.

"It's good to be home with you." I press a kiss to his cheek.

"It's so good to have you in the house again. I put fresh linens on your bed. If you want to crash, be my guest. I bet you're exhausted after the flight." He squeezes my shoulder then leaves me alone while he goes to get the rest of the bags.

I climb the stairs to my room. A smile tugs at the corners of my mouth because it's exactly how I left it, except the comforter and sheets are different. I exhale as I collapse onto my bed. The exhaustion of travel settles over me. My mind wanders to Acyn as my eyes grow heavy. I forgot to power on my phone when I got off the plane. The excitement to see my dad blocked out everything else.

Harlow: Made it.
Acyn: Good! Glad you didn't miss your flight.
Harlow: Why are you living in the past?
Acyn: LMAO enjoy your time with your dad!
Harlow: Wish you were here.
Acyn: Me too.
Harlow: I'll text you in a bit. I need some sleep.
Acyn: Pack your bags the night before and you wouldn't be so tired.
Harlow: I like to live life on the edge.
Acyn: Get some rest, grandma.
Harlow: I'm going to remember this for when I'm back.

Acyn: Shakin' in my sneakers, Sunshine.
Harlow: LMAO. To think I thought I missed you.
Acyn: You do even if you don't admit it.

I send him the middle finger emoji and put my phone into Do Not
Disturb mode. I didn't think I was tired, but now a nap seems appealing.
My dad brings in my bags, but I'm half asleep and don't say anything. He
kisses the top of my head before he leaves my room. It feels good to be
home.

The next morning, my dad and I walk along the beach. It's one of the
things I've missed about living here.

"Have you spoken to Hendrix?"

I don't immediately respond even though I expected the question. I've
tried not to think about seeing Hendrix again because it distracts me
from enjoying the few days I have with my dad.

I let out a sigh. "No, we don't really talk like we used to. I think it's
for the best." I may be filled with uncertainty, but I can't deny that it's
been good for Hendrix and me to take a break from talking all together.
Trying to be in each other's lives post-breakup probably wasn't the best
idea.

"He's asked about you every time I've seen him over the past few
months. I'm telling you this because I think he still has hope that
somehow you two will end up together."

Ever since I came home crying after our breakup, my dad and I talk about so much more than just surface things. I tell him practically everything now like I used to when I was younger.

"I know he does but... I don't believe he and I will ever be compatible. I want to be my own person, and he wants me to follow him around," I say. "I didn't think it would be an issue for me to be back here seeing him again, but it's a lot easier to think that when someone isn't in close proximity."

"If you don't want to go to the party tomorrow, we can do something else."

I smile at my dad because I know he just wants me to be happy. I squeeze his hand. "Thank you, Dad, but I'll be okay. I'm not the same girl I was when I left here six months ago."

That's what I'm telling myself, anyway. My fear is that I'll look at him and realize nothing has changed at all. I don't want to fall back into old ways because familiarity is so comforting.

"You're not, and I'm proud of you, Kiddo."

Later that afternoon, I get a text from Kyrell asking if I want to get together for Hendrix's pre-birthday bash today. Since Hendrix and I are only twenty-four hours apart, our parents would alternate which day we would actually celebrate our birthdays. The years that our birthday bash doesn't fall on his birthday, he throws a pre-birthday bash. He started that when we were sixteen. It tends to be a wilder party than the birthday bash that our parents put together for us.

Harlow: Who will be there?
Kyrell: Everyone.

I roll my eyes because everyone means all their high-school buddies they really don't give a shit about. But they all like to party, so I guess it works out. Marisa and Quinn are my only real friends that are attending the party tomorrow. Besides, Hendrix will be there. I don't know that I voluntarily want to hang out with him before I have too.

> *Harlow: I think I'll pass. That's not my scene.*
> *Kyrell: Ah, c'mon, Harls.*
> *Harlow: I'm good love, enjoy.*

If this were before I had moved to Seattle; I would have said yes without hesitation. I'm channeling Acyn at this moment, because I'm not going to say yes to shit I hate. I hate hanging out with people who don't give a damn about me and who I don't give a damn about. Why pretend?

> *Kyrell: LMAO fine, can I stop by after I'm done?*
> *Harlow: I don't care but don't bring anybody from high school.*
> *I don't want them at my house.*
> *Kyrell: You're so friendly.*

I ignore his last text because he knows that I don't talk to those people. Not that my high school experience was terrible, but they weren't people I cared to carry on lasting friendships with. Hendrix and Kyrell were really my only two friends. I didn't it mind it that way because I liked to keep to myself. I was "friends" with everyone else by association.

My phone rings, and it's someone that I actually want to hear from. I answer the video chat.

"Hey, Sunshine."

"Hi," I say, smiling brightly. "Are you done with work already?"

"Yeah, today was a chill day." He sits down in the tattoo chair. "What are you doing?"

I sigh and cradle my chin in my hand. "Kyrell wants to hang out later."

"That's right." He nods. "I forgot he's good friends with your ex."

Acyn never calls Hendrix by his name. He has dubbed him *the ex.*

"Yep." I smile. "But enough about me. What are you doing this..." I look at the time because he's two hours behind me. "Afternoon?"

"I..." He gets distracted by another call. "Hey, let me hit you back. You should go out and have fun while you're there though. Forget everyone else."

"Alright." My mouth curves into a smile. "Talk to you later, and I'll consider." He chuckles, gives me a two-finger salute, and ends our call.

I tap my fingernails on the counter, trying to decide whether I want to go to this party with everyone or not. It would be nice to get out of the house and enjoy the beach, but I can't get past all the people I know will be there. Then I'll have to deal with them tomorrow too.

I text Marisa and Quinn to see if they want to go shopping for a birthday outfit with me. They both immediately respond in the group text that they'll meet me at the mall in an hour. Apparently, Acyn was right. I would end up buying stuff here instead. He knows me well.

✦

I gaze at my birthday outfit for tomorrow as it hangs in my closet. It's a floor-length, sheer tulle skirt paired with a bodysuit embellished with rhinestones. One can never go wrong with a little extra sparkle on their birthday. Excitement buzzes through me. I've always loved celebrating my birthdays. I thought maybe the glamour of them would wear off as I got older, but it hasn't.

I didn't celebrate the first few years after my mom passed away. It was hard to do things without her. I also felt like I was betraying her by doing happy, exciting things. Sometimes I still do. Except now, I do things in honor of her and to celebrate her. My very existence is a celebration of my mother, even if she isn't physically here with me.

I hear our doorbell chime at the same time my phone does. I ignore my phone to go answer the door.

I see Kyrell through the glass. "Hey!" I say, pulling him into a hug. "I didn't thi –" my words get lost in my throat. I see Hendrix stepping out of the car behind him. I narrow my eyes at Kyrell. "Are you trying to ambush me?"

He cringes, looking remorseful. "I texted you."

"You sent the text after you rang the fucking doorbell!" I whisper-yell at him.

He mouths, "I'm sorry," as Hendrix gets closer to the door.

Hendrix looks good, maybe better than the last time I saw him. His black curls are a little longer, and he's built more muscle. The corners of his mouth turn up as he approaches me. Yep, he still has a smile that sort of takes your breath away.

"Hey, Harls. Hope you don't mind me being here with Kyrell."

Kyrell is now looking awkwardly between Hendrix and me. If I had telepathy, I'm sure he would be apologizing for doing me like this.

"Hey Hendrix," I say clumsily. "You look good." *Wait... what the fuck?* My eyes widen, surprised I let that thought slip past my lips.

Kyrell looks at me with raised eyebrows, probably hopeful that I won't kill him later. I knit my eyebrows together as I give him a look of contempt. His eyes find the floor once he realizes that I'm still not happy about this surprise tag-along visit from Hendrix.

"You look gorgeous," Hendrix says, bowing with a nod of his head. I can only watch him because what do you say to a person who you know is still in love with you?

"Um, thanks." I tuck a stray curl behind my ear. "Um... lemme go get my bag and we can go somewhere that isn't here." I close the door, so they know to stay on the porch and not come inside, but Hendrix interrupts me.

"I asked Kyrell to bring me with him," he spits out. "He mentioned he was going to skip the get-together tonight and come hang out with you so – "

"You thought you'd tag-along?" I ask with a quirked brow.

"Yeah, so don't be mad at him."

Kyrell gives me a silent plea in the form of a smile. Instead of responding, I roll my eyes and shut the door in their faces. Maybe they'll think I'm not coming back and leave. I mean, I know I could just tell them to leave, but they already know that I'm not doing anything tonight. I sigh as I slowly climb the stairs to my room to get my bag and phone. I don't know why my brain didn't consider this scenario earlier when I gave Kyrell the greenlight to stop by. I expected him to stop by much later than this. The sun hasn't even set for the day yet. I wonder why Kyrell didn't want to go the get-together. He loves shit like that.

I alert my dad that I'm going out with Kyrell and Hendrix. He gives me a look of surprise. I wave him off with my hand. "I know, I know. He tagged along and well... he's here now. I'll be back in a few hours. Love you."

I exit the room before he can ask me any questions. There's nothing to say anyway. I would have to see Hendrix eventually. Our birthday party is tomorrow. May as well rip it off like a band-aid.

We eventually find ourselves sitting in the backyard of Kyrell's parents' house. They're out of town, as usual. His parents weren't around a lot growing up and apparently, they still aren't. The third time we went over to his house while we were in middle school, I finally asked him where they were. He shrugged and said he didn't know. I remember thinking his life must have been lonely in a house this big. When we were younger, most of his time was spent with Hendrix or me. They really only started hanging out here when they realized it was cool to throw parties in high school. What better house to throw a party than one where parents are rarely home?

I settle into the plush pillows of a hanging swing. Kyrell offers me a brownie bite. I gladly take it because hopefully it will take the edge off of my nerves. Or maybe I'll need some nerve. Too late, I think as I swallow the bite. Hendrix refuses because he could be fined for using marijuana.

"You're such a buzzkill, Hendrix," Kyrell says with a mouthful of brownie.

He isn't wrong, I think to myself. *Wait, be nice Harlow.*

"How have you been, Harls?" Hendrix asks.

"Good." I nod. "Working at Holy Shot and taking on photography gigs wherever I can." I pick at the fray of my cut off jean shorts. I'd rather look anywhere but at him right now.

"How's the photography thing going?"

I stop picking at the frayed strings and look at Hendrix. I'm shocked that he's showing interest in something that I'm doing. "Great, actually." I smile. "I just had a shoot in LA."

He flashes me a smile. "That's amazing! I'm happy for you."

All I can do is blink at him because I'm not sure how to react to him being genuinely happy for me. I can tell by his tone that he's being sincere. Maybe he has changed with a little time and distance.

"You were in LA and didn't bother to text me? I'm hurt." Kyrell holds his hand over his heart.

"It wasn't for pleasure." I reassure him. "Well, it was pleasurable for me, but I was there for a job with not much downtime. Besides," I say, shrugging. "We're supposed to hang out in two weeks anyway for our tattoos."

Hendrix leans forward, resting his forearms on his thighs. "You two are getting matching tattoos?" he asks with his brows furrowed.

"Yeah, bruh. I told you about this. Her friend is doing them," Kyrell says matter-of-factly.

"Who?" Hendrix asks when I know he already knows the answer.

I only have one friend with tattoos that I hang out with. "Acyn..." I say.

"Oh, that's cool. Maybe when I have more downtime, instead of a day or two, I can hit him up for one."

I blink and then look at Kyrell, who is also looking at Hendrix like he's gone mad.

"Um... you," I say, pointing my finger at him, "want a tattoo from Acyn?"

Hendrix shrugs. "Yeah, you two are friends, right? Any friend of yours is a friend of mine."

Kyrell is now looking back and forth between us as if we're playing a game of tennis. I wasn't expecting this reaction from him. I also can't help but feel like he asked about us being friends for him to know whether Acyn and I have become more.

"I'm sure he would be down." I know that's a lie. From what I've gathered, Acyn doesn't care too much for Hendrix. He's never spoken poorly of him but will make remarks here and there.

"Will you take me to the sunflower fields next time I'm in town?" Kyrell asks casually as if he's not adding kindling to a fire.

I'm not sure if he's trying to elicit a response from Hendrix or not. Knowing him, he probably is. I know Hendrix saw all of those pictures because he liked every single one.

"Uh yeah..." I side-eye Hendrix, who still seems unbothered. "Acyn would have to take us though because I was blindfolded the whole way there."

"Aw, fucking sweet," Kyrell says, giving me puppy dog eyes. "Hendrix," Kyrell slaps his arm. "Did you hear that?" I don't understand why he likes to bother Hendrix so much. They usually end up fighting at the end of it all.

"A field of sunflowers..." Hendrix nods, almost as if he's contemplating whether he wants to comment or not. "He seems like a nice guy."

I'm not sure how to take this side of Hendrix. I thought it would be difficult to be around him and that he would throw a fit if Acyn was brought up. Maybe he really does want to be in my life now. I guess the problem is I don't know if I want him in mine. There's so much history there, and I'll always wonder if he's being genuine or just hoping I'll let my guard down. Kind of like I am now.

"You guys cancelled your birthday party?" I ask, wanting to change the subject.

"No, we showed up for a little bit and then left." Hendrix shrugs. "It's not fun like it used to be. People and priorities change," he says, looking into my eyes.

"They do." I nod and watch the fan whirling above my head.

Kyrell and Hendrix talk while I zone out. My body is physically here, but my mind is on my birthday party and Acyn. I can hear the boys talking, but I'm only half listening and responding when necessary. Hanging out with them hasn't been as bad as I was anticipating. I don't know what I expected from Hendrix, but it wasn't this... more mature version of him.

My phone rings, bringing me out of the trance the fan had me in. The edible must have kicked in. I steady myself as I stand; Hendrix reaches out his hand to help me, and I grab it before I topple over. We hold hands for a few seconds longer than necessary before I remove mine from his.

"Thanks." I smile and get my phone from my bag. "Damnit," I mutter when I see I missed a call from Acyn. I haven't heard from him all day, and I kinda missed him... a lot.

"Everything okay?" Hendrix asks.

"Yeah." I chew my thumbnail as I look at my phone because I get Acyn's voicemail. "Just missed a call."

He runs his hands through his curls as he does when he's annoyed and doesn't say anything in response. I'm sure he knows who it is. I've posted pictures with my other friends in Seattle, but Acyn is the one person I'm with consistently.

I look at the time and realize it's getting late. Deciding I don't want to look like a zombie tomorrow, I ask Kyrell to take me home. "Hey, Kyrell. Do you think you could run me home? I have a lot to do in the morning before the party tomorrow."

"Yeah, whatever you want, Harls. Lemme go find my keys." Kyrell leaves Hendrix and me alone for the first time all evening.

"It's been good to see you in person and not just in pictures," Hendrix says, leaning against the counter of the outdoor bar.

He's awfully close now. I can smell his cologne. "Yeah." My voice is a squeak, and I quickly clear my throat. "This went better then I imagined it would."

"Why?" He chuckles and tucks a stray curl behind my ear. The action causes me to meet his gaze. It reminds me of old times. For a second I get lost in his eyes like I used to. The familiarity of them, the warmth. His eyes travel down to my lips as he licks his own. I glance quickly at Kyrell who is walking towards us holding the keys in his hands. When I look back at Hendrix, his lips meet mine.

My eyes are wide open as I stare at his long, black lashes as his mouth is pressed to mine. The way I was just looking in his eyes I thought this kiss would elicit more of a response from me, but... it doesn't. I don't feel the same way I used to. I place my hand on Hendrix's chest and push him back. I initially look down at my feet unsure of what to say. I glance at Kyrell who is staring between the two of us.

"Hendrix..." I take a few steps away from him. "I don't feel the same way you do." An apology is on the tip of my tongue but again, I swallow it. I'm not going to apologize for something I'm not sorry for.

"Is it because of Acyn?" he asks bluntly.

"No," I lie. Acyn is the first and last person on my mind every single day. Even with Hendrix's lips on mine, I was thinking of him. Wishing I was kissing him instead of Hendrix. I think... *I'm in love with Acyn.* Or maybe I've known this whole time and this kiss just confirmed it.

"Then what is it?"

"People change, Hendrix. Feelings change." I wrap my arms around myself. "We've changed. I'm not the same person I was six months ago, and neither are you." Kyrell is still staring at us as if he's watching a soap opera.

"But you're still the same girl I've always been in love with." He grabs my hand, but I slide it out of his.

"I –" There is nothing more for me to say. No matter how I package the delivery of the words, he's still going to think that we will somehow mend things. Instead I turn to Kyrell. "Can you take me home now, please?"

"Uh... yeah, yeah, sure. C'mon."

I quickly walk away from Hendrix and past Kyrell making a beeline for the car.

I let out the breath that I was holding during that whole exchange as I lean against the car door. Kyrell reappears moments later, unlocking the door for me to get in. I slide into the seat and shrink against it as I see Hendrix walking towards the car. Kyrell stops him and talks to him for a moment before he comes to the car. Hendrix stands there staring at him, and I can tell that he's contemplating doing whatever Kyrell just told him not to.

Kyrell gets back in the car. "He wants to know if you'll still be at the party tomorrow?"

I sigh. I kind of forgot about the party tomorrow. "Uh, yeah... I guess I have to go."

He gives Hendrix the thumbs up, and he responds with a smile before he disappears back into the house. "Kyrell, what the fu- "

The engine revs to life as he turns the key and begins to back out. "Harls, listen, I had no idea that was his intention or I wouldn't have let him tag along with me."

I cross my arms and stare out the window. "What did you tell him in the driveway just now?"

"He wanted to come with to drop you off so he could talk to you. I told him I think you need some space."

I could have all the space in the universe from Hendrix and it still wouldn't be enough. Now, I'm dreading the party tomorrow. I let out a groan. "Kyrell, why does he always do this? Why is his timing always fucked up?"

His eyes remain on the road and the music is the only sound between us. "Hendrix will go after whatever he wants because he's used to getting whatever he wants. He's having a hard time understanding that you don't want him like he wants you. He thinks that if he tries a little harder that maybe you will change your mind."

I bang my head against the headrest in exasperation. "If I were going to change my mind, I would've done that months ago." I enunciate every word as if he's in the car with us.

"I know that." Kyrell taps his fingers on the steering wheel. "So you and Acyn, huh?"

I look out the window, pretending to be more interested in the moonlight dancing across the ocean. "Why are you bringing him into this?"

"Thought I'd ask to see what kind of reaction I got from you." I don't say anything in response. "You know, I've watched you go from making everything about Hendrix to being your own person and creating your own life. I'm fucking happy for you."

I place my hand over my heart. "Aw, Kyrell," I say it jokingly, but I can feel tears forming in my eyes. "That's really nice of you to say."

"I have my moments." He smiles, pulling into the driveway. "Don't worry about tomorrow. I think it will still be fucking amazing."

"I won't." I smile and give him a kiss on the cheek. "I'll see you tomorrow." I shut the door behind me and run up to my front door. Kyrell waits for me to unlock it before he pulls back out. I wave as he leaves.

Once inside, I rest my back against the door. Hendrix's actions tonight didn't shock me, but I had hoped we could be around one another without him feeling the need to profess his undying love. I really hope that he doesn't pull that shit tomorrow.

I pull my phone from my bag to see if Acyn texted or called me. He didn't. Knowing him, he's probably passed out on his uncomfortable couch with Six-Two-Six. Letting out a sigh, I climb the stairs, wishing I were home with him.

22

Acyn

Harlow hasn't been gone that long, and I'm already concerned because I miss her so much. I really need to get a fucking grip.

I just finished up with a client and decide I may as well call her to see how things are going in Texas. She picks up almost immediately and it's so good to see her face. You don't notice how much time you spend with someone until they aren't there with you. She seems happy, like a ray of fucking sunshine, to be home with her dad.

She's in the middle of talking about hanging out with Kyrell when I get a call from the client I'm seeing tomorrow. He's been coming to see me since I first started when I was eighteen. I'm pretty sure he has more tattoos than I do. I end the call with Harlow and switch over to talk to him.

"Hey, Ace!"

"Hey, Elijah, what's up man? Everything good with you?" I hope he didn't interrupt my call with Harlow to shoot the shit with me. We'll have plenty of time to do that tomorrow.

"Yeah, I had a family emergency come up, and I won't be able to make it tomorrow."

I pinch the bridge of my nose in annoyance. Why the fuck couldn't this family emergency have happened days ago so I could have been at Harlow's party. Oh shit, wait. He's still on the line.

"Damn, is everything alright?" I try to sound concerned.

"Oh yeah, just some things I need to handle."

"I can have Riley call you and set up another time if you want." My annoyance is growing with each word that comes from his mouth.

"Yeah, sounds great. Sorry to cancel last minute."

"No worries. I'll see you another time." I end the call and squeeze my phone in my hand. Harlow and I are just friends. I shouldn't be annoyed that I'm missing her birthday when – wait... unless.

I pull up flights from Seattle to Houston. Maybe I can still make it there in time for her party. "Yes!" I shout and Riley's head snaps up to look at me from behind the counter. There's a flight that leaves tomorrow morning at 8a.m. and arrives at 2p.m. in Texas. I would need to get a hotel so I could shower and change. Excitement builds when I realize I can do this. But I have one fucking problem. I don't have her address. I think of asking her uncle, but they aren't in town either, and I don't have his number.

I stare at my phone as if it's going to give me an answer. Then I remember that Harlow said she was going to hang out with Kyrell later. I bet he knows her address. Luckily, we have been texting back and forth about the tattoo he wants to get in a few weeks. I pull up his texts with a smile on my face.

Acyn: Hey. I need your help.
Kyrell: You name it and I got you.
Acyn: I need Harlow's address. So I can surprise her at her birthday party.

Kyrell: My man Acyn! Let me ask her because I only know how to get there. I don't know the actual address. I'm with her right now.

While I wait for him to text me the address I purchase the ticket before the last few seats are taken. He texts me back a minute later with her address.

Kyrell: The party starts at 6. She's going to lose her shit!
Acyn: Thanks man! Are you going to be at the party?
Kyrell: Hell yeah! See you tomorrow.

I hop up from my seat and stop at Riley's desk before I dash out the door.

"I'm going out of town tomorrow, and I'll be back on Monday."

"Are you okay? You're smiling more than usual."

"Yeah, I'm fucking great! I'll call Hunter and let him know that I'm going to be out of the shop and unavailable for a few days. He knows what to do."

"Okay," she says, looking confused. "Where are you going?"

"I'll see you Monday." I walk out the door before she can ask any more questions. She may have helped me with Harlow's birthday present, but that doesn't mean I'm ready to tell her anything that I don't have to.

Once in my car, I make a mental list of everything I have to do before I leave tomorrow. I call Harlow but she doesn't answer. Maybe it's best I don't talk to her until I see her because I'm sure I would let it slip that I'm on my way to her. I don't know how the hell I'm going to sleep tonight because adrenaline is already pumping through my veins. Once

I'm home, I text Sevyn to let her know where I'm going and to ask her if she can take care of Six-Two-Six. Of course she doesn't hesitate to say yes.

Harlow is more than just a friend to me. We started off there, but it's developed into more. I think she knows it, too. Sometimes I can see it in her eyes when she looks at me. I'm sure that she sees it in mine. There have been a few times over the past few weeks where I've wanted to kiss her but I haven't. When she talks about her ex, even though she tries to be indifferent, I can tell her feelings about him are mixed. I don't think she knows how to feel about him.

I find myself not wanting to wait anymore.

I step out of the shower at the hotel. I'm not sure how people survive the humidity that's already sticking to my skin. I have about an hour before the party starts. She may be worried about me at this point because I haven't wished her a happy birthday or responded to the messages she's sent me. She'll understand once she sees me, though.

The GPS tells me my destination will be on the right in a quarter of a mile. I'm fashionably late. It's not something I intentionally do, but I'd rather skip the awkward early party phase of sipping drinks and staring at one another. My heart rate picks up because parties aren't really my thing, but there isn't anything I wouldn't do for her. It's apparent which house is her dad's because the decorations are generous. I find a spot, park, and grab her present from the back.

I send Kyrell a text.

Acyn: I'm here. Should I just walk in?
Kyrell: I can meet you out front. I want to record her reaction.

I head towards the house and Kyrell comes out seconds later. He throws his hands up in the air to greet me. "Acyn! I never thought I'd see you in the great state of Texas!" He wraps his arm around my shoulders as we enter the house.

"Neither did I." I chuckle. I'm doing a lot of things I wouldn't typically do since I met Harlow.

"C'mon, everyone is out back. Do you want a drink or anything before we go back there?" he asks as he gestures towards the kitchen were passing.

My mind is on Harlow. Drinks can wait. "Nah, I'll worry about that later."

"Let's do this then," he says with a grin and pulls out his phone.

We enter the backyard that's packed with people, but my eyes find her instantly. *She is stunning.* Her hair is in a braid that wraps around her head. It gives the fitting illusion she's wearing a crown. The sun illuminates her skin, and she's fucking perfection. She's standing in the middle of a group of people. A guy is with her, and from the pictures I've seen, I can tell he's her ex. He has his arm around her shoulders as they talk to the people around them. To my surprise, she graciously moves out of his hold and stands between two girls instead. One whispers something in her ear, and she laughs.

No one laughs as much as she does. Harlow is genuinely carefree and fucking happy. I've learned that laughter is her medicine. If it were bottled up and sold, I would buy a lifetime supply.

Her friends are talking to her but she scrolls through her phone and chews on her thumbnail. It makes me realize she must be wondering why she hasn't heard from me on her birthday of all days. The guy to the right of her is trying to get her attention but she doesn't listen to what he's saying.

"I can't wait until she realizes you're here. She's gonna flip," he says as he continues recording. We haven't been standing here longer than two minutes.

Then as if she senses someone is looking at her, she looks up and scans the crowd. At first, her eyes pass over me but then they snap back to me and she blinks a few times. Harlow gawks at me as if she isn't sure whether I'm there or not. I smile and wave at her.

She takes off running towards me as fast as she can. Everyone around her looks at her like she's crazy. I toss the gift to Kyrell. I brace myself to catch her so we don't both fall on our asses. She crashes into me, and I pick her up off her feet and spin her around.

"Acyn!" she squeals with her arms wrapped tightly around my neck.

"Hey, Sunshine. I thought I would come say happy birthday instead of doing it over the phone."

"I told you today would still be amazing," Kyrell says with a grin as he continues to record.

Harlow's feet touch the ground, and she stares between us with a shocked expression. "You knew?" she asks Kyrell with her hand over her heart.

"Yeah, I knew since yesterday." He stops recording. "But Acyn wanted it to be a surprise."

She hugs me again. "Wait, did you know you were coming?"

"No." I hold my hands up. "I didn't know until yesterday when my client for today canceled. That's why you haven't heard from me. I had to get ready and then I was on the plane."

"I'm not sure what to do with all these surprises, Acyn." She places her hands on her cheeks. "You're here!"

The two girls she was talking to before walk towards us. She smiles at them as she grabs my arm, pulling me towards them. From their weekly video chats and photos back at her place I know that they're Marisa and Quinn.

"Guys," she practically squeals, "this is Acyn! Acyn this is Ma – "

"Marisa and Quinn. I've heard so much about you two." I extend my hand out to both of them, and neither of them look sure of what to say.

Quinn eventually finds her words. "You're clothed."

Marisa nudges her, and Harlow slaps her hand over her mouth as she looks at me. The guy who I think is her ex has been glaring at me but is standing within earshot now. And he looks pissed.

Kyrell gives me a curious look, glancing between me and Harlow's friends. "You have an OnlyFans or something, bruh?"

I open my mouth to respond, but Harlow interrupts. "It's an inside joke, right you two?"

"Yep, you definitely wouldn't understand," Marisa says. "It's nice to finally meet you in person. Harlow has told us everything about you." She shakes my hand. "You have such nice arms. I mean tattoos."

"Wow, so this is what it's like to have embarrassing friends," Harlow says, covering her face with one hand and holds onto my arm with the other. The ex is still lurking. I've never had someone stare at me this hard without wanting to fuck me.

"C'mon, you can meet my dad!" She pulls me along behind her.

"Harlow..." the ex says as he steps in front of her. He looks from her to me as if he's making a silent demand of her.

I pull Harlow towards me, and she settles against my chest. I wrap my arm around her neck as if it's second nature. She doesn't pull away from me like she did with him. Instead, she relaxes into me and places her hand on my forearm.

"Uh, Hendrix..." She looks back at me. "This is Acyn." She keeps her eyes on me. "Acyn, this is Hendrix." I don't make any movement to extend my hand. Neither does he...initially. Then he reaches out his hand, and I glance at it for a few seconds before I shake it.

"Nice to finally meet you. I know you two spend a lot of time together." His tone is slightly accusatory.

"We do," is all I give him. What Harlow and I do or don't do is none of his business. Even though he so badly wishes she were still his business. I lean forward a little so my mouth is next to her ear. "Let's go find your dad, Sunshine."

"Yeah, he's going to love you." She grabs my hand and sidesteps the fuckboy. I smile smugly, walking past the ex. The fake-ass smile he had on during the introduction is now a sneer.

We find her dad at the grill. I'm a little nervous to meet her dad. Now I know how she felt when meeting my parents. Harlow was right; he and West could be twins, except Harlow's dad seems more traditional. She taps his back, and he turns around to face us.

He gives me a genuine smile when he realizes who I am and shakes my hand. "Acyn. Nice to meet you in person."

"A pleasure to meet you, sir."

"You made it! Harlow had said you weren't going to be able to join us."

"A fortunate change of plans happened for me." My stomach growls. I haven't eaten anything since yesterday. I've been running on pure adrenaline.

"It's great to have you here. I'm sure Harlow will show you around, but enjoy your time. We can catch up later."

It went better than I expected meeting her dad. I didn't really know what to expect because I've never intentionally met someone's parents. In the past it was more of a "stay away from my daughter" type of thing. I wasn't a "bad" kid, I simply didn't care for rules. I like to push boundaries. Her dad's boundaries are ones I don't want to test, though.

"Have you not eaten?" Harlow asks.

"Nah, I was just focused on getting here. I haven't bothered to eat," I admit.

"I won't have you starving on my account. Let's get some food. You met all the important people... well three important people."

We sit underneath the gazebo to eat with Marisa, Quinn, and Kyrell. I notice that there are a lot of people here but they seem to be here more so for her ex than her. She hasn't bothered to introduce me to anyone else. Now I see why she wasn't initially thrilled about the party.

Harlow nudges my arm as she sits next to me. "I'm glad you're here." She briefly rests her head on my shoulder before she looks at me and smiles.

"Me too, Sunshine."

"Aww," Quinn squeals. "He calls you, Sunshine?" If the heart eyes emoji were a person, it would be the look on Quinn's face as she looks between us.

"He's always called me that. I don't know why you're squealing about it," Harlow says with a shy look as she glances at me.

"I know, but it's different hearing it in person."

"What's wrong with Harls?" her ex asks, taking a seat no one offered him. Everyone's eyes snap to his as if he's an intruder. It makes sense now; he must have given her that nickname.

"I don't like it," I answer honestly. "I think Sunshine is more fitting for who she is as a person. Especially after the first night we spent together. It just... stuck. You know what I mean?"

Everyone is looking between me and the ex who is now glowering at me. I guess he didn't know how much time we spend together. Whoops. Harlow is trying her best to hold back a laugh. He opens his mouth to say something but Quinn interrupts him.

"Do you have any brothers by chance?" she asks me hopefully.

I chuckle. "No, no brothers. I only have sisters."

"Damn," she mutters, crossing her arms. Marisa and Harlow cackle.

"How come I've never met your sisters, Ace?" Kyrell asks with a mouthful of food.

"Would you want me to introduce your sisters to a guy like you?" Everyone laughs, even Kyrell.

Kyrell shrugs. "Touché."

Two of my sisters are too old for him, and Sevyn is married. It doesn't matter though, because even if I did have single sisters his age, I wouldn't introduce them. He isn't a bad guy, but I can see myself in him. I wouldn't have wanted my sisters to meet a guy like me when I was going through the phase he's in now. He's looking for a good time and that's it.

We all continue to talk while her ex observes us all, not saying anything. Kyrell says something funny, and Harlow buries her face in my chest as she cracks up. Her ex looks like he wants to try and break my neck in that moment. I get the sense he's used to Harlow doing what he wants because it made things easier for both of them, while I simply want to be in her company and will take her anyway I can get her.

"Are you two ready to open gifts now?" her dad asks.

"Yeah," she says and then looks at her ex. "Are you ready?"

He stands and holds out his hand to her. "Yeah, c'mon."

"Oh..." She glances at me and then back at him. "Um, I'm going to stick with Acyn since he doesn't know anybody."

I can see his jaw flex with annoyance. "Right." He gives me a curt smile. "Wouldn't want him to feel lonely."

"Don't mind him," Kyrell says. "He's just realizing his place."

"C'mon." Harlow pulls me by my hand towards the table that's covered with gifts. She stands next to her ex once we reach the table. He gets ready to place his arm around her, but she pulls me next to her and he stops. I smirk because she wants me around and I know that bothers him.

"Thank you all for coming for the twenty-fourth birthday of Harlow and Hendrix," a woman who looks like her ex announces. "We're so grateful to have both of you home and are proud of who both of you have become."

She gives Harlow an appraising look as she says this as if she doesn't mean it for her but has to say it because people are around. This has to be the ex's mother then. "Let's open gifts. Then we can drink and dance the night away."

Everyone applauds and they pass gifts to them.

Harlow gets a lot of stuff that isn't really her. It's shit you would buy someone you don't know very well. I understand that she didn't have a big circle of friends, but she grew up here. I would think that the people she grew up around would know her a little better or at least have an idea of what she would like.

"This is for you," her ex says as he holds a gift out for Harlow. She hesitates before she takes it from his hand.

"Thank you, Hendrix. I didn't think we would be getting each other gifts this year..." Her words hang between them. "I feel bad now." She gives him a sympathetic smile.

"It's just something that reminded me of you, Harls," he says.

She slowly unwraps the box in her hands. Everyone's eyes are on her, and its apparent she's uncomfortable, but she handles the situation with grace. Harlow opens the box and looks inside. She looks at me, then at the box, and then at her ex. Then she pulls out a... *baseball*.

"Oh...um..." She's damn near speechless, and so am I.

When she turns it around in her hand, I can see that he signed it. It takes everything in me to not fall out laughing.

"It's a baseball..." Harlow awkwardly holds it up for everyone to see, and they act like it's the best gift in the world. "Thank you, Hendrix." She puts it back in the box and her ex gives her this awkward hug and tries to kiss her cheek but she pulls away.

"Is that all the gifts?" she asks.

"Oh shit," Kyrell yells from the back of the crowd. "No, hold on. There's one more I set down inside." He disappears inside the house and reappears with my gift. A grin pulls at my lips because the timing of this is just too perfect. "It's for Harlow from Ace."

Harlow turns around to face me with her eyes wide. "You got me something else?"

"Yeah, nothing major." I shrug. "Just something that reminded me of you." May have been petty to say that, but it's true.

She grins and takes the package from Kyrell.

"Sorry my wrapping skills are shit," I say, but she playfully swats my arm like she always does when she thinks I'm being ridiculous.

Her fingers tear at the wrapping paper, and she instantly knows what it is when she sees the box. Her hands still for a moment as she glances at me and then continues unwrapping it. Once it's completely unwrapped, she places her hands over her mouth as she stares at it.

"Acyn..." She's looking at the box like it holds everything she's ever wanted.

"What is it?" Kyrell asks.

"The camera that I love." She looks at me again and has tears in her eyes. Then she wraps her arms around me in a tight hug. "Thank you."

I hug her back. Everyone is staring at us, but we don't fucking care.

Quinn breaks the ice. "So does this mean we're getting professional photos before you leave? I mean, I wasn't gonna ask but since we're here..."

The tension subsides and Harlow gives Quinn of a look of appreciation for not making things awkward. I can't help myself and I wipe a tear from her eye. The gesture garners a look of disdain from her ex, who now looks like I just stole his favorite toy from him.

"Uh yeah..." Harlow says. "I can take photos of you guys... and anyone else who would like a professional photo."

The woman who looks like the ex speaks, "Okay, gifts are done. Enjoy the rest of the evening, everyone. The servers will be around with cake if you would like some." She glances at me, and I give her a look of annoyance that matches her own. I can tell she wasn't expecting that and clears her throat. "And make sure to talk to Harlow if you would like a picture."

As the crowd disperses, Harlow says thank you to those who gave her gifts.

Kyrell approaches her. "I didn't get you anything because I already paid Acyn for our tattoos."

She smiles and hugs Kyrell. "Guess I can't back out of this now, can I?"

"Fuck no. Sealed your fate months ago when you agreed to my wild idea." He pulls her into a hug. "Happy birthday, Harlow. It's good to see you genuinely happy." He walks off without saying another word, and the ex follows behind him. I can hear him asking questions about Harlow and me but Kyrell just shrugs him off by giving him bare minimum answers.

"And you." She turns to me. "Thank you for making this so much better than I thought it would be."

"What else are friends for?" I ask her, sitting on the edge of the table.

She stands between my legs and grabs the collar of my shirt. My heart thumps in my chest at the simple gesture. "I think..." She raises the camera to her eye. "We may be..." She snaps a picture. "Past that."

"Past what?" I ask her. I think I know what she's going to say but I want to hear it from her lips.

"Past –" We're interrupted when Marisa and Quinn come up to us and wrap their arms around Harlow.

"We're ready for our closeup, babe," they announce.

Harlow smiles as they strike exaggerated model poses. "You know, you guys could have just asked me to take pictures whether Acyn gave me a camera or not."

"Yeah." Marisa shrugs. "But you're here for fun and we didn't want to ruin that."

"Are you kidding? I love taking pictures. It's gotten worse now. Ask Acyn."

I chuckle and look at her. She looks so fucking happy. "Uh, yes. She goes nowhere without a camera. Which makes me wonder. Why weren't you taking pictures of your birthday party?"

"I didn't have a reason to. Now I do," she says, kissing my cheek before walking off with Marisa and Quinn.

23

Acyn

HARLOW SPENDS THE REST of the evening snapping photos of everyone and anything she can. I take a few photos of her with her friends and her dad. I'm even nice enough to take a picture of her and Kyrell that her ex sneaks into. After a while, Kyrell appears with some edibles and joints once the older people have gone home.

Harlow eats half of a cookie and then feeds the other half to me.

"So, what do you two do back in Seattle when you hang out?" her ex asks.

Everyone is having a good time, but this dude looks salty as hell. She doesn't bat a lash as she shoves the other bite of cookie in my mouth and laughs when frosting gets on my lips. Using her finger, she wipes it off my lip, and then licks it off her fingertip.

"Umm... when we're home..." She looks at me and giggles. "I guess it would depend on which house we're at. We call each other's houses home." It's clear the edibles have hit her. She doesn't censor herself like she does when she isn't lifted. I'm not gonna stop her from telling him what we do if he wants to know that damn bad. "We hang out a lot." She shrugs. "And do whatever we feel like really. It's always fun to get together with his family and –"

"You've met his family?" he asks as he tugs at his hair. It doesn't seem to take much to annoy him.

"Oh yeah," she says, nodding. "I'm really good friends with his sister too. That's how we met. Then he recently introduced me to his mom and dad, who I love, a month or so ago." Harlow doesn't seem to register that this is making him upset. Or maybe she does and just doesn't give a fuck. She turns towards me and asks, "Do you wanna dance?"

"Sure, Sunshine." I stand and reach my hand out to her. "Excuse us," I say to the glaring ex as we walk past him.

"Wait for me," Kyrell says as he pulls Quinn and Marisa towards him. "No offense, Hendrix, but you're a fucking buzzkill lately."

It seems like Kyrell is the only person who is honest with him. Maybe that's why she stayed with him for so long. He's used to getting his way, and it seems like he makes things difficult when he doesn't. Harlow grabs a glass of champagne from a server as we head towards the dance floor. It's her birthday, and she's finally acting like it.

Harlow's hand is linked with mine as she pulls me into the center of the dancing crowd. She downs the rest of her champagne and wipes her mouth with the back of her hand, giving me an appraising look. "Can you even dance?"

I look her up and down. "Can you keep up is the real question?"

Harlow presses her body into mine. I place my hand on the small of her back, pulling her closer, as she starts to move to the beat. I match her movements, and she looks at me with surprise.

"I meant what I said."

The song switches and the rhythm changes to a quicker pace. She spins around, pressing her back into me. Okay, wait, let me rephrase that. She grinds her ass on my dick. I respond by gripping her hips and moving with her. She lifts her arms, and her fingertips caress the side of my face, trailing down my neck, and then she runs them down her own body.

Goddamn, she's killing me. My body is focused on hers, but my mind is imagining her legs wrapped around me as she calls out my name.

I'm so lost in the movement of her body and my own dirty thoughts that I don't notice the song ending until she releases the pressure she was just applying to my dick and turns around to face me. She rests her cheek on my chest as the tempo of the song slows. I lift my arms to wrap them around her when someone taps my shoulder. I turn to the left to see her dad next to me. Oh shit, great, he just saw me feeling up his daughter in every way possible.

"Can I cut in?" he asks politely as the song switches to something slower.

Thank fuck because I really was about to tell him I had absolutely no regrets for feeling on his daughter if that's what this was about.

"Be my guest," I say as I lift her hand to his and bow out.

Harlow smiles at me and begins dancing with her dad.

I make my way off the dance floor to find a drink. Kyrell and the ex are standing next to the table. This should be interesting. I would avoid the situation entirely, but I need something other than alcohol and weed in my system. Kyrell greets me while the ex is looking sour. *Shocking.*

"Enjoying the party?" Kyrell asks.

"Yeah, it was worth the flight," I say as I down the bottle of water. "When are you heading back to LA?"

"I head back tomorrow. I hate this fucking place," he says bluntly.

I don't think I've ever heard something negative leave his mouth before. I side-eye him and he chuckles.

"A story for another time," he says.

I nod, deciding to leave it at that. If he wanted to tell me, he would. I turn my attention to Harlow and her dad as they dance.

"I'm going to go take some pictures of Harlow with her dad," I say. I can feel the ex's eyes on me, and if Harlow isn't around, I'm not going to watch what I say. Hell, even if she is around. But I'd rather not start a fight and ruin a party she's just starting to enjoy.

"Being a good boyfriend." Kyrell nudges my arm.

I don't try to correct him, but the ex does. "They aren't even dating," he scoffs and sneers at me.

I pick up Harlow's camera from the table where she left it. I contemplate whether I should say something or just let him have his moment. "Yet..." I say, turning on the camera. "We aren't dating *yet*." I do that douche bag shooting gun movement towards him, using my pointer finger and thumb, making a clicking noise with my tongue.

"Excuse me while I go take pictures of my gorgeous ass friend for now." I don't even know how Harlow feels about me, honestly. Sometimes I can see it in her eyes, but I haven't heard it from her, so it makes it hard for me to believe. Her ex doesn't know that though.

I walk away and hear Kyrell telling the ex to chill. If he wants to throw it down here I will. I'm sure he thinks because he's a professional athlete he has the upper hand. I don't go to the gym and run daily for nothing. Once I'm closer to Harlow and her dad, I take lots of pictures. I have no clue if they're good, I just shoot and hope for the best. When the song is over, I take some of them standing together. She thanks me and asks her dad to take her camera inside.

She wraps her arms around me as another slow song starts. It must be getting later. They aren't playing dance music anymore. I wrap her in my arms as she rests her cheek on my chest.

"You smell good," she says. "I mean you always smell good... or maybe I just missed you." Her arms wrap around me a little tighter.

I chuckle. "You could also be a little bit tipsy and on cloud nine right now too..."

"That too." She pats my chest. "That too. But it was all worth it. I've had fun tonight. May feel differently tomorrow depending on the severity of my hangover in the morning, but tonight... I'm fucking happy."

"I'm happy for you, Sunshine." I kiss the top of her head.

Harlow and I dance for a few more songs. We aren't really talking, just holding onto each other and slowly swaying.

"Acyn..." she mumbles against my chest. I think she's falling asleep.

"Yeah?" I stop us from moving and look down at her.

"I'm tired," she says with a yawn. "And my feet hurt from dancing in these fucking heels."

I kneel down and take them off her feet. I'm honestly surprised she's kept them on this long. She's either barefoot or in flats most of the time.

"Take me to bed, please?" she asks with her arms outstretched, waiting for me to carry her.

I pick her up in one fluid motion, carrying her bridal style, and she wraps her arms around my neck.

"Thank you for coming. You were the best surprise." Her lips brush against my neck. My body responds as it always does to her touch.

I stop when I come toe-to-toe with the ex, who now looks outright murderous.

"Harls, are you okay? Do you want me to take you upstairs to your room?" he asks.

He's bold and has me fucked up if he thinks I'm going to pass her off like a fucking relay baton. I guess if she says yes to him I don't really have a choice, though.

She lifts her head and her eyes focus on him. "Acyn's got it, Hendrix. Thanks, though."

Then she buries her face back into the crook of my neck and wraps her arms a little tighter around me. I smirk at the ex who now visibly looks ready to lunge at me. His fists and jaw are clenched. I'm sure the only thing stopping him is that I'm holding Harlow in my arms.

It looks as though every hope and dream he had with Harlow is slowly being crushed by *me*. I'll continue to stomp on them, fucking dance on them, if I have to. His eyes bore into mine, and I maintain my cocky grin I know he so badly wants to wipe off of my face.

"Are you sure about that, Harls?" he asks.

She groans, "Acyn and I sleep together all the time, Hendrix. He's got it."

"Yeah man," I say with a serious face. "We sleep together all the time. I've got this." I throw him a wink.

I move past him and Harlow calls out, "Night, Hendrix. Good seeing you again."

I'm an asshole, so I turn back around and address him by his name for the first and last time. "Night, Hendrix. Good meeting you."

All he can do is stand there, gawking at us as I take the woman of his dreams inside with me.

"Where's your room?" I ask once we're through the door.

"Upstairs, second door on the right," she mumbles.

I make my way through her house and climb the stairs. Once I find her room, I enter and kick the door shut behind us. I gently lay her on the bed and toss her shoes next to her suitcases strewn all over the floor.

"Uh... are you wearing that to bed?" I ask as she tries to get comfortable to fall asleep, but she's wrapped up in her skirt.

She groans, sitting up to strip off her skirt. "I was going to but this shit is itchy."

Underneath it is something that looks like a bathing suit. She removes the straps from her shoulders with her eyes half closed and then peels the top down over her breasts. I wasn't ready.

"Fuck..." I mutter to myself.

"Get me a shirt from my drawer please," she says casually as if her breasts aren't out.

I open the drawer and of course it's her panty drawer. I slam it shut and, thankfully, the next drawer has shirts. I grab one and throw it at her face. She falls back against the bed dramatically when it hits her, and she laughs. I fucking love that sound.

"You jerk." She giggles. "I'm intoxicated. I could have suffocated!"

"Right, you really were in danger with a light cotton shirt hitting your face," I say as I take off my clothes.

It's 3a.m. and it's still fucking hot as hell. She takes off the thing that looks like a bathing suit and tosses it at my face. When I remove it from my eyes, I'm met with a view of her ass cheeks as she crawls up her bed to her pillows. I'm momentarily rendered speechless and unsure of what to do with myself. I don't think I can sleep in just boxers like I normally do because... well now my dick is at full attention. She flops down onto her bed and pats the spot next to her. I stand there, contemplating my options. I can lie next to her, or I can take a shower and rub one out.

"Acyn, lay with me," she says.

So, I do.

I would rather be buried inside her, but I also don't want to make a move on her when she's drunk and half asleep. I want her to be fully aware of everything I'm going to do to her body. Every single touch, stroke, suck, lick, and moan – *all of it*.

I try to think of anything other than the fact that she's half naked next to me. Harlow cuddles up to me when I get comfortable. She doesn't say anything but places her hand on my chest for me to hold. I really hope she doesn't try to sling her leg over me because she's going to feel my dick that's still fully erect. Not sure when that will go away. Or if it will go away.

Harlow sits up. I hope she isn't going to puke on me. I can tell she's looking at me in the dark with her face silhouetted by the silver moonlight coming through the window. She doesn't puke. She straddles me, and I'm not sure whether I should stop her or see what she does. Placing her hands on my chest, she slowly spreads her legs as she lowers herself onto me. A moan escapes her when her pussy presses against my dick. I can't help that it twitches in response. She rakes her hands down my abs as she slowly rocks against me. I inhale sharply and move my hands up her thighs until I'm holding her hips. I should stop her. But I don't. I will follow her lead, though.

She suddenly stops and lays her head on my chest. "Just let me listen to your heartbeat. It reminds me of home," she mutters.

I hold her as she drifts off to sleep...wondering if she'll remember this when she's sober.

24

Acyn

WE SPEND OUR LAST full day in Texas with her dad because that's all she wants. Her dad has plans to come visit Seattle for the holidays and that makes Harlow happy. I know she loves her dad, but I also know that she no longer considers Texas home. Since we bought our tickets to Texas at separate times, I change my ticket to match hers for the trip back home.

On the flight home, we talk about everything other than what happened in her bed. I don't want to press her into talking about it, but I'm also not going to forget it. It isn't about just sex with her. It's about the fact that I can't see myself without her in my life now. I've never been in love before, but I imagine this is what it feels like.

"Home sweet home," Harlow says as we enter her place. "Ah, never thought I would have ever loved having my own place, but it turns out I do," she says as she sets her phone and bag on the kitchen counter. "Thank you for flying all the way to Texas for me."

"No need to thank me, Sunshine. It was pleasure to meet your dad." I set her unnecessary bags on the living room floor. Yeah, I still gave her shit because she filled half of my suitcase with stuff she bought while she was there.

"He loved you by the way," she says as she slips her sneakers off of her feet. "Everything will be 'Acyn this' and 'Acyn that' from now on." A smile tugs at her lips even though she pretends to be annoyed. "I'm gonna go shower now. Feel free to stay and make yourself at home like you always do."

"I'll wait until you're done. I may shower here. I've just barely stopped sweating from all the humidity we've been in the past few days."

She give me a dramatic eye roll. I hear her call out, "Weakling," right before she shuts the door and locks it. Smart move on her part because I probably would have gone in there after her.

I flip on the TV and rummage through the fridge while some murder show plays in the background. Her phone rings, and I turn around to see who it is. Surprise, surprise it's the ex. I have to chuckle because she changed his name to "The Ex" and replaced the eye-roll with a zombie emoji. After it goes to voicemail, I resume my mission for food when her phone rings again.

"Give up," I mutter to myself as I watch it until it stops.

Why does he call her like that? When it goes to voicemail, a text comes through seconds later and... I read it.

I know I shouldn't, but I can't help myself.

The Ex: I loved spending the night with you and kissing those lips again.

I knit my eyebrows together and read it again before her screen goes black. She... spent the night with him? When would this have – oh, when she hung out with Kyrell. I think she had said he would be there. But she tried calling me back when I tried calling her. When I texted Kyrell, he said he was with her. She even sent me texts but... maybe she did hook back up with him.

At her party, she didn't seem like she did. It looked like she couldn't be bothered to give him the time of day. Maybe that's because I was there. I don't know how their reunion went. I didn't even bother asking. I figured if there was anything of importance she would have told me.

I know I don't have a right to be annoyed or even angry... but I am. We aren't even together, but I still can't help but feel fucking disappointed. At the end of the day, we're just friends. I don't know that she would tell me if she did sleep with him. Because again, it really isn't any of my business.

They have a lot of fucking history. Maybe I need to give her space to sort herself out. Fuck... I still want to be in her life. Even if that means I have to give her space to try and get my feelings in check. Fuck. Fuck. Fuck.

She comes out of the shower in just a towel. "Are you okay?" she asks.

I'm at war with myself. I want to rip her towel off of her and claim her in every way I can, but I also can't stop repeating the words from that text in my head.

"Yeah," I lie. "I'm just tired. I think I'm going to go home to shower, sleep, and check on Six-Two-Six."

She looks slightly disappointed, and I hate to be the cause of that look.

"Alright." She smiles. "We did just travel and I'm sure Six-Two-Six misses you."

I can't help but chuckle in spite of feeling... disappointed, angry? For reasons that aren't even valid because she isn't mine. We're just fucking friends. "I'll text you." I know I said I want to give her space but all I can do is physical space right now.

"Okay." She approaches me and stands on her tip toes to give me a kiss on the cheek. "Tell Six-Two-Six his human pillow says hello."

I smile. "I will." I want to ask her what happened between her and the ex but I don't. I leave it there and head home.

Harlow

I grab my phone to text my dad but roll my eyes when I see a text from Hendrix on my screen. Delusional is the only word that comes to mind. I send him a text back.

Harlow: Hendrix, things are over between you and I. Don't make this any more difficult then what it has to be.
Hendrix: He isn't going to love you like I do Harls.
Harlow: That's the whole point. I don't want him to love me like you do. I want him to love me in only a way that he can.
Hendrix: He isn't right for you.

I don't have time for this. I try to be cordial but it's hard when he's being pushy.

Harlow: Neither were you but I'm still standing. I'm none of your concern any longer. Let me go.

I block his messages and calls. I'm *not* going there with him again. He needs to accept that I've moved on. I smile to myself. It feels good to finally be able to say that to myself.

It's been a few days since we've arrived home from Texas, and I can't help but to feel like Acyn is avoiding me for some reason. He stopped into Holy Shot the morning after we got back, but I haven't seen or heard too much from him since. I'm trying not to be clingy but at the same time I want to know what's going on with him.

Harlow: Hey. Do you want to hang out after work today?

I've never been nervous to send him a text but I can feel that something is… off. I rack my brain as I wipe down tables, wondering what could've happened between Texas and home. Or even over the past few days. I thought everything was good. In fact, everything felt better than good because I knew there was nothing holding us back anymore.

Unless… maybe he – my phone chimes. I have to keep myself from running across the shop to get to it.

Acyn: I can't tonight.

My shoulders slump and I feel like an idiot for being so disappointed. I let the feeling settle in my stomach, twisting it into knots. No explanation. He has been saying that for the past four days. It's been almost a week. At first I thought that he was just tired and then busy with work. I can respect that and give him space to do whatever he needs to do. But now I feel like he's intentionally avoiding me.

I check the time to see that there are only five minutes left of my shift. I start on his favorite cup of coffee after deciding that I'll stop by his shop so he has to give me a real answer instead of these three-word texts.

I see him through the window of his shop and he isn't even busy. In fact, he's sitting in the chair scrolling through his phone. I enter the shop and Riley gives me a smile from behind the desk.

"Hey Harlow! How was your birthday?"

I force a smile because I really don't want to talk to her. "It was good. Thanks for asking." I look over at where Acyn is sitting and he's still on his phone. I see from here that he has earbuds in. I turn back to Riley, "Can I go in?"

"Like you have to ask. Go ahead."

My heart thumps in my chest. I don't know why I'm so damn nervous; I've been here a thousand times. But those thousand other times, I knew that he wanted me here. Now I'm not so sure. I stand in front of him and hold out the cup of coffee. He looks up from his phone and into my eyes. I don't think he expected me to stop by because he looks slightly shocked that I'm standing in front of him.

I offer him a smile. "Thought I would stop by and see you."

He removes his earbuds. "What are you doing here?"

I blink and my smile fades. I wasn't expecting that question from his lips. My confusion must show because he tries to correct himself. "I mean... I have a client in twenty minutes and—"

"I just wanted to stop by and bring you a cup of coffee since we haven't been able to hang out this week." He then looks at the cup of coffee in my hand and almost looks afraid to take it. "It isn't poisoned...," I joke, trying to lighten the mood.

A smile tugs at his lips as he takes it from my hand. It reminds me of the first time I gave him a cup of coffee. The electric feeling of his fingertips brushing against mine. His fingers linger a little longer this time before he takes it from my hand.

He clears his throat. "Thanks Sun – Harlow."

My brows knit together. He's never corrected himself when he calls me Sunshine.

"Do you maybe want to get together this weekend?" I shift uncomfortably to my other foot. "If you're not busy."

His eyes don't meet mine. "I can't, Harlow."

I nod and swallow the lump that's forming in my throat. Why is he being like this?

"Oh, okay...um –" The door opens, and a woman with waist length jet black hair walks in. That must be who he's waiting on. She stands at the desk with Riley for a few minutes and then makes her way over to us. Acyn smiles at her which makes me quirk an eyebrow. I try to keep my emotions in check because this is his client after all and jealousy has never been my thing. I sure feel like making it my thing now, though.

"Ace," she says as she walks towards us. She gives him a hug and a kiss on the cheek... like I do. "I'm so glad we got to catch up the other night."

His eyes flit to mine as she takes a seat, unaware of the fact that we are now in the middle of a stare-down. So this is why he hasn't been talking to me. He's been going out and meeting people. I nod my head slowly as tears prick my eyes.

She turns to me. "Are you his apprentice? You're learning from the best, you know."

Acyn looks like he doesn't know what to say. It's clear that he didn't mean for me to know about her.

"I'm no one." I answer for us both, trying to ignore the sadness settling over me. "I'll see you around." I don't bother looking at Acyn.

I walk as fast as I can without running as I exit his shop. I can't help but look at him through the windows. He's still staring at me and holding the cup of coffee, while the woman talks to him animatedly as if nothing is going on. He didn't have to say anything to me. I force myself to look away from him. I can take a fucking hint.

I don't cry on the way home or when I climb into a hot bath. I don't even bother checking my phone. I turn it off instead. For the first time in a long time, I simply want to be alone.

I toss and turn that night like I always do when something is heavy on my mind. Ripping the blankets off, I make myself some hot tea and sit on my couch in the stillness of the night. I can either take this time to focus on myself or do what I know how to do so well: focus on someone else. I'm not trying to make my life about Acyn, but I do want him in my life. He doesn't have to tell me that he's seeing other people. We aren't together.

Maybe I've been reading our relationship all wrong this whole time. This really could just be a friendship. But I can't ignore the chemistry between us. Perhaps I took too long to sort out my feelings with Hendrix and he got tired of waiting. Or he could've never been waiting in the first place, and the feelings I feel aren't mutual.

What the fuck do I even feel? Sadness, loneliness, hurt... *love*?

All of the above.

I don't understand why he wouldn't just talk to me. The funny thing is, everyone makes communication sound so easy when it clearly isn't. I rub my temple with my fingertips, letting out a long sigh. I think about turning on my phone, but if I do that I for sure won't be able to sleep. I don't even bother with my tea. I pour it down the sink. The only thing I can do right now is focus on myself. I can't make someone want to be with me and I *won't*.

Sevyn stops by Holy Shot with Eli and Emery. I haven't told her anything about what's been going on, and I doubt that Acyn has either. The twins wipe that thought from my mind as they climb up the barstools to hand me a piece of paper.

"What's this?" I ask them with a grin. I tear through the twenty stickers they used to close the paper.

"It's a surprise," Emery says.

"Yeah, a surprise. Open it! Open it!" Eli chants.

I open it and read the paper that I see is an invitation to their third birthday party. I gasp. "You can't be turning three! You're too little," I tease them.

"We are turning three!" they say, giggling.

"Can I please have a hot chocolate and a muffin?" Emery asks. She's always straight to the point.

"Me, too," Eli adds.

"Can you come?" Sevyn asks me.

I think about Acyn. He wouldn't miss their party for anything in the world. "Um... yeah." I smile as I make the twins their hot chocolates.

"What's up with you?" She sits on the stool beside Emery.

"Nothing." I shrug but I don't meet her eyes.

She narrows her eyes at me. "I'll ask again. What's up with you?"

"Why are you giving me the mom glare?" I try to match her energy, but she's mastered it and her eyes are the same color as Acyn's. "Fine," I let out a sigh. "Acyn and I aren't really on speaking terms."

She cradles her head in her hands. "Don't tell me he fucked this up."

I don't respond. I just shrug because I really don't know that anyone is to blame.

"I'm going to kill him," she says.

I hand the twins their hot chocolates and muffins.

"No." I raise my hand. "Just leave it. It's fine. I'll still go to the party, but I don't know that I'll stay for the entire thing."

Sevyn raises her hands up in exasperation. "I was rooting for you!"

Laughter tumbles from my lips because it reminds me of the Top Model episode where Tyra Banks yelled that.

She lets out a sigh. "I won't say anything, but I'm for sure going to be a subtle bitch to him."

"Thanks Sev. I appreciate your loyalty," I joke even though I really do. "I couldn't miss Eli and Emery's party, could I?" I ask them.

"Are you bringing presents?" Emery asks.

"Of course I am," I reassure her. "What would you like?"

"Oh God, she wants the world. Don't ask them that. They really are happy with anything," Sevyn reassures me.

Eli and Emery are now busy telling me all that they want. I hear requests for a unicorn and an alien.

"A wha– " I forget my words when Acyn walks through the door.

Sevyn follows my line of sight. "Oh, yeah," she cringes, "I told him to meet me before I knew you two were at war."

His steps momentarily falter, but he makes his way towards us.

"It's fine," I say as I slip my apron over my head. "I'm off anyway. I'll see you and the little ones this weekend." I smile at her and disappear in the back to grab my things.

When I reappear, Acyn is looking at me, but I don't keep my eyes on him. I wave to the twins and Sevyn. As I walk past Acyn, he touches my arm, and I glare up at him. It must say enough because he releases me as though I've singed his fingertips.

As I'm walking out the door I hear a loud *whack*.

"Argh!" Acyn yells. "What the fuck was that for?"

"Language!" Sevyn retorts. "And you know what it was for!"

Celeste puts me in touch with one of her friends in NYC who's looking for a photographer. When she first suggests me for the shoot, I tell her there are tons of photographers in NYC and ask why they'd want to reach out to me? She replies that while there may be a ton of photographers in NYC, I'm not there and I need to put more value in my work.

"When will this be?" I ask her during our phone call.

"Wednesday through Friday of this week. All expenses paid and of course generous compensation. All you have to do is show up. I'll be there, too."

I look at the calendar and see that Kyrell and I are supposed to get our tattoos on Thursday. I contemplate whether or not to take the shoot. I really don't want to say no to this opportunity, but I also don't want to leave Kyrell hanging when we've had this planned for months.

"Uh... yeah, sure, I'll be there," I say in a rush before I change my mind and end up staying here just hoping to see Acyn.

"Perfect," Celeste replies. "I'll email you all the information."

I end the call and look around my place. I haven't picked up my camera since we got back from Texas, mainly because Acyn gave it to me and also because I haven't been in the mood for pictures. This will definitely be a good way to get back in the groove of things. NYC is one of my favorite cities although I doubt I'll be able to enjoy it because I'll be so busy.

Keeping myself busy, I pack my bag. It doesn't take long because I don't pack much. I chuckle to myself because Acyn would probably be proud of me but at the same time, *fuck him*. I'll talk to West after he gets home later tonight. He's never said no to me requesting time off because I'm the only employee he has that's willing to work any shift.

My phone chimes with a text at the same time someone knocks on my door. I already know who it is.

"Kyrell!" I fall into his hug. "Why do you always text me before you knock?"

He shrugs. "In case you're running around naked or something."

"Only you would think of that."

He flops down on my couch as if he owns the place.

"You're here early." I disappear into my room, returning with my suitcase.

"Are we going somewhere?"

"No, I'm going to NYC," I say, avoiding his eyes. "I have a photoshoot."

"Are you breaking up with me?"

A smile tugs at my lips. "I could never."

He sits up on the couch and pulls out a joint from behind his ear. "What are you running from, Harls?" He lights up the joint and takes a pull as he observes me.

I give him a blank expression and shrug. "I don't know what you mean."

He nods and scrubs his hand down his face then holds the joint out to me. "I've noticed every time something happens that affects you in a major way... you do something drastic. So–" he leans forward " –I'll ask you again, what are you running from? I've known you since sixth grade. It isn't like you to dip on me. I expect that from everyone else, but not you."

His words sink into me. I peer at him and then look at the floor. It just occurred to me that Hendrix was never my best friend. It's *always* been Kyrell. I think back on our friendship. Kyrell spent more time with me than Hendrix did after my mom died. I remember Kyrell telling me that it made Hendrix "uncomfortable" to be around me when I was sad. Not Kyrell though, he'd sit with me for hours, not even talking, just to keep me company.

Then when Hendrix and I did get together, Hendrix always called him for advice. It's clear now that Hendrix realized Kyrell knew me better than he did. Most of the gifts that he got me were because Kyrell had suggested them. Then, when I moved here to Seattle, he was with me a lot those first few weeks because he knew I needed the support.

The night we went out dancing, I told him that I was considering going back home. He told me not to do that because I would eventually regret it. That I just needed to get used to being here and meet more people. Shortly after that, I met Acyn.

I sit next to him on the couch and take the joint from his hand.

I take a hit and hold it for as long as I can before I let out a steady exhale. "Acyn and I aren't talking," I admit.

"What happened?" he asks with genuine concern.

I don't look at him because I really don't want to cry over Acyn again. I've cried enough. I shrug. "I don't know... everything was fine when we came back from Texas and then it wasn't." He props his feet up on my coffee table and I lay my head on his lap.

"There has to be a reason," Kyrell says.

"Really?" I ask him. "Why does there have to be a reason? He could have just got tired of waiting for me."

"Nah, not with the way he looks at you and the lengths he goes to for you. There is a reason he's pushing you away. Not that a reason makes it acceptable, but there has to be one."

I don't say anything and he runs his fingers through my hair while he thinks. At this point, I don't know that I care to know his reasoning. He could have simply talked to me.

"What do you want me to do?" he asks after a few minutes. "Do you want me to punch him in the balls?" I almost inhale the joint from laughing. "Cause I'll fucking do it."

"No, no don't do that."

"So does this mean I can't get my tattoo? Are we just saying fuck him?" That's one thing about Kyrell. He won't allow you to stay down for long.

"Get your tattoo. I know you've been looking forward to it." Silence falls between us. After a moment, I say, "I'm sorry to leave you."

"I get it. Sometimes you just got to get the fuck away. Why do you think I moved out to California? We've gotta do what's best for us, Harls. No one else fucking will."

He's right. At the end of the day all we have is ourselves.

25

Acyn

THE PAST TWO WEEKS have been fucking awful. Not having Harlow in my life has made shit almost unbearable. Yet, I still can't find the courage to talk to her. Especially not after the look on her face when Isabella mentioned that she and I caught up the other night. Harlow has never looked at me with such disappointment and contempt.

My intention was to give myself some space to reel my feelings in if she wanted to kick shit off with her ex again. I want all of her, not just pieces of her. I've never shared well, and I don't want to play ping pong with her ex. I've typed out thousands of texts since I last saw her and haven't sent a single one.

After I saw her at Holy Shot and she gave me a look of loathing, I knew a text wasn't going to do it. I probably shouldn't have walked in there like I owned the place or tried to touch her after pushing her away, but I'm fucking drawn to her.

The only reason I'm going in today and not saying fuck it all to hell is because she and Kyrell are getting their tattoos today. Maybe I can grow a pair and actually talk to her. Even Six-Two-Six misses her. Since she hasn't been coming home with me lately he ignores me and goes back to laying on my bed. My entire life is a fucking mess. To top it off, Sevyn has been more passive aggressive than usual, at least since she dropped off the birthday invite to Harlow.

I scrub my hands over my face and get out of bed to start this shit show of a day. Maybe I should stop by Holy Shot and gauge how she's feeling so I know whether to hide sharp objects.

⁂

To my surprise, I don't see Harlow at the counter. It's West.

"Acyn, it's been awhile." Oh fuck, he knows. "Your usual?" I let out an exhale when I realize he doesn't know.

"Uh yeah... where is Harlow?" I ask as I peer around the coffee shop, waiting for her to come up behind me wielding a pot of hot coffee.

"She didn't tell you?" he asks as he hands me my cup of coffee. "Harlow's in New York for a few days for a photoshoot. I dropped her off at the airport yesterday. I think she said she'll be back tomorrow but she said she was thinking of staying for a while longer because she loves it there."

Regret washes over me. She was so excited to get that tattoo with Kyrell, and I fucked that up for her, too. Apparently Ace the ass is a more fitting nickname than I thought. I nod as I pick my coffee up off the counter. "Thanks, man. I'll see you around." He waves me off as I head to my shop.

I'm proud of her for getting a shoot in NYC, but I also know that she's there to avoid seeing me. Fuck.

⁂

I told myself I wasn't going to ask Kyrell about Harlow. That lasts for about five minutes.

"Have you talked to Harlow?" Fuck that shit. I want to know how she's been. He knows her better than anyone else. I try to sound casual, but I know I don't.

"Yeah," he says, "she said she thought it best not to come today. But what I want to know is what happened after Texas? Because it seemed to me that you two would finally get off that friends bullshit, bang, and make it official. How did you possibly fuck that up?"

Typically, I can carry on a conversation while tattooing like it's as natural as breathing. I can't though when he asks me this question. I have to stop and look at him.

I really don't want to admit that I saw the text or that it's what started this hell on earth. But it's the honest truth and the only valid answer. Maybe he can tell me what happened that night if anything. I shake my head, trying to clear it, and let out a sigh.

"When we got back–"—this sounds ridiculous now that I'm about to say it out loud "–I saw a text from her ex that said something along the lines that he had a good time with her the other night and enjoyed tasting her lips again. Or some bullshit like that..."

I shrug and resume working on his tattoo again, not only to give myself something to do but so I don't have to look at him.

Kyrell snorts, which startles me, and then falls out of the chair laughing. He inhales as soon as he sits back up in the chair but is still chuckling to himself. I really want to be let in on what he finds so funny, because I have no idea.

"Hendrix said that?" He sucks his teeth. "Man, you're a dumbass. You believed that funky ass text message?"

"That's what the text s—" I say before he interrupts me.

He sucks his teeth. "Fuck that text. You realize you could have avoided this whole situation if you would have just texted me and asked me what happened?" A chuckle escapes him and now I feel really fucking stupid. "I was there the whole night with them. Matter of fact, it wasn't even the whole night. Harlow only stayed until midnight because she had all the shit to do for the party the next morning. Hendrix kissed her, and when he did, she pushed him off." He looks at me. "She said she didn't feel that way about him anymore. That's it. Case closed. She didn't fuck him. She didn't kiss him back."

I place my head in my hands as my heart races. *I fucked up big time.* I really fucked up. How the hell am I going to fix this? Kyrell sees the distress written all over my face.

He rests his hand on my shoulder. "Look, you fucked up. It happened. One thing I know about Harlow is that she's forgiving to those she loves."

I arch an eyebrow, "Loves? Did she say that?"

"No," he sighs, exasperated. "I see the way she looks at you and the way you look at her. I'm an observer, and I spent a lot of time with her and 'the ex,' as you call him. She never looked at him the way she looks at you. I knew she loved him–" he shrugs "–but not in the way she loves you. Don't fuck this up over some exaggerated text from Hendrix fucking Moore."

I shake my head, annoyed with myself. "How the hell do I even fix this?"

"I don't know," he says sarcastically. "Maybe you should try doing what you should have done in the first place and *talk* to her."

I chuckle in spite of my despair.

"If all else fails... grovel."

I really should've just talked to her, but we're here now. I go back to his tattoo but my mind is fucking reeling.

"You feel like a dumbass, don't you?" he asks, side eyeing me.

"Yeah man, I do."

I shoot a text to Sevyn to have her come help me carry in the gifts for Eli and Emery. I got them the electric cars they've begged me for every time we've gone to Target.

Sev: I'll be out in a second let me change their outfits.

I toss my phone onto the seat and see Harlow for the first time in days walking across the lawn. My stomach feels like it drops to my feet. I have to talk to her now or I may not get another chance.

"Fuck," I mutter to myself.

I hop out of my car, opening the back door to try and make it look like I was busy and wasn't just staring at her. When I hear her approach, her steps stop for a few seconds, but she moves to walk past me.

"Sunshine..." I croak out. She keeps walking past me as if she didn't hear me and then she stops between our cars. Scoffing, she looks up at the sky and then whips around to face me. Her eyes flash with anger.

"Oh, it's Sunshine now? Fuck you, Acyn."

Okay, at least she spoke to me. She turns around to open her car and I reach out to her. "Wait... can I talk to you?"

Her eyes meet mine. "What could we have to possibly talk about right now?"

"Everything." Even though she looks like she could set my soul on fire, I don't break our eye contact. She crosses her arms and leans against her car. I relax a little because at least she isn't trying to leave now.

"I'm sorry...." I start. She scoffs, but I continue, "I'm sorry for pushing you away."

"It doesn't matter." She shrugs as she looks anywhere but at me now.

"It doesn't matter?" I ask her.

"Yeah. It doesn't matter now. I don't want your apology. Is that what you wanted to talk about?"

"No," I run my hand down my face because this isn't going how I thought it would go, but at least she's talking to me. "I was distant because –"

"I really don't give a damn why you were distant, Acyn. That's your own personal business. Why the fuck would you want to share that with me now? Or did you forget I tried to talk to you multiple times?"

"I know." I guess the only way to get all this on the table is to blurt it out. "The day we came home from Texas, I saw a text from your ex talking about spending the night together and that... he kissed you." Her brows knit together as she looks at me with confusion and then it must register what text I'm referring to. "I know I don't have a right to –"

"Why does that matter to you?" She scoffs. "Tell me how it matters when you're spending the night catching up with people, too. You know if you wanted to see other people, I would have been okay with it. I could have handled it. But you didn't give me a chance to handle it at all."

I regret, with every fiber of my being, asking Isabella to come to the shop that day.

"Because... you're mine," My eyes lock onto hers.

She narrows her eyes at me. "I belong to –"

Before another word is out of her mouth, my lips are on hers. I pull away just enough to mutter, "Me," against her lips.

I want to devour her. I grab the back of her neck, pulling her towards me greedily. Claiming her mouth again. Claiming all of her. She responds by wrapping her arms around my neck, pressing her body into mine. She moans into my mouth. I run my hands along every curve of her body, gripping her ass before grabbing her legs. I pick her up and wrap them around me, pressing her against the car.

Her hands grip my shoulders as she grinds against me. I'm completely lost in the taste and feel of her. She tastes sweet, like cake and mint. As intoxicating as I imagined her to be. I need to taste all of her. I release her legs from around me and trail kisses down her neck. I'm aware we're outside, but I don't give a fuck at this point. I want a taste. I back her up so she's flush against me and the garage door. Hopefully, the only person coming right now is her. I kneel down, thankful she's wearing a dress, and rip her panties off. She gasps and looks at me with wide eyes. "Acyn there are people and –"

"Tell me you want me to stop, Sunshine, and I will."

She bites her lip as she looks down at me. Fuck, she's beautiful. I hike her leg up over my shoulder, waiting for her to respond. It doesn't take her long to make up her mind and she shoves my head into her pussy. I run my tongue along her slickness, tasting every last drop. I flick at her clit. She grips my hair tighter as she moans. I suck, flick, and lick her center until her legs start to shake. She's grinding against my face as I hold her up against the garage door.

"Acyn, Acyn..." It's a mix of a moan and cry. My name sounds so good spilling from her lips.

"Acyn I'm gonna cum..." She pants as she wraps her other leg around my shoulder and thrusts her pussy into my face. I don't let up. I quicken the pace of my tongue as she comes for me. A shiver runs through her, she stills for a moment, and then releases, crying my name. I continue to suck on her as she relaxes against the garage door when another voice cuts through everything.

"What the fuck, Acyn?" Every word is enunciated. It's Sevyn's voice.

Harlow pushes me back hard enough that I stumble backwards from where I'm kneeling and smack my head against the bumper of my car.

"Acyn!" Harlow gasps. "Are you okay?" She kneels down next to me.

"Yeah, I'm great," I reply. Better than great, actually.

Harlow remembers Sevyn is standing there. "Sevyn, I can explain – we – I... " she holds up her hands and cringes, "I'm sorry."

"It's a good fucking thing I made the kids stay inside because they would have been traumatized forever. Harlow, put your fucking panties on." She points to the ripped material wrapped around her ankle.

Harlow looks completely satisfied and horrified all at the same time. She kicks them off into my direction, I gladly catch them, but she refuses to look Sevyn in the eye.

"You two better stay for the entire party now and help with clean up afterwards. You can fuck on your own time." She doesn't say another word as she carries one of the presents inside.

I forgot I texted her to come help me before I saw Harlow heading towards me. It wouldn't have stopped me from eating her for lunch the way I just did, but I got completely lost in the moment. Harlow looks at me with wide eyes.

"I can't go in there," she says, shaking her head. Her cheeks are flushed, not from embarrassment, but from the orgasm I just gave her. I can't wait to see this look on her more often. "I'm serious, Acyn, I can never see her again." She covers her face with her hands.

"Sunshine." I pull her hands away from her face. "Trust me. Sevyn doesn't give a flying fuck about what she just saw. I walked in on her and Zane one time at my house on my bed. We're even now." She stares at me with wide eyes and then erupts with laughter. "If you're wondering, I made them buy me a new bed. She'll just have to live with a defiled garage door."

I pull her into a hug, and she wraps her arms around me. "I'm sorry I pushed you away," I mutter into her hair.

"Apology accepted," she says. "On one condition..."

I give her a curious look "What?"

"All future apologies need to go this way. Minus Sevyn interrupting."

"Whatever you want, Sunshine."

26

Harlow

ACYN AND I STAY for the rest of the party out of fear that Sevyn will rain hell fire down upon us if we don't. I still can't believe she caught us, but at the same time I don't regret it. When we got back into the house, Sevyn had already told everyone that we were together. Thankfully, she didn't tell them the dirty details.

His mom hugged me and told me she was so happy while his dad told Acyn it was about time. Apparently they all saw this coming before we did. We did, too, but I think we were too scared to face it. The past two weeks of stress are gone thanks to finally being with him and that expert tongue of his.

"I'm so happy for you two," Sevyn says as we clean up the mess in their kitchen and living room.

I give her a foolish grin. "Thank you. I'm happy too."

Eli and Emery run into the living room followed by Acyn chasing after them. "I tried to stop them, but they're so fast," he says, slightly out of breath.

"And you go to the gym for what?" I ask, sarcastically.

He gives me a lopsided grin as he approaches me. "I'll show you later." I squeeze my thighs together with anticipation.

"Acyn, what is wrong with you? The kids!" Sevyn scolds.

"Sev... it's not like they know what I'm talking about. Do you?" he asks the twins while Sevyn glares at him.

"Harlowww. Can you read us a bedtime story?" Emery asks me as she motions for me to pick her up.

"Of course, I would love to read a bedtime story to you," I say as I scoop her up in my arms.

"Me too?" Eli asks as he grabs my hand.

"Two stories then." I glance over my shoulder at Acyn, and he smiles.

"I'll be up to get you in a minute. I guess I'll be nice and help Sev after we fucked up her garage door." Sevyn punches his arm and he cowers away.

The twins and I cuddle up on Emery's bed, and they're out before I even get to the third page. I'm not surprised, considering how much they ran around at their party. They both fell asleep on me, and I don't want to move out of fear of waking them. I close my eyes, too.

I wake to Acyn whispering my name. "Sunshine, c'mon."

"The kids," I whisper. I look for them, but Acyn already moved them. He holds his hand out to me, and I grab it. "Was I asleep long?" I ask rubbing my eyes.

"Nah, only like an hour. Let's go home." His fingers interlace with mine.

I don't even bother asking him which one because, wherever I go with him, I know that I'll always be home.

⋆⊱✿⊰⋆

As soon as I step through the door, Six-Two-Six wraps himself around my legs and meows. "Aww, Six-Two-Six you missed me didn't you? Acyn is mean, isn't he?"

I follow Acyn into the kitchen where he sets out more food for Six-Two-Six who is now purring in my arms, completely uninterested in what he has to offer. "You've deprived us of cuddles for two weeks. He needs time to adjust."

"I'm trying to cuddle you right now," he says. "I never thought a cat could be a cock blocker." He leans against the counter.

I set Six-Two-Six down in front of his bowl. "There. I'm all yours," I say, standing in front of him, placing my hands on his chest.

"Are you?"

"What?" I ask, knowing perfectly well what he's implying.

"Mine..." He slowly rubs his thumb along my bottom lip. "I want to hear you say it." His voice is hoarse, and his eyes look like they're on fire, and I become very aware of the growing need between my thighs.

I hold his gaze. "I'm..." I grab his hand and place his thumb in my mouth, twirling my tongue around it. He inhales sharply. I slowly suck and then release. "...yours," I say as I look into his eyes.

I pull him towards me until his lips meet mine. The kiss starts off slow but quickly becomes fevered. He backs me up into the living room. I stumble over something but he doesn't let me fall. His lips never leave mine as his hands roam over my body. We bump into the wall in the hallway, and he presses me against it. I grope at his shirt, wanting it off of him.

I take a moment to admire his abs as he pulls it over his head. I run my fingertips along his tattoos like I've been craving for months. Once his shirt is off, his lips are back on mine. He hoists me up, and I wrap my legs around him. I hear the ripping of fabric as he tears my dress off of me. I bite his lip as he mumbles, "I'll buy you a new one." I couldn't give a damn about that dress. My panties already bit the dust hours ago.

In his room, he sets me on the bed and trails kisses down the length of my body before standing up to remove his jeans. I lick my lips in anticipation as he grabs the hem of his boxers, pulling them down. His dick springs free. All that I can think about is riding him into the sunset. He's all mine, and I want to feel every inch of him.

"Spread your legs for me," he commands. I do as I'm told. I slide my fingers over my clit, rubbing slowly, as my moan fills the space between us.

"Fuck..." He mutters as he drinks me in, slowly stroking his dick from root to tip. My pussy is dripping, and all I want is for him to be buried in me. He kneels on the bed, trailing his hands up my legs. "You couldn't be any more perfect," he whispers.

He sucks my nipple into his mouth, gently grazing it with his teeth. I surrender to him as he slowly kisses his way down to my center. My heart rate quickens with anticipation. I cry out and tangle my fingers in his curls as his warm tongue meets my pussy. He makes slow circles around my clit. Each swirl is bringing me closer to the edge of ecstasy. Moaning and moving my hips, I beg him not to stop. I need this release so badly. With one more swirl of his tongue, my toes curl, and I come undone. I buck off the bed, but he holds me in place as he continues to suck every last possible drop from me.

He kisses his way back up my body, and I bring his lips to mine, eager to taste myself on him. I suck on his lip and murmur, "I want you inside me."

Acyn responds with a growl and sits up to position himself at my entrance. My eyes lock onto his. He rubs the tip of his dick against my sensitive clit, and I let out a moan as he dips it into my wet center. Then he takes it out, rubbing it over my sensitive bundle of nerves again. He does this repeatedly, rubbing and dipping. I'm caught somewhere in between pleasure and torture, craving a release. The pressure he applies on my clit with the tip of his dick mixed with entering me slowly brings me closer to the edge.

"Are you going to cum for me?"

I nod as I pant, letting out a moan, and my breath hitches as he enters me and buries himself as far as he can go.

"Acyn..." I cry out. I see stars behind my eyes as I enter euphoria. He keeps the pressure on my clit with his thumb as my orgasm shivers through me. I open my legs wider so he can go deeper and then he starts to move. His strokes are slow, and my God, they feel so fucking good. He's stretching me out, giving me the perfect mix of pleasure and pain.

"You feel so good. Tell me you're mine," he commands through gritted teeth.

"I'm yours," I cry out as he picks up the pace of his thrusts. I wrap myself around him and my pussy clenches as another orgasm hits me like a wave. I call out his name, biting his shoulder and clawing at his back. He pulls me tighter against his body as he thrusts into me.

"Fuck, Harlow, I'm gonna cum..." His voice sounds strained.

"Cum inside me..." I moan into his ear.

That pushes him over the edge into euphoria. A shudder ripples through Acyn as he spills into me, letting out a low, rough growl. His hips stutter, and after a few more languid strokes, he kisses my neck before resting on top of me. I keep my legs and arms wrapped around him, rubbing my hands along his back as our hearts pound together.

After a few minutes, he lifts his head to kiss me. "You're all I've wanted," he says.

"And you're all I've needed," I reply.

I tangle my fingers in his curls and deepen the kiss as we warm up for round two.

I open my eyes as I feel Six-Two-Six's paws on my face and hear the clinking of glasses. The corners of my mouth turn up when the activities of last night replay in my head. Acyn and I stayed up exploring each other until the first light of morning filtered through the windows. I roll over in bed and wipe the sleep from eyes. When they refocus again, Acyn is coming back into the room with a tray of food.

I blink because it isn't like him to be up before me. Apparently sometimes he *is* a morning person. My stomach growls when the smell of pancakes fills the room.

"Morning, Sunshine!" he says and then stage dives next to me. Clearly much hasn't changed. I glare at him.

"Breakfast in bed?" I ask, sitting up to get a good look at what he brought in. There's pancakes, bacon, fruit, orange juice, and a single sunflower in a vase.

"Yeah, you've been upgraded to the full boyfriend experience," he says with a lopsided grin, looking proud of himself.

"Where's my phone? I have to get a picture of all of this."

He hands me my phone, and I snap pictures of the breakfast, of him, of us. Of everything. These are moments I would never want to forget.

"Can we eat now?" he asks after I spend five minutes taking pictures.

"Yeah." I set my phone aside. "We can. I need my strength to keep up with you."

He winks. "I told you I would show you why I work out."

He showed me over and over... and *over* again last night. I check the time on my phone and realize it's 1p.m.

"It's late. What time did you get up?"

"Only an hour or so ago. You didn't work today, did you?"

"No," I shake my head. "I took the weekend off. And after last night–" I take a sip of orange juice " –there's no way I'm going anywhere today."

He presses a kiss to my temple. We eat breakfast, chatting in between bites. The pancakes are perfectly airy and melt on my tongue. When we're done, I gather our plates, but Acyn insists I stay in bed while he cleans up. He won't hear a single complaint from me. Getting comfortable under the covers again, I grab my phone to upload the pictures I took to Instagram.

"Making this internet official?" He lays beside me, watching me scroll through the pictures.

"Yeah... wait, unless you don't want me to."

"You've been posting pictures of me since I first met you. Now that I have you naked in my bed, you think I give a shit?"

Giggling, I lay on his chest. "I was trying to be courteous."

"We're past that, Sunshine."

"Thank you for breakfast." I sit up enough to press a kiss to his lips. "I'm enjoying the perks of the boyfriend experience.

"Not much has changed, just get to be buried inside you now."

I playfully swat at his chest. Looking through my camera reel, I see a few he took of me snuggled up sleeping with Six-Two-Six. I scroll a little more and see one he took of our intertwined hands. This is where I was always meant to be. I choose to upload a mix of photos he took and some of mine.

I add the caption, "I've been upgraded to the boyfriend experience courtesy of Acyn DeConto." I tag him and then click the blue checkmark to upload the pictures. Within seconds people comment and like the photos.

Kyrell is one of the first to comment: ***"Finally y'all banged and made it official! #teamacyn."*** I show it to Acyn.

"Fucking Kyrell." He shakes his head with a smile.

My heart almost stops when Hendrix likes the photos. I... *forgot* about him. I had blocked his calls and texts but didn't think about Instagram because I haven't been using it over the past couple of weeks. I side-eye Acyn when I see that Hendrix has the gall to leave a comment: ***"Happy for you, Harls."***

"Um, I can block him if that makes –"

"I'm good," he says as he types something out on his phone. "He can watch us be happy."

I look at my phone after he stops typing, surprised to see he left a comment. Acyn's only ever commented on the first picture I took of him in the coffee shop. He doesn't see the point in commenting if he was there or can tell me himself.

I read, *"All I've wanted."* I climb on top of him as I pin the comment and reply, *"All I've needed."*

I toss my phone to the side because all that matters is underneath me.

He places his hands on my hips as I straddle him. I feel his dick getting hard beneath his me and I decide to let it free. I leave a heated trail of kisses down his abs. He watches me hover my mouth over him. I slowly lick from the base of his dick to the tip as he lets out a moan. I wrap my lips around him, swirling my tongue as I do. He grips my hair with his hands as he slowly guides my mouth up and down. I wrap my hand around him as I continue to suck, moving my hand and sucking harder as I pick up the pace.

He's matching my sucks now with the thrust of his hips. "Baby..." he chokes out, "I'm gonna cum..."

I suck a little harder as he looks at me. "Fuck, Harlow... you want me to cum in your mouth?"

I respond by not releasing him. He tosses his head back against the pillow, gripping a handful of hair, and lets out something between a growl and grunt as he comes. I pop my mouth off his dick as I swallow his release and straddle him again. He gives me a dazed look, his skin glistening with sweat, as his eyes focus on me.

His hand cups my face as he rubs his thumb along the side of my mouth, wiping away his cum. I lick it off of him and see the fire flash in his eyes. He flips both of us over in one fluid motion so that he's on top of me.

"Welcome to the girlfriend experience." I press a kiss to his lips. "Want to shower with me?"

"Is that even a question?"

27

Harlow

THIS MAN IS FLUENT in my body language. He worships me. I've never experienced this level of pleasure in my life. It isn't only a physical pleasure, but an emotional pleasure as well. The pleasure of knowing someone wants to know every curve, thought, and detail of you so they can take you to a state of bliss only they can.

I've lost myself in him but in exchange have also found myself in him. We're sprawled out on his bed watching some show that I'm half paying attention to. He's tracing small circles on my thigh with his finger, and all my attention is focused on that one spot. You would think that spending all day together would be enough but... it will never be enough with him. I'll always want to be wrapped up in him.

My phone rings, cutting through the bubble we've created for ourselves. I'd almost forgotten the outside world exists.

"Mmm... who is it?" I mumble lazily against his chest.

He reaches for it. "It's your dad."

I sit up because I forgot today is Sunday. This is our usual catch up day to make up for the short conversations we have throughout the week. "I need a shirt," I announce as I scramble off the bed and grab one of his.

"Chill, Sunshine." He watches me slip on the shirt. "You look gorgeous and freshly fucked."

Sitting on the bed, I playfully shove his arm, fix my hair, and smile as I answer. "Hey, Dad." I'm sure I look a mess. Acyn pulls me against his chest, and I relax, forgetting about my looks.

"Hey, Kiddo. Just calling to check in on you. I tried calling earlier."

My mind immediately replays all the positions Acyn and I have been in since we got home last night.

"I was... busy." Acyn coughs to cover a laugh and I elbow his side.

"Hi, Acyn. What are you two up to?"

"Oh nothing, Mr. Shaw. Just enjoying the company of my girlfriend." My whole being lights up when he calls me his girlfriend. I kiss him. Not caring if my dad is watching.

"That's gre–" His mouth falls open. "You two are finally together?" he asks, pointing at us.

"Why do you have to say 'finally' like that?" I ask, faking offense.

"Because I thought you two were together already. I didn't want to ask because I try not to be a 'nosy dad' as you like to call me."

I haven't called my dad nosy since middle school. "Dad, you can ask me anything you want."

"No, no. I try to let you be an adult. I know you're in good hands, and it's clear that you're happy. That's all I need to know." He gives me a warm smile. A timer goes off in the background. "I've gotta get the food out of the oven, Kiddo. Game day. Love you," he says excitedly. My dad loves his sports.

"Enjoy." I blow a kiss at the camera. "Love you." He pretends to catch it before hanging up the phone.

I wish he lived closer. It would be fun to hang out with him and watch a game. Acyn isn't really into sports, but it would be nice to spend regular evenings with them together. Usually, we get together with

Acyn's family, but since we got together yesterday, we're staying home tonight.

"I'm hungry. We should order food so we can lay in bed," I say.

"You're really not going to leave this bed today are you?" he asks with a chuckle. My only response is wrapping myself up in a blanket and snuggling closer to him. "Alright, what are you in the mood for?"

"I could eat anything right now. Surprise me."

An hour later, Thai food arrives. I keep true to my statement and don't leave the bed. I wrap the blanket around my shoulders and dig in. On the show we're watching, a girl with waist-length jet-black hair appears on screen. She reminds me of the girl from his shop. The one he spent the night with. I freeze with the food halfway to my mouth and stare at the woman on the screen.

"You don't like it?" he asks.

I put the bite of food into my mouth and chew it slowly as I continue to watch the TV. Then I turn my attention to him. "Who was the girl at your shop?"

My palms become sweaty, and the food suddenly isn't so good anymore. I shouldn't have swallowed that bite because now I feel it sitting in my stomach as I await his answer. We weren't together then, but... I still want to know if he was spending his time with someone else.

"Isabella?" He takes a sip of water, seemingly unbothered.

I want to wipe that grin off of his face.

"Oh, she has a name?" I reply haughtily.

I set my food down and lean against the headboard. Funny how he already knew who I was talking about. "Did you sleep with her?"

"Isabella?" He scrunches up his face. "No. She isn't into me like that."

I knit my brows and give him a scrutinizing look. "How would you know she isn't into you like that? She sure seemed happy to see you."

His eyes widen and his mouth falls open. "Aww, Sunshine, are you jealous?" He tries to cup my face with his hand, and I move away.

I'm trying to keep my growing annoyance at bay. "No, I just want you to answer the damn question."

"She isn't into me like that –"

I raise my hands in exasperation because I simply want to know if he was fucking her or not. I know I'm being petty because he wasn't mine then. Well, he was, but he just didn't know it yet. "Acyn, answer the question..."

"Isabella isn't into me because she's into girls," he admits.

I repeat the words in my head and then my eyes widen. I put my hand over my mouth as I gawk at him. "She is?" Relief pours over me.

Acyn's shoulders shake with laughter . "I was trying to tell you. Look, I know I'm handsome..." I scoff, rolling my eyes. "But not everyone is into me. She also asked me about you after you stormed off."

I splay my hand across my chest. "Excuse me, stormed off? Can you blame me? You didn't volunteer any information, and she is gorgeous."

"Well, she thinks the same about you."

"Me? Well what did you tell her?" I resume eating now that I know he wasn't seeing anyone else.

He shrugs. "That you're my girlfriend."

I freeze with my fork in the air. "But I wasn't..."

"Yeah, but she didn't know that, and what is that shit you always say? Speak it into existence or some bullshit like that?"

I've been teaching him about manifesting and the law of attraction. "I didn't think you believed in that stuff..." I say, nudging his arm. "To be honest..." I let out a sigh. "I thought you were tired of me."

His brows knit together. "Tired of you? No, I could never tire of you. If the past twelve hours haven't proven that already. I find you annoying but –"

I shove him playfully, and he grabs my wrist, pulling me towards him. "But," he continues on, "you're my annoyance." I smile like a fool. "It's just you, Sunshine."

I sit up and press my lips to his. Suddenly, I'm not so hungry for food anymore.

28

Harlow

ACYN AND I HAVE been together for a couple of months now. I swear he and I must have known each other in a past life because we get each other in a way that only we can. I mean, yeah, he still gets on my nerves, but that's what partners are for, right? They know every button to push but you wouldn't want anyone else pushing those buttons but them.

Kyrell texted me shortly after we got together. He asked if we could get our tattoos now that Acyn and I are "banging," as he called it. We have plans to get them today. I'm still working at Holy Shot, and West is slowly stepping away from the business as Ava nears her due date. I've taken on the role of temporary assistant manager while he finds someone he's comfortable with to fill the manager position once their daughter is here. He wanted me to continue working there, but it isn't where I see myself a year from now.

My photography business, Vision & Vibe, is taking off. What started as a hobby is turning into a real business. Even though West would love to have me stay on at Holy Shot, he also knows that I'm pouring every ounce of creative energy I have into my photography.

Acyn has been helping me get the business side of things sorted out. At first I mentioned the idea of renting a space for a photography studio in passing. That weekend, he took me around Seattle to see different lofts.

By the end of the day we contacted an agent to rent one that surprisingly isn't too far from his tattoo shop.

That's one of the many things I love about Acyn. I'll say something in passing, but he picks up on the sense of longing in my tone and will do everything he can to help make it happen. There's still a lot of work to be done, but I look forward to putting in the work to see my dreams materialize.

Acyn is also joining a friend as a silent partner for a tattoo shop in LA. Hunter is Acyn's right-hand man at Crown Ink, and he asked Acyn if he would be willing to invest in his shop. He couldn't refuse because he knows Hunter will be successful wherever he goes, even if it isn't in one of Acyn's shops. After agreeing to help him with the startup, he and Hunter travel back and forth to LA a lot. Sometimes I go with them, but this time I stayed because of work. I'll see him this afternoon, with Kyrell, for the first time in a couple of days.

But first, I have a date with Sevyn.

I'm sitting solo in the cute café Sevyn told me to meet her at... twenty minutes ago. My phone chimes with a text.

Sevyn: I'm one light away. I'm perpetually late. But you know this.

She may be late to everything, but she's reliable. We get together at least once a week for what we call "luxurious girl dates." Friends are soulmates too, after all. Last week we went to a spa for facials, and today we'll catch up at a French café.

I hear the click of her heels before I see her. Sev is always dressed to the nines. She thinks she's a hot mess, but she always looks like she just came from a photoshoot.

Sevyn sits down with a huff. "Emery bawled her little eyes out because she wanted to come on our date. Eli doesn't care where I go as long as he has his shows and fruit snacks."

"Aww, poor Emery. Maybe I can take her on a date."

She puts her hand over her heart. "She would faint with excitement if you took her out."

Our server comes and takes our order. We get chocolate croissants, bowls of fruit, and mimosas.

"How is Vision & Vibe going?" she asks as she shimmies her shoulders with excitement.

I almost choke on my mimosa laughing at her. "Good," I say, nodding. "I think I found a space for the studio, but I won't know whether I got it or not until next week."

"You'll get it," she says without hesitation.

"Are you signing up for school?"

She shrugs. "I don't know if I can do it with the kids and Zane."

"Oh, that's cool. Use them as excuses," I say nonchalantly, taking a bite of my croissant.

"You bitch!" She gapes at me.

"Look, those are valid reasons to be hesitant, but if not now, when? Zane and the kids will always be there. One thing I've learned is that you have to do things for yourself, too. Like these dates. We do this for us."

Over the past few months, Sevyn has expressed a desire to go back to school for fashion design. I've never met someone as fashionable as she is. She *lives* for it. She started a YouTube channel and already has a decent following but wants to further her education so she can work in the industry.

"I know but... what if I can't do it?" she asks, her voice laced with uncertainty.

"Sev, I know change is scary, but I also know that this is what you're passionate about. You need to ask yourself what happens when this all works out. Shift your perspective, babe."

She gets up from her seat and hugs me. "Thanks for believing in me."

"You can and will do this. I've always got your back." I hug her a little tighter. We break the hug when our server arrives with another round of mimosas. "So, when are you signing up?"

"Tonight." She smiles. "I can sign up for spring quarter."

"Yes, you can!" I exclaim. "If you don't, I'm stopping by your house and cutting all the straps off your designer bags."

She gasps. "The mere mention of that made me have chest pains. We would have to physically fight."

I clink my glass against hers. "Then chase that dream, babe."

After my date with Sev, I head to Acyn's shop for my appointment with Kyrell. We decided on a tattoo of a wave with a sun behind it to remind us of where we came from and to always look forward to the better days on the horizon.

I see Acyn through the window when I walk past and can't help but smile. He still makes me feel like butterflies are coursing through my veins. Riley doesn't even bother looking up from her computer. She just waves now. I beeline for Acyn.

"Sunshine." He plants a kiss on my lips and pulls me into a hug. "Did you miss me?"

"A little." I grin. "How was your trip?"

I plop down into my usual chair in the window. He busies himself with setting up his station. I take a picture of him and post it to my stories on IG, tagging Kyrell with the text: "Kyrell is always late." He responds almost immediately and says he was busy with a *lady friend* and he'll be here in less than a minute.

"LA is too fucking hot," Acyn says. "I'm glad he'll be living there and not me. But the shop is going to be dope when the renovations are done. Makes me want to renovate my shops here. Are you ready to get tatted today?"

"Yes. I –" I stop mid-sentence because someone walks in that looks like Kyrell but... he doesn't have his locs. I stare at him as he walks toward us.

"You cut your hair?" I ask in disbelief. He's had his locs since I met him in middle school. This is a huge change for him.

He shrugs as if it's no big deal. "Figured it's time for fresh beginnings and all that. What do you think?"

"You look good." I give him a hug. "I just wasn't expecting this." I run my hand over his low-top, curly fade.

"Nice cut, man." Acyn bumps his fist against his. "Who's going first?"

Kyrell looks at me and says, "ladies first," with a bow.

"Is this going to hurt?" I ask as I take my seat in the chair. I wasn't nervous until this very moment. I decided to get mine on my ribcage on the left side of my chest. I'm second guessing the placement now.

"You'll be fine, Sunshine. Not like you can't handle a little bit of pain," Acyn says with a wink. My eyes widen as I look at Kyrell.

"Oh, y'all are freaky, freaky?" He does a body roll each time he says "freaky".

I cover my face with my hands. "Can we just start the tattoo, please?"

They're the worst together. I didn't expect Acyn and Kyrell to become friends. I thought that maybe it would be weird given the fact that he's so close with Hendrix. But I'm glad they have a friendship because Kyrell is someone who has been a constant in my life since I met him. He's been with me through a lot, and I couldn't imagine him not in my life.

Acyn gets about halfway through my tattoo, which doesn't hurt as bad as I was anticipating.

"Did you see Hendrix has a girlfriend now?" Kyrell asks.

Hendrix doesn't take up space in my head anymore. I wasted too much time on him to continue when I'm happy.

"Nope. Have you met her?"

Kyrell shakes his head. "He and I had a falling out."

I look at him because he and Hendrix were almost like brothers. For them to not talk anymore, that's crazy. "What happened?"

He sighs and scrubs his hands down his face. "Do you remember Aubrey? The girl I was spending a lot of time with over the summer?"

I already don't like where this is going but wait for him to continue on.

"Well Hendrix came out to visit and met her. Long story short... that's his girlfriend now."

I gasp. "What the fuck?"

Acyn shakes his head and scoffs.

"Why didn't you say anything?" I grab his hand, squeezing it.

"What is there to tell? Besides, you were going through your shit with Acyn at that time."

I glare at Acyn who pretends like he suddenly doesn't have any hearing. "This was recently then?"

"Yeah, I found out they were hooking up a day or so before I saw you last. But I just saw today that they're actually together and not just fucking."

"That's really shitty, and I'm sorry you felt like you couldn't talk to me but... fuck him. And fuck her too. Clearly she isn't someone you would want to be with if she switched up so easily," I say.

Acyn finishes up with my tattoo. "I would have broken his jaw," he interjects, "but that's just me. He definitely isn't a friend, and both of you are better off without him."

I kiss him and get up to check out my tattoo in the mirror. I grin; it's beautiful with the waves and the sun behind them. The words "rise & fall" are written beneath in small lettering.

"I love it!" I exclaim when I turn back around to face Acyn.

"My tattoos look good on you, Sunshine," he says with a grin.

"Rise and fall... that's all we know how to do, huh, Harls?" Kyrell fist bumps me as he gets ready to sit in the chair next.

"That's just life though isn't?" I shrug. "The rise and fall, the ebb and flow... at least we have each other, right?"

"Damn right," he replies.

29

Harlow

"Harlow..."

He only uses my name when he's trying to be serious. I'm too busy kissing and sucking his neck to give a damn.

"I'm going to miss my flight..." he mumbles.

I tug at his belt. It's cute he thought he was going to get out the door unscathed looking as fine as he does. He has a black button up on with the top few buttons undone and black slacks with a black Louis belt. He smells delicious.

"Mmm..." I bite my lip, meeting his gaze. "We can be quick." I kiss his lips.

We won't be apart for long. He's going to LA for the grand opening of Hunter's tattoo shop. I'll meet him there tomorrow. He has to leave today to help with the finishing touches. I'm staying behind because they start the renovations on my photography studio today.

"Harlow..." He inhales sharply.

"Yes?" My hand is in his pants now.

"Why are you like this?" he groans. His eyes close and his head rolls back as I stroke him.

"Because... I want you to fuck me," I mutter against his lips.

That's all it takes. He flips me around, smacking my ass as he does. I gladly assume the position with my ass in the air. He rubs his fingers along the slickness and then licks them.

"Always so wet for me, Sunshine."

My breath hitches and my fingers fist the sheets as he thrusts into me. His hand palms my ass while the other one finds my clit.

"This is what you wanted?" he asks through clenched teeth as he pulls out slowly and then slams into me. Acyn wastes no time finding his rhythm. I spread my legs further apart, giving him ample access.

"Yes!" I cry out. His thrusts and the way he's playing with my clit have teetering on the edge. Gripping the sheets, I pull them off the bed.

"Then cum for me..." he commands.

I feel the tingle start in my toes and travel up to my center. I see stars behind my eyes as I fall into ecstasy calling out his name. After he ensures that every last drop of my orgasm is all over his dick, his hands grip my hips as he thrusts into me.

I meet his fevered strokes, throwing it back for him as he grabs a handful of hair. "Fuck..." He stills momentarily and lets out a grunt, finding his release. For a moment, the only sound between us is our labored breathing. Acyn leans forward, pressing a kiss to my shoulder before pulling out. I collapse onto my belly, turning over with a satisfied smile on my face.

"You're unbelievable." He chuckles, zipping up his pants and buckles his belt. I place my foot on his chest. He leaves a trail of kisses that start at my foot and end at my lips. "I'll see you soon."

I pull him back to me by his collar and kiss him again. "See you soon. Go before you're late. You're turning into me."

"It was worth it." He winks, grabbing his bag.

I'm looking forward to meeting Acyn in LA in a few hours but first I have stuff to do at my soon-to-be office. Excitement settles in as I walk around the studio with Ava. When I told her that I was renting a space for my photography, she didn't hesitate to offer up her services. There are perks to having a highly sought after interior designer for an aunt.

She assures me that the studio won't need much work. There's a lot of natural light with floor-to-ceiling windows and hardwood floors throughout. When we walked into this loft, I knew it was the one. Ava is working on getting my office space and waiting area presentable. The idea of my own photography studio seemed farfetched initially. I didn't think that I would need or want one. After a bit of research, I realized that it's more beneficial to have one than not. Now to see this farfetched idea actually happening makes me happy.

"Okay, I was thinking we could –" Ava stops abruptly and rubs the side of her belly.

I glance up from the mood board she's showing me to see her wincing in pain.

"Ava, are you okay?" I rest my hand on her shoulder. She's close enough to her due date that she could be in labor. I've never been around someone in labor, and the thought alone causes my heart to race. What am I supposed to do if she is?

Her eyes flutter open and she smiles. "I'm fine. Just Braxton Hicks contractions is all. As I was saying, we could—" Her sentence is cut short again, and this time she grips my hand.

I wince in pain from her grip being so tight. Her breathing becomes labored, and she breathes deeply, inhaling and exhaling. "I think we need to call West."

"Um, shouldn't I just take you to the hospital? You could be in labor. I just would hate for you to have –"

She nods her head vigorously with her eyes closed as she continues to breathe deeply.

I don't have time for panic to settle in because my only focus is getting Ava into my car. I put her arm around my shoulder and head for the elevator. She has more contractions on the short walk from the office to the elevator. I think my hand may be shattered from her grip at this point.

I call West as soon as we're in the car and tell him what's going on. Panic is present in his voice as he tells me he'll meet us at the hospital.

Ava looks at me with tears in her eyes. "I can't do this. I don't know what the hell I was thinking, wanting to be a mom."

"Ava, you're going to be the best mom. Stop talking like that. Besides, it's too late to return her now."

The smile that spreads across her face quickly turns into a frown as another contraction takes her breath away.

"Hold on, we'll be there soon," I assure her, knowing that Ava and West will be amazing parents.

After arriving at the hospital, I dash inside to get a wheelchair and alert the doctors that Ava's in labor.

"I think she's coming soon. West better get here," she says through gritted teeth.

"He'll be here. Don't worry." They wheel her inside, and Ava has a death grip on my hand, pulling me alongside her. I guess I'll see my cousin be born today.

Once in the delivery room, everyone moves in fluid motion around Ava. West arrives a few minutes later, eyes wild and hair a mess.

"Harlow," he says, hugging me. "Thank you."

He rushes to Ava's side. She looks happy to see him but also like she wants to kill him. Watching her go through contractions, I don't blame her at all. I fade into the background as they get her ready for labor. About an hour later, she starts pushing. I go between wringing my hands and chewing my fingernails. I silently ask the universe for the baby to make it here safely. They have waited so long for her. After what feels like forever, the smallest cry fills the room and tears prick my eyes because it's the most beautiful sound.

She's finally here.

West and Ava are crying. "Hi, Mercy," they whisper to her. Even though Ava had a hell of a time during labor, I know that one day I want this moment for myself.

After they tend to Ava, and Mercy is snuggly in a blanket, West hands her to me. I look at him with wide eyes because I've never held a human this small before.

"You won't break her, Harlow," he reassures me.

I cautiously take her into my arms. She's the cutest thing I've ever seen. I walk around the room in total awe of her. It makes me wonder if my mom were still here, if I would have had a sibling.

My phone vibrates in my back pocket. I slowly walk towards Ava, as if walking too fast will disturb Mercy, and place her in her arms. "I'll be back," I whisper.

I pull my phone out of my pocket once I'm out of the room, expecting it to be Acyn. It's a number I don't recognize, but I answer it anyway because it could be a potential client.

"Hello?"

"Hi, is this Harlow Shaw?" a woman says on the other end of the line.

"This is she. May I ask who's calling?"

"I'm Sarah, from Galveston Hospital. I'm calling about your dad..."

My heart rate picks up, my vision gets blurry, and I feel like I can't breathe. This feels like my mom all over again.

ACYN

I walk around Hunter's shop. The grand opening is later today. It will be a red carpet event that Harlow is ecstatic about. I glance at my phone, waiting for her message. I'm supposed to pick her up in an hour, but she hasn't texted or called me since this morning when she was on the way to her studio. I know she's busy with the renovations, and knowing her, she's probably frantically packing last minute.

"You ready, man?" I ask Hunter.

"As I'll ever be." The corners of his mouth turn up. "Thank you for all the support. I couldn't have done it without you."

Hunter started off as my apprentice at eighteen, and he's twenty-two now, opening up his own shop in a prime location in LA. I didn't hesitate to invest when he asked. His work ethic is like mine. I know he's going to make himself, and me, a lot of money. It isn't just about the money, though. It's about jumping into something that you love and giving it your all. If you have the passion and drive then nothing else matters.

"I always got you." I give him a hug. "Alright, I've gotta get to the airport to pick up Harlow. Traffic is a bitch right now. I'll see you in a bit."

I arrive at the airport right when she should be getting off the plane. I wait by the baggage claim designated for her flight. I wonder how many bags she packed this time. The plan is to attend the opening tonight and then go to Palm Springs for a few days tomorrow. I never really used to travel before I met her. She lives for travel and going to new places. It doesn't matter where.

People appear out of the gate from her flight. I'm looking for her smile... but I don't see it. I check the time and the flight number again. I have it right, so I try calling her phone but it's off. I wait for a few more minutes because maybe she had to use the restroom or something. Time ticks by and still no Harlow.

I check my phone to see if maybe I missed a call from her. I didn't. I try her phone again and I get her voicemail. I tap my phone against my hand, trying to think of what to do. It isn't like her to not show up. I know she was supposed to be with Ava today. Maybe West knows where she is, or maybe she actually missed a flight taking forever to pack her sixty-seven bags.

I tap West's name, and he picks up after a couple rings. "Acyn –" I hear the cry of a baby in the background.

"The baby is here?" That would explain why she's late.

"Yeah, yeah. She's here." I can hear the smile in his voice. "But Harlow. Her dad. He had a heart attack..."

The smile fades from my face. "What?"

"Yeah, she got a call shortly after Mercy was born. I was supposed to call you. I'm sorry but I've been trying to figure out how to go see my brother and –"

"No apologies necessary. Is he okay? Is she okay?" I scrub my hand over my face, looking around the airport. I can't imagine what Harlow is going through right now. All I know is that I've got to get to her.

"They didn't tell Harlow much else. She's his emergency contact, and she took the first flight she could find."

"Alright, uh..." My mind is racing, "Thanks, man. Sorry this is such a bittersweet day for you guys." I end the call. "Fuck..." I mutter to myself.

I make up my mind to try and buy a ticket now in hopes that I can at least be there shortly after she arrives. I really don't want her to be alone right now. Especially if West isn't able to make it because he just had his daughter. I head to the first counter with someone behind it. I explain to her what is going on and that I need a ticket to Texas today with a rental car if possible. Harlow must be in the air right now because her phone is still off when I try her again.

"We have one that leaves in thirty minutes." Man, am I grateful to be at an international airport.

"I'll take it." I don't hesitate. I don't give a damn about the price. I just hand over my card and my ID while she sorts the rest of it out.

A few minutes later, she hands me my stuff along with a ticket. "I hope he's okay."

"Yeah, me too."

I try Harlow's phone one more time before the plane takes off. It goes straight to voicemail. All I can hope is that she and her dad are okay. I shoot her a text in hopes that she'll see it when she's able to turn on her phone.

30

Harlow

I HAVEN'T STOPPED CRYING since the phone call. I stare out the window as the pilot announces that we're finally landing in Houston. This has been the longest flight of my entire life. My mind is racing with possibilities. I debated catching a flight as soon as possible or waiting to see if there was more news. I knew once I was in the air I wouldn't know what was going on, and it's been torture.

I only know that I want to be with my dad. Waiting for them to pull the plane to the gate after it lands is excruciating. At this point, I barely have much of a thumbnail left. Once we're told we can exit the plane, I push past everyone. The only thing on my mind is my dad.

I rent a car and speed all the way to the hospital. If they were to try and stop me right now, they would have to engage in a high speed chase because I'm not stopping for shit. Thankfully, I don't get pulled over. I run inside the hospital and wait at the nurse's station for someone. It's later in the evening so no one is there. I pace back and forth, finally seeing someone.

"Hi, I'm here to see my dad. Felix Shaw. Can you please tell me what room he's in? Is he okay?" I'm wringing my hands together, and I'm sure I look an absolute mess.

"Shaw..." She checks her charts and pulls his. "He was awake a couple of hours ago, honey, and he was alert. You can go back and see him. Room two-twenty-eight."

My body relaxes for the first time in hours when I hear that he's awake. I give her a smile, trying not to run down the hallway to his room. I reach his door and try to steady myself. I lean against the wall trying to breathe even though it's hard. I'm hunched over, dry heaving in the hallway, when the nurse who was at the desk places her hand on my back.

"Oh honey, this is a lot. Sit down. Inhale."

I take a deep breath and hold it.

"Okay, exhale."

I do as she says and let it out slowly.

"Do that a few more times for me. Focus on your breathing. Your dad will be okay and so will you."

People really underestimate the power of kindness.

"Are you ready to stand now?"

I nod as she reaches her hand out to me and helps me stand. I feel much more stable than I did when I first arrived at his door.

"Will you be okay?"

"Yes." I nod. "I just – this is a lot for me, and I was expecting the worst, but he's alive. Thank you." I turn and place my hand on the doorknob.

"Let me know if you need anything. My name is Evelyn. I'll be the nurse on tonight."

I go still as a chill runs through me. Evelyn, "Evie" to everyone who knew her, was my mom's name. I turn around to face her. "Thank you. I will."

My dad doesn't wake when I enter the room. He looks just how I remember him. I prepared myself for him to be dead, but he's still here with me. I quietly pull up a chair next to him and sit down, grabbing his hand. He stirs. I stare at him to see if he'll wake, and his eyes flutter open.

"Harlow..."

"Dad, it's me." I stand giving him a kiss on the cheek. "Sorry it took me so long to make it."

"You didn't have to come for me, Kiddo." His eyes are already closing again.

"I'm already here, Dad. Sleep and we'll talk in the morning."

He's already asleep again before I finish my sentence. A few minutes later, Evelyn comes in and hands me a few blankets for myself. Hospitals are always so cold. I forgot my bag and phone in the car. I think of Acyn and wonder if he talked to West. I wonder how they're doing with the new baby. I told West I would call him as soon as I landed but seeing my dad was the only thing on my mind. I curl up in the chair and wrap the blankets tighter around me. It's late there too and I don't want to disturb them. I'll call him when I wake up again. I already feel myself drifting off to sleep. My dad is okay. He's still here with me. That's all I could ask for right now.

I wake to a kiss being pressed to my forehead. Opening my eyes, Acyn comes into focus. I blink a few times, a little disoriented. The beeping of the machine monitoring my dad's heart rate reminds me of what happened. I wrap my arms around Acyn's neck.

"Hi, Sunshine," he whispers.

I look over at my dad, who is still asleep, and point to the hallway. Acyn waits for me to get up and follows me out. He wraps me tightly in a much needed hug. I melt into him, letting him hold me for a while without saying a word. Tears prick my eyes, and I don't even know why. My dad is okay, so it must be from all the stress I've experienced since the phone call. I feel safe in Acyn's arms. I'm sobbing now but I can't stop. He doesn't say a word. He just holds me and that's all I need.

After a few minutes of crying, he holds my face in his hands and wipes my tears. He gives me a kiss despite the fact my nose is running.

"I'm so glad you're here." I wrap my arms around him again. "When did you get here? What time is it?"

"About forty-five minutes ago, and it's—" he glances at his watch "—four-thirty a.m. How's your dad?"

"Good. Stubborn. Told me I didn't need to be here."

"I'm sure he's feeling a lot of emotions right now, Sunshine. It's nothing against you."

"I can't just leave him here alone now... you know that, right?" I was thinking about it on the plane ride that I can't and won't leave my dad living here alone. If he would move to Seattle with us that would be great, but I don't know if he'll be up for that. I don't even know if a long distance trip like that would be wise given his current health situation.

"I know, and I wouldn't expect you to. I'm here for whatever you need, Sunshine. You name it."

I hug him tighter. "I know, and that's all I need."

My dad wakes a few hours later. He beams at me when he sees me, and I'm finally able to give him a real hug. "You look amazing for just having a heart attack dad," I tease.

"I told you I'm fine. There was no reason for you to stop your life for me." My smile fades as I try to process why he's shutting me out.

Acyn clears his throat. "Uh... I'm going to go get breakfast. I'll be back." He plants a kiss on top of my head and exits the room.

"Dad... what's going on with you?"

He won't look at me and instead focuses his attention on the television screen. I reach across him for the remote and turn it off. I know my dad is my dad but this isn't something we're going to avoid talking about. His health is at risk. Perhaps my reasons are selfish because he's all I have left, but that's all the reason I need. He lets out a sigh, looking defeated. I've only seen this look on my dad's face when my mother passed away.

"I've known since shortly after you moved that I have high cholesterol. I saw a doctor for the diagnosis but didn't follow the care regimen." My mouth falls open and he holds up his hand. "I know, I know. I kept telling myself that I would get to it when I get to it. I'm pretty active as you know, and I didn't think this would ever be a problem for me. I've been stressed at work but haven't retired because..."

I look at him, expectantly waiting for him to finish his sentence, but he doesn't. I lean forward. "Because... what, dad?"

"Because..." He lets out a sigh. "I–things haven't been the same since you left. The house is empty. It's the house you were born in, raised in, the house we created memories in with your mother," he says, his voice cracking. "When you left, I didn't think it would be that bad... but then you were gone. I hate being home in an empty house with so many memories. So even though work is stressful..." He shrugs. "It's better than being at home alone."

"Dad..." My tears fall into my lap. I had no idea that he felt this way. Whenever I talked to him on the phone he was always happy. When I saw him a few months ago he seemed fine. I guess that's the problem: *I assumed*.

"Why didn't you talk to me? I would have –"

"What?" He shrugs his shoulders. "Stopped living your life when you have turned into this amazing young woman? No, you're meant to have your own life. Not be worried about me."

"I still want you in my life, Dad. I constantly daydream what it would be like for you to live in Seattle. You would be near West and me. There is nothing for us here, Dad, but memories. And –"

A nurse comes in, announcing that she needs to check my dad's vitals and saying his cardiologist will be by shortly as well. I lean back against my chair as my mind reels with this information. I had no idea that my dad felt so... lonely. The thought didn't cross my mind that there was nothing left for my dad here, either.

The cardiologist tells my dad that while he's doing well, he still needs to take this event seriously. I almost want to applaud him but I keep my mouth shut and listen to what he has to say. His heart attack was mild and his heart didn't suffer any severe damage. The small amount of tissue that was damaged should fully heal within eight weeks. In spite of all of that, he still wants to keep my dad for a few days of monitoring.

Silence falls between us after he leaves. After a few minutes, my dad speaks first. "I don't want you to feel like you have to take care of me, Harlow..."

"Then don't give me a reason to feel that way. I hate to pull the guilt trip card, Dad but...when you're not taking care of yourself –" Tears well up in my eyes. "You're all I have left." I squeeze his hand. "Please consider moving to Seattle. I would take care of everything. From listing the house to finding you a place to live. You wouldn't have to worry about a single thing." He opens his mouth to speak, and I interrupt him. "Please, Dad, just consider it. I'm an adult now. I can handle things. Let me handle things."

He squeezes my hand as he smiles. "I sure am lucky to have you as a daughter. I'll consider it. I'm going to get some rest, and you need to rest, too." He pulls me into a hug. "I'm grateful you're here."

I squeeze him back before I release him. "Do you want me to bring you some food when I come back?"

"That would be nice." He nods, closing his eyes, settling in for his nap.

I step out into the hallway and see Acyn walking towards me. "I need a bed..." He gives me a devilish smile . "I mean we can do that but I need clothes, a shower, sleep, food. Everything."

He wraps his arm around my shoulders. "I got you."

Steam rises around us as we sit in the bathtub filled to the brim with bubbles. Acyn massages my back as I sit between his legs. The water trickling off his fingers as he lifts them out of the tub is the only noise between us. I'm hopeful that my dad will choose to move to Seattle after given some time to think about it. Moving there was simpler for me because West already had a fully decorated guest house. I let out an exasperated sigh as I think of all that I'd have to do if he does decide to move. I don't mind it; I just hope that I can make it all happen like I said I could.

Acyn kisses my back and rests his chin on my shoulder. "What's on your mind, Sunshine?"

I melt into his chest. "I told my dad he should move to Seattle to be close to me and West. Then I started thinking about all that has to be done if he agrees. The most important thing is him having a place to live. I doubt he'd want to live with me. He already feels like he's intruding on my life even though I've assured him he isn't. So now... my mind is racing with ways to make this happen. Surprisingly, I'm not at all worried about selling the house if he does say yes."

He intertwines our fingers. "What if you moved in with me?" I whip around to face him, sloshing water over the sides of the tub. "That way, your dad could move into the guest house, and we could live together... like we already do."

"You *want* me to live with you?" I never considered us actually living together until now. Moving in together would seem like a major step for so many people. For Acyn and me, it feels... right.

"Yes," he says without hesitation. "We're always either at your place or mine but we haven't spent the night apart in a while. If you moved in then at least that would free up the guest house. Even if he only wants to stay there temporarily."

"I would love to move in with you." I wrap my arms around his neck. "This could actually work. I'll have to call West and –" My eyes widen. "Shit, I forgot to call West!"

"I've talked to him. I told him that your dad is okay but you should still probably call him so he can hear it from you."

I hold his gaze in awe. I wasn't expecting him to take care of anything. It feels good to have someone to lean on that can support me when I feel like I can't support myself.

"Thank you, babe."

He kisses my forehead. "You never need to thank me. I got you... always."

This is what it feels like to fall in love... to *be* in love. He's all I've wanted. All I've needed.

31

Harlow

THE DAY BEFORE MY dad left the hospital, he decided that he would move back to Seattle with me. I tried my best not to bring it up after I initially did. I knew that he needed to come to the decision on his own. After talking to Acyn about moving in with him, I set things in motion in case he said yes. I called West and told him about my dad moving into the guest house, and he happily agreed. West wasn't able to physically be here, but he has done as much as he can from afar.

Ava had people from her office move my things and redecorate the guest house so that it suits my father's style. It's perfect for him even if he decides to only live there temporarily. I contacted a real estate agent who assured me that our house will sell quickly, given the neighborhood, and she wasn't wrong. Within the first week of the house being listed, we received multiple offers.

It's been a bittersweet time for my dad and me. This is the house he bought with my mom; I was born here, raised here. These walls hold so many memories. Our hope is that the family who bought the house will be able to create their own treasure of memories. It's time for us to move on and plant roots elsewhere.

My dad is sitting with me in his office, sorting through papers while I pack boxes.

"Should we have a going away party?" he asks, peering at me over the top of his glasses. We leave next Monday for Seattle. I'm a little surprised my dad wants to have a party. He's always acted like they were a nuisance before, but this is the place we've called home for so long. It would be a nice farewell.

"If it's a party you want…" I do a pirouette. "A party you shall have."

He smiles at my playfulness. "I'm grateful that we'll live near each other again."

"Me too." I beam. "You'll love Seattle. Mercy is a doll. Ava sends me pictures daily, and she's already grown so much over the past six weeks. My heart couldn't be happier."

I wasn't sure how my dad would react to living in his brother's guest house, but he seems to be really excited about it. I know that he's always wished he and West had a closer relationship. Hopefully, this move helps that happen.

Later on that day, my dad texts me the list of people he would like to have over for lunch on Friday. He didn't want to have a dinner because in his words, "I don't want to have people over all night." I told him he was getting old.

I quickly glance over the list and see that Hendrix's parents are on it. I can only hope that he's busy with something. He has a girlfriend now, so I doubt he'll try to attend. The rest of the people on his list are colleagues and friends. This will be a retirement and going away party rolled into one.

Acyn will be back tomorrow evening. He's been racking up frequent flyer miles with how much he's flown here over the past six weeks. He's been so understanding and supportive throughout this whole process. Even though I feel like I'm falling apart, he comes along behind me and helps me put all the pieces back into place. Digging through stuff in the house has brought up a lot of emotions, and he's been my soft landing space to process it all.

"Do you want me to do it? I mean, I'm enjoying the view..." Acyn's referring to my tennis skirt that's giving him the best views as it flies with the wind. "But I'd rather you not break your neck."

I'm standing on a step stool, stretched as far as I can go, trying to hang a banner up for the party happening later this afternoon. "I..." My fingertips finally loop the banner on to the hook. "Got it!" I face him and bow with a satisfied smirk. He holds his hand out for me as I step off the stool. "How does everything look?" I turn on the spot, admiring all the navy and gold decorations we just put up.

This time with my dad has felt like a whirlwind. He's at an appointment with his cardiologist this morning. I'm trying my best to give him space and not be a helicopter. He had to gently remind me that I'm his daughter and not his caretaker. At first I was hurt by his words, but Acyn reminded me that I need to give my dad the space to heal. He needs to resume his regular activities, and he can't do that if I'm doing everything for him. It's been a learning experience for us both.

"It looks great, Sunshine. I think your dad will love it." He drapes his arm over my shoulders, and I snuggle into him.

"I do," my dad says from behind us as he joins us out on the patio. He wraps his arm around me, too. I feel like the luckiest girl in the world standing between the two most important men in my life.

"How was your appointment?" I ask.

"Great. I'm doing great. He even set up an appointment with a cardiologist in Seattle for once we get there. I'm ready, Kiddo." I give him a tight hug, and he squeezes me back.

I step away, wiping tears from my eyes. "Acyn and I are going to pick up the cake and the party platters I ordered. We'll be back in about an hour. Make sure you're ready, Dad." I point an accusatory finger at him. "Don't plop down in front of the sport's channel."

"It's my party," he says. I look him up and down with my hand on my hip. "You look like your mother with that glare." The corners of his mouth turn up. "Okay, I'll go get ready," he concedes.

The party is in full swing, and my dad is enjoying himself. It's nice to watch him carry on with everyone. I invited Marisa and Quinn who seemed happier to see Acyn again than me. They were sad when they learned that my dad and I would be permanently moving out of Texas but also understood why. I've gone through a rollercoaster of emotions over the past month and a half. It's hard to leave behind all that you've known, but the horizon of new beginnings has a gorgeous view, too.

We're in the middle of a conversation when Quinn's face falls. I stop mid-sentence and peer over my shoulder, searching for what caused her reaction. My eyes meet Hendrix's gaze; there's some girl on his arm and he looks... unkempt. After Kyrell told me what happened, I can only assume that this is the girl who switched up on him. I turn back around, giving the girls a look.

"Did you invite him?" Marisa whispers.

Acyn looks over his shoulder and waves at Hendrix. I jab him in the side, and he grunts, pulling away from me.

"What? I'm just being friendly." He insists.

I roll my eyes at him and turn my attention back to Marisa. "My dad put their family on the list. He's best friends with his dad after all." I let out a sigh, regretting sending them an invite. It was naïve of me to think that Hendrix wouldn't show up if given the opportunity.

Quinn is talking out of the side of her mouth. "He's coming over here. He's coming over here."

"Shut up!" I hiss as Hendrix comes to stand in our circle as if he belongs.

"Hey, man," Acyn says. "Good to see you again."

I narrow my eyes at him, knowing he's full of shit.

"Yeah, you too. Happy to see you two... thriving," Hendrix says as he extends a hand towards Acyn, but his eyes are on me. Could this be any more awkward?

"Who's your little friend?" Quinn cuts through the awkwardness as she eyes the girl on his arm.

"Oh, this is Aubrey." The girl offers a friendly smile that I don't return. "Aubrey, this is Harlow... and her friends."

"Boyfriend." I splay my hand across Acyn's chest plastering a fake smile on my face. "This is Marisa and Quinn, my best friends. We're just missing Kyrell. You already know him though, don't you Aubrey?" I narrow my eyes in her direction.

She shifts uncomfortably and looks to Hendrix, who offers her no comfort. Acyn looks at me with a mixture of caution and admiration. He interlaces his fingers with mine as silence settles between us.

"And this..." My dad cuts through the silence as he brings a friend of his into our circle. "Is my beautiful daughter, Harlow"—I smile, extending a handout to his friend— "and her boyfriend Acyn." The man extends his hand out with a warm smile. "I wouldn't have been able to get through this without either of them."

Hendrix has a sour look on his face as he disappears into the crowd of people, leaving his current flavor of the week trailing behind him. The rest of us fall into conversation about what the future holds for each of us. It's been a pleasant afternoon filled with food, amazing conversation, and my dad looks satisfied and happy. I was a bit skeptical when he first suggested a party but now I see he just wanted one last get together with friends.

"I'm going to get some more platters for the food table." The party is dying down, but I still want there to be food available for the last people who may trickle through.

"Do you need help?" Acyn asks.

"No." I kiss his lips. "I got it. It will only be one anyway. I'll be right back."

"We'll keep him company," Quinn says.

I don't doubt they will. There's nothing in the fridge other than food for the party, so it doesn't take me long to find it. As I turn around with the platter in my hands, I see Hendrix's face. I let out an exasperated sigh, looking behind him to see if his girlfriend is anywhere in sight.

"Where's Ariana?" I ask, knowing damn well that isn't her name.

"In the bathroom." He leans against the counter. "You and Acyn are pretty serious, huh?"

I tip my head to the ceiling, asking the universe why this is happening now. "Does it matter?"

"Everything matters with you." He takes a step closer to me.

I take a step back. "What do you want, Hendrix?"

"You."

Sneering, I scoff. "You have Audrey! Remember? Your girlfriend that you ruined your best friendship for. What is going on right now?"

"She doesn't matter, Harlow. All she does is satisfy a need."

I feel the sting of bile rising in my throat. To think I spent so much time with him makes me sick.

"Well..." I swallow the vomit threatening to come up. "Let her fulfill your other needs, too. I'm not the one for you." I make a move to step past him, and he blocks my way.

"Do you really think he can love you like I can? Provide a life for you like I can?"

"Hendrix," I say sharply, "I'm in love with Acyn. I love Acyn. You've gotta move on. Let me go..."

His honey brown eyes are locked onto mine. "I don't want to let you go. I love you, Harlow." He steps closer to me. I can already tell what his intentions are. I back into the fridge as he runs his fingers down my arm.

The puke I just swallowed is threatening to come back up. "Stop, Hendrix," I warn him. I'm ready to hit him with the platter of food but he flies back. I blink with confusion as I see tattooed hands connecting with Hendrix's face.

ACYN

I'm only half listening to what Marisa and Quinn are carrying on about. Harlow has been gone for a few minutes now. Maybe she needs help.

"Excuse me, ladies. I'm going to see if Harlow needs help," I say, excusing myself from the table.

As I enter the kitchen, I hear Harlow's voice.

"Hendrix, I'm in love with Acyn. I love Acyn. You've gotta move on. Let me go..."

My steps falter. I know she didn't mean for me to hear this. I don't know if I should keep walking into the kitchen or if I should pretend I never heard anything and wait for her. Movement from the hallway catches my eye, and I see that the ex's girlfriend is listening in on the conversation, too. They must have been talking for a minute. The ex professes his love for her. Not fucking surprising. I'm on high alert when I hear Harlow tell him to stop. I round the corner to see her backed against the fridge as he runs his hand along her arm.

There he goes touching what's mine again. I snap.

I rip him away from her and my fists connect with his jaw. Multiple times. I've been wanting to do this for a while. My fist slams into his nose. I'm satisfied when I hear a crack. He cries out in pain.

I cock my fist back ready to punch him again when I hear Harlow's voice. "Acyn, this isn't what it looks like, I was trying to –"

"Oh..." I stand up with my chest heaving. "I know, Sunshine, but he needed to learn to stop putting his hands on what isn't his." I give him one last swift kick to the ribs and then turn around to face her.

There is a wild desire in her eyes when my gaze meets hers. She doesn't pay notice to the pile of shit writhing around, screaming expletives beneath my feet.

"Did you hurt your hand?" she asks as she pulls me towards the stairs.

"I don't think so." It doesn't really matter if I did or not because it was worth it.

We reach the bathroom, and she pulls me inside, locking the door behind her. I lean against the counter, she stands between my legs, and her lips crash into mine. I'm stunned for a second because this isn't the reaction I was expecting for beating the shit out of someone. I'll fucking take it, though. Her hands fist my shirt as she kisses me with a sense of urgency. I pull her closer to me, feeling her heart beating wildly in her chest.

She pulls away only to peel her jeans off. I grip her ass while kissing her neck and slide my hand between her legs to feel her panties, and they're soaked. I stand up and flip her around so we're both facing the mirror. Her eyes lock onto mine as I bend her over and pull her panties to the side. All she wants is me, and I'm going to happily give myself to her.

I slowly push into her wetness as I watch her face in the mirror. She moans as she closes her eyes, biting her lip, as her pussy clenches around my dick. When she opens her eyes again, I lean forward, kissing her shoulder and her neck as I savor the feeling of being inside her. I grip her hip as she hikes her leg up on the counter. I thrust into her as her own hand travels down to her clit. We watch ourselves get lost in each other in the mirror. I wrap my hand around her throat, applying light pressure, as I thrust into her. I feel her pussy clenching around my dick. I know she's going to cum, she doesn't have to tell me.

She lets out a cry, saying my name with a look of complete ecstasy on her face. I don't slow down; I want her release all over me. Her eyes flutter open once she's ridden out her orgasm and the look of... *love* in them sends me over the edge right after her. Both of us are sticky with sweat, and she gives me a lazy smile as she brings her leg down from the counter. I reluctantly pull out of her. It's my favorite place to be. She turns around to face me and I bring my lips to hers.

"Violence is not okay..." Her voice is hoarse just from screaming my name.

"Violence is not okay." I nod, repeating her words, trying to be serious. She rolls her eyes, biting her bottom lip to keep from smiling.

"But... watching you beat the shit out of him turned me on, and I needed you inside me." Pulling her toward me, I kiss her neck . "How long were you standing there?"

I know she's asking because she wants to know how much I heard. I'm going to let her tell me she loves me when she feels the time is right for her. I doubt that's the way she wanted me to hear it.

"I didn't hear much. Just him professing his love for you." She lets out an exasperated sigh. "Maybe he'll think twice about assuming everything is his."

"Oh my God." Her eyes snap to mine. "Your hand; is it okay? It sounded like you broke something."

"I doubt I did. I'm sure he broke something running into my fist like that." I bring my hands up between us, and my knuckles are raw.

"Can you move them?"

"Harlow... I just fucked you into oblivion. You tell me?" I wrap my arm around her waist, pulling her flush against me. "Are you okay, though?" I ask, searching for any indication that she isn't because I'll beat his ass again.

"I'm good." She presses a kiss to my lips. "C'mon, we should rejoin the party." I take her hand, knowing the smile on her face is genuine and that she truly is okay.

Once we're back outside, Harlow's dad approaches us. "Would either of you happen to know why Hendrix had a broken nose and a possibly dislocated jaw?"

"Did he?" Harlow asks, clearing her throat. "That's... not surprising."

"He doesn't know how to keep his hands to himself," I say bluntly. I would do it all over again, and he's lucky that's all he got.

Felix pats my shoulder. "Hopefully, he learned his lesson."

I nod, confirming the ex learned several lessons, and if not I'll be more than happy to teach him again. Harlow wraps me and Felix in a hug. He's welcomed me with open arms from the beginning. I'm grateful that he trusts me to take care of his daughter when and if she needs it. I don't think she needed it today, but it sure felt good anyway.

32

Harlow

Walking into Holy Shot, I'm met with a sight that makes my heart swell. Acyn is sitting with my dad, Ava, Mercy, and West, engaged in a lively conversation. I can't help but smile watching them all together. I'm elated that my dad decided to move to Seattle. He's only been here for three weeks, but he's so happy here.

We are so happy here.

I feel myself relaxing as I approach them. I love photography, but that doesn't mean my days aren't tiring. Vision & Vibe is flourishing. It's nice to have a studio and not have to run around the city, meeting people for shoots. I still travel if a client asks, but it isn't a necessity now.

After sitting down in Acyn's lap, he pulls me towards him and kisses my temple. "Hey, Sunshine." Those words will always give me butterflies and put a smile on my face.

West and my dad are going back and forth about something while Ava bounces Mercy on her knee. This has become normal for both our families, gathering at Holy Shot.

"Do you two want to come over for dinner tonight?" my dad asks.

I love hanging out with them, but tonight I just want to be home snuggled with Acyn and Six-Two-Six.

I hesitate in responding. "We have plans, but we'll be there this weekend," Acyn says which surprises me because I wasn't aware that we had plans. "Are we still on for hiking Saturday morning? Maybe West won't sprain his delicate ankle this time." Each of us try not to laugh as West stares at Acyn with his mouth open.

"He does have a good point," my dad says, chuckling.

Last weekend, West sprained his ankle getting out of the car before their hike and they tease him about it every chance they get. "It was a serious injury..." West defends himself.

"Let's go Sunshine," Acyn says in my ear as they continue to carry on. I say goodbye to them all and let out an exhale as soon as we're out of the shop.

"We have plans?" I intertwine my fingers with his.

"Nope, you hesitated. I could see on your face that you need a chill night at home."

I hug him as we walk to his car. "I love spending time with them," I admit, "but I also like being with just you."

Acyn opens the door for me and I slide in. "What do you want to eat?" he asks, getting behind the wheel. "Or do you want me to make you something?"

"Surprise me," I say, resting my head against the seat.

"Bet. I'll drop you off at home so you can shower while I go get the food. Sound like a plan?"

"A perfect plan."

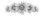

I slip into my silk robe after a relaxing bath and head for the kitchen. My steps slow when I hear slow music. Walking into the living room, I see Acyn has made a space for us to have dinner in front of the fireplace. He appears behind me with plates of food from our favorite Thai restaurant. We settle onto the plush fur rug and oversized pillows.

"What did I do to deserve this?" I take the plate he's holding out to me.

"You exist. That's all you need to do." His ember eyes meet mine.

"I love you..." I blurt out before I even think about it.

The overwhelming feeling of the love I have for him can't be contained any longer. I've known since the sunflower. Maybe even before then, but that's when I knew without a doubt that I had fallen for him. He slowly chews his bite of food, eyes locked on me, as he sets his plate aside. His eyes don't leave mine as he grabs my plate from my hands setting it beside his.

"I'm sorry, Sunshine... I don't think I heard you." I see a smirk threatening to appear on his lips. He's inches from me now.

I glance at his lips briefly. "I said..." I look into his eyes again. "I love you." My heart thumps in my chest.

His hand comes up, brushing against my cheek, tucking a loose curl behind my ear. The simple gesture makes me hyper aware of his close proximity. His lips meet mine. It's a soft kiss. One that leaves me hungry for more when he pulls away.

"I love you, too," he says, holding my gaze.

I crash into him, pushing him back onto the pillows. Straddling him, Acyn pulls at the ties of my robe, causing it to slip off and pool around my hips. I tug at his sweats, pulling them down and letting his dick spring free. Positioning myself over him, I slowly sink down, and his head drops back against the pillows as he enters me inch by inch. I toss my head back, reveling in the feel of him.

Kneading my breasts, I ride him while he rubs my clit. I spread my legs further, welcoming the pleasure he's giving me. Each tantalizing wind of my hips elicits moans from Acyn's lips. The sound brings me closer to the edge. My breath hitches as I feel the flood gates of my orgasm slowly opening.

"Acyn..." is all I manage to get out before my pussy clenches around him and the tidal wave of my release spills.

He sits up, pulling me flush against him, wrapping his arms around me as he matches the wind of my hips with his thrusts. I can tell he's near his release as his thrusts become more fevered and he drives into me. Acyn takes my nipple into his mouth, teasing it with his tongue before he pulls off, grazing it gently with his teeth. I sink my fingers into his curls, tugging them, feeling myself on the cusp of another release. His thrusts become deeper and harder, unraveling the knot of tension building in my core. My breath hitches when the tension snaps. He grips my waist, watching while I come undone for him. Sliding his hand around the back of my neck, he brings my lips to his. Moaning into my mouth, he finds his release seconds later. His thrusts slow as he spills into me. We kiss languidly, keeping our connection long after the waves of pleasure washed over us. Slowly, we come down from our high.

"I love you," I whisper in his ear.

Pulling away, he meets my gaze. "I love you, too."

33

Acyn

HARLOW HASN'T STOPPED ASKING me what I want for my birthday. I told her all I want to do is spend a few days with her on the Oregon Coast. She growls in frustration every time I tell her this. I know she wants me to give her some generic, material answer but what I want for my birthday isn't material. I knew she was desperate when she enlisted the help of Eli and Emery to find out what I wanted for my birthday. I jokingly told them that I wanted a black 1966 Mustang GT.

When she pulls up in front of my shop, driving that exact car, I think I'm fucking dreaming. She steps out looking like a goddess, flipping her waist-length twists over her shoulder. Her eyes meet mine through the window with a grin on her face.

I meet her outside. "Is this mine?" I'm almost afraid to touch it.

"All yours." She slides her shades down her nose. "Me and the car."

"You've been mine since that first shitty cup of coffee." Laughter tumbles from her lips as I press a kiss to her temple. Pointing at the car, I ask, "How?" I don't know whether to thank her or fuck her... or both.

She shrugs nonchalantly as if she isn't gifting me my dream car. "It helps when your dad and his friends have a love for old cars and can help you find them at reasonable prices. So yes, she's all yours."

She leans against the hood, dressed in an all-black skintight jumpsuit with black heels that I'd love to see draped over my shoulders. The only thought on my mind is thanking her by fucking her on the hood of this car.

That's exactly what I do. I drive us to somewhere secluded, where she can scream as loud as she wants, and dick her down. It's a fine start to my birthday week. But the real present awaits us at the coast.

"I'm glad you brought us here. I forgot how gorgeous it is," Harlow exclaims with the night sky reflected in her eyes as she stares at all the stars. It's a perfect night; there isn't a cloud in sight. She's sitting between my thighs with her back against my chest as we sit snuggled up next to the fire.

"I brought you here for a reason..."

"Not to throw us in the ocean again, I hope." She'll never forget that. I can't blame her because I won't either.

"No." I chuckle. "But that was a good memory."

She sucks her teeth. "For who?"

"Me. It was the first time I saw you naked."

"I thought you were going to say something sweet!"

I intertwine my fingers with her. "This is also where..." I plant a kiss on her hand as I bring it to my lips. "I realized that I was in love with you."

She turns around to face me. "Really?"

"Yeah, I thought you were mad at me the next morning, remember?"

"Yes. It was hard for me to pretend to be mad at you."

My heart rate picks up as I get closer to the reason. "I realized then that I would do anything to make you happy. I knew I was fucked... and completely in love with you."

Her eyes are glistening now. I fumble around in my pocket and bring out a small yellow ring box with shaky hands. Her eyes widen with recognition as she stares between me and the box. I open it to reveal a glittering, two carat, round cut diamond ring.

"Harlow Shaw..." I press a kiss to her lips. "You're all I've wanted and all I've needed. Will you marry me?"

"Yes! Yes!" She holds out her hand. "I love you so much, Acyn."

"And I love you."

I slip the ring on her finger. "You gave me the best birthday present, and you didn't even know it."

She looks from the ring, sparkling on her finger, to me in disbelief. I pull her towards me and kiss her slowly because I know I have a lifetime to savor her.

There was no one before her.
There will never be another after her.
There is only her. Only us. All I've wanted. All I've needed.

Epilogue

Harlow

MY RING GLITTERS AS I tangle my fingers in Acyn's curls. A smile begins to spread as I stare at it, still in awe that this man is all mine.

A chuckle rumbles from his chest. "Staring at your ring again?"

"Yes. How did you know?" Our bodies are intertwined after getting lost in each other... *repeatedly*.

"Because you stopped massaging my head."

"Look at it," I say as I hold up my hand in the moonlight. "It's hard not to stare."

He looks up at my hand, interlaces his fingers through mine, and brings my hand to his lips. "It's perfect, but you know we have to be up in three hours?"

"Excuse me." I splay my hand over my chest. "I'm not the one who has trouble keeping my hands to myself. I was perfectly fine going to bed."

"Bullshit. You wear one of my t-shirts to bed every night, and tonight you somehow end up in lacy lingerie. Not that I'm complaining, but it takes two to tango, Sunshine."

I can't stop the giggle that escapes me. "I wanted to see what it looked like on."

"And I wanted to see what it looked like off," he says, kissing my neck.

We spent the past two weeks on the Oregon Coast celebrating his birthday and our engagement. We love our families, and they're very involved with all that we do, but for this moment, he wanted it to be us two. We spent time relishing in our engagement and each other. I didn't think it was possible to continuously fall in love with someone. But I find myself falling deeper in love with him every day.

"It's going to suck going back to reality tomorrow." I sigh. "Sevyn and Ava are apparently already planning our engagement party."

"Sevyn is going to be a force to be reckoned with until we say 'I do'," he says. "This is the moment she's been waiting for since we first met."

I snuggle closer to him. "What do you think of my coffee now?"

"It still tastes like shit."

I gasp, swatting at his chest. "*Really*? Even now that we're engaged you won't admit that I know how to make coffee?"

He plants a kiss on my forehead. "Apparently I'm a sucker for shitty cups of coffee."

Life has been a blur with our work schedules and planning our engagement party and wedding. With the engagement party only a few weeks away, there's a lot that needs to happen. I've been missing the two weeks we had alone. It feels like a distant memory even though it was only a month ago.

It's Friday, and all I can think about is spending the entire weekend wrapped up in my future husband. I inhale the scent of plastic gloves, ink, and green soap as I enter his shop. It's a mixture of smells I never thought I'd find comfort in. Acyn doesn't bother looking up as I enter and sit down on my usual bench in front of the window.

"Hey, Sunshine. I'm almost done."

"Is this your fiancée?" his client asks.

The sound of fiancée makes me feel warm and tingly.

"Harlow, this is Elijah. Elijah, this is my future wife."

Butterflies course through my veins, and I can't help the foolish grin on my face. "Hi. Nice to meet you."

"Do you remember when I almost missed your birthday?" Acyn asks.

"He's the reason I almost missed it."

Elijah lets out a roar of laughter. "Throw me under the fucking bus, huh? It all worked out though, didn't it?"

"It did." I assure him. "Acyn just loves to give people shit."

Acyn winks in my direction, sitting up straight. "You're done for today, Elijah. I'll see you again soon."

Elijah stands up and puts his shirt on. He turns to me and extends his hand. "Pleasure to meet the woman who can put this son of bitch in his place."

"Pleasure is all mine." I place my other hand over my heart, bowing slightly.

"Yeah, yeah. Get out of here, Elijah," Acyn says as he steers him to the front doors. Elijah's laughter echoes through the shop.

"I like him."

"Elijah's been good to me. Even if he is an asshole."

"So, what does that make you?" I ask.

"An asshole who's about to be your husband." He leans closer, waiting for me to kiss him.

I press my lips to his. "Damn right."

Putting my feet up on the bench, I watch him clean up his station. I've had an idea bouncing around in my head since he proposed. "Acyn..."

"Yeah, Sunshine?"

"Can we get tattoos on our ring fingers?"

He gives me a heart-stopping smile. "Now?"

"Why not? Or we can do it another day if you just want to go home."

"Home is wherever I'm with you. Let's do it now. Do you know what you want?"

"Yeah, I want the ace symbol."

He stills for a second as he studies me. "I thought you said you didn't like my nickname."

"Oh, yeah." I sit in his tattoo chair. "I said that because you were being rude. I still prefer Acyn but... you're my ace."

He leans forward, sweeps my curls out of my face, and kisses me. "I love you," he says as he runs his thumb across my bottom lip. "But I still think your nickname is fucking horrible. Harls? What the fuck is that? Sounds like someone is hacking. I have to suppress the urge to correct anyone who calls you that."

I fall into a fit of laughter, leaning against his chest. "Only you could make an insult sound sexy. Sorry we can't all have–" I make air quotes "–edgy and cool nicknames."

"Who said that?" He scrunches up his face.

"*You,*" I exclaim and do my best impersonation of him, making my voice deep and copying his mannerisms. "You can call me Ace," I say, rolling my eyes. "With your stupid lopsided grin."

He lets out a belt of laughter. "I don't sound like that. Stop that shit."

"Yeah, you do. You know you do. That's why you're laughing!"

"Wow." He catches his breath. "I had no idea you had so much pent-up frustration about my edgy and cool nickname."

"I don't. I just thought you were ridiculous for telling me to call you Ace."

"Well now look. You're getting an ace tattooed on you."

"Happily."

"If you get it where your ring sits, you won't be able to wear it until the tattoo heals. Do you want it above it or do you want to take your ring off?"

I clutch my left hand to my chest. "I'm not taking off my ring."

"Above, got it." He preps my skin for the tattoo.

I open my mouth remind him to take pictures but he beats me to it and pulls out his phone to take a picture of me before he begins.

"You know me so well."

"It's second nature now," he says, handing me his phone to look at the pictures. I don't even flinch when he presses the needle to my skin.

It doesn't take him long to finish. It's small, black, and sits just below my knuckle. I move my hand side to side to admire it and grin. "This is perfect."

"I don't think that there is anything about you that isn't perfect," he says.

I press a kiss to his lips. "What are you putting on yours?"

"I already know what I want." He says as he pulls out a small sketch that he won't let me see.

"You already have one drawn out?" I ask in amazement.

"Of course," he says nonchalantly. "It shouldn't take long."

I watch, mesmerized, as his tattoo gun meets his skin. Watching him work is one of my favorite things. He looks so serene. The stencil he applied moments ago is coming to life.

"What do you think Sunshine?" he asks once he's done and holds his hand out to me.

I take it and stare at the sunflower that looks like the sun. The only thought running through my mind is, *this is my husband. This is my husband. This is my husband.*

"It's beautiful," I say, looking up at the ceiling, telling myself not to be ridiculous as tears sting my eyes. But it doesn't matter; a tear escapes and falls down my cheek. Acyn kisses it away and pulls me into a hug.

"I love you," I whisper against his neck.

"I love you too, Sunshine."

We stay like that until he breaks the silence. "We should lock up and get home. It's getting late. We can chill by ourselves this weekend. Sevyn can live without two days of wedding plans."

I let out a long, low sigh. "That's exactly what I need."

Planning our wedding is exciting, fun, and exhausting. Even though Ava and Sevyn are handling all the details, it's our wedding, and I want to make sure it's what we want. "Let me take a picture of us first so I can brag about how amazing my husband is to the internet."

Acyn smiles, shaking his head while I set up my portable tripod and position it in front of us.

"Ready?"

"Always."

"It's on a –"

"I know the drill Sunshine." He says as he holds his ring finger up to the camera and pulls me into a kiss. I follow his lead and hold my ring finger up to the camera too.

While he cleans up, I scroll through the pictures. I can't help the grin that's on my face. I choose to upload two. One where we're locked in a kiss holding our ring fingers up to the camera and the other where I'm looking into his eyes like all the answers to the universe are in them. I type the caption: *the beginning of forever.*

"Ready, Sunshine?" he asks with his hand held out to me.

"Always," I say as I interlace my fingers with his.

We're all deserving of happiness and of a love that's so deep that you only discover the depths to which it goes with each passing day as your love grows.

I squeeze his hand a little tighter as we walk into the night because I know I'm holding onto my forever.

Keep In Touch

Thank you for reading. If you enjoyed this novel, please consider leaving a review on Amazon, Goodreads, and wherever else you can so other readers can enjoy it, too!

Visit my website or take a picture of the QR code below to subscribe to my newsletter, get exclusive updates, explore my other books, follow me on social media, and to stay up to date!

www.aevaldez.com

Also By A.E. Valdez

All I've Wanted, All I've Needed
Colliding With Fate
The Beginning of Forever
A Worthy Love

Three Kings Billionaire Series:
Snow King Catches His Snowflake

Thank you

To my endlessly supportive husband, I love you. Thank you for cheering me on in every single thing I do. You knew how much this meant to me and told me to go all in. And I did.

To my sweet boys, life would not be life without you. Thank you for reminding me to play and to never grow up.

Maria, thank you for treating me like one of your own and for always being there for me. I love you and your amazing family!

Christina, thank you for being my friend for the past twenty-one years. You've believed in every single dream and have been alongside me for everything. I really have no clue where I would be without you. Guess I made it through the portal after all.

Emily, thank you for making the cover I imagined come to life. You a truly talented and amazing artist.

Thank you to all my friends and family who reached out, celebrated me, and sent me words of encouragement.

To the readers of my visual stories, Lost In Parris & Corban X Cross, thank you for supporting me and my characters for two years. I went from telling little, episodic stories to writing a book. As always, sending big love.

To my readers, thank you for picking up my book and reading it. This is only the beginning!

Made in the USA
Middletown, DE
25 October 2024

63247653R00183